DRAGON GAMES

DRAGON GAMES

STEPHEN MERTZ

FIVE STAR
A part of Gale, Cengage Learning

Detroit • New York • San Francisco • New Haven, Conn • Waterville, Maine • London

GALE
CENGAGE Learning

Set in 11 pt. Plantin.
Printed on permanent paper.

LIBRARY OF CONGRESS CATALOGING-IN-PUBLICATION DATA

Mertz, Stephen, 1947–
    Dragon games / Stephen Mertz. — 1st ed.
        p. cm.
    ISBN-13: 978-1-59414-872-9 (alk. paper)
    ISBN-10: 1-59414-872-4 (alk. paper)
    1. Olympic Games (29th : 2008 : Beijing, China)—Fiction. 2. Beijing (China)—Fiction. I. Title.
PS3613.E788D73 2010
813'.6—dc22   2009050648

First Edition. First Printing: April 2010.
Published in 2010 in conjunction with Tekno Books and Ed Gorman.

Printed in the United States of America
1 2 3 4 5 6 7 14 13 12 11 10

This novel, our "first born," is for my Elda, dedicated from the heart with undying love.

PROLOGUE

It was a lousy day for a funeral.

Black thunderheads hugged the surrounding hills like a smothering blanket. The morning air was warm and still, heavy with humidity. Cicadas chattered. It had rained earlier, and the grass of the hillside cemetery was slippery, the rows of simple gravestones tattooed with dampness. A stand of willow trees hunched under the weight of accumulated moisture, their drooping branches dripping audibly.

Further up the hill from where a fresh grave had been dug, McCall stood watching, well removed from and unheeded by the small group of mourners listening to the young pastor read from the book of Psalms. The *drip-drip* of the weeping willows melded with the preacher's voice, making him barely audible to McCall. *Maybe this is a perfect day,* he thought. It was as if nature Herself shared in his grief.

He was dressed in somber gray. A well-proportioned man of forty-three, he was a shade over six feet, with thick black hair that was just beginning to turn gray at the temples. He did not know the mourners, and he had never been to this place before.

He only knew the one they were burying.

A man in his eighties was flanked by a young couple in their twenties. The father, accompanied by grandchild-and-spouse. The old man wore an ill-fitting suit of indeterminate age. His thatch of silver hair was neatly combed, but his leathery features and broad, sloping shoulders spoke of a hard life spent toiling beneath a merciless sun. His rough, farmer's hands were clasped before him. His lower lip trembled. His rheumy old eyes held a depthless sadness that matched what McCall was feeling.

A fine mist began to fall as the casket was lowered.

McCall thought, *so it ends here, on a rainy hillside so far from the pageantry, the defeats and the glories of Beijing.*

Memories washed over him.

He had not been present for the very beginning of what was ending here, but he now knew exactly when and how it all began . . .

CHAPTER 1

August 8, 2008. The Olympic Green, Beijing, China

The Olympic Green, where more than half of the 2008 Summer Olympic competitions would be held, and the Olympic Village, home to the largest number of athletes for the longest duration of time in the games' history, had been constructed on the ancient north–south axis that bisected the Forbidden City and other imperial landmarks, and once represented the Chinese emperor's central position in the nation. Now, it was the center of a smoggy, urban sprawl with a population twice that of New York.

The Beijing National Stadium, centerpiece of the Olympics, dominated The Green. The stadium was the world's largest enclosed space, three hundred yards long by two-hundred-and-sixty yards wide, with seven levels, consuming sixty-five acres, towering at two-hundred-and-thirty feet against a skyline of modern skyscrapers side by side with centuries-old architecture.

Commonly referred to as "the bird's nest" because of the unique lattice-like, interwoven concrete skeleton that formed the stadium, and the curved steel-net walls that enclosed it, tonight the National Stadium resembled a living organism of incredible proportions that raised its raucous roar to the heavens while gorging itself on the endless stream of humanity swarming about it. The radical, postmodern design allowed shafts of light to peer out from between the concrete and curved steel, giving the giant organism the appearance of hundreds of bright eyes.

It was the most God-awfully *ugly* piece of man-made rubble Dan Price had ever seen.

The pulsating thunder of the opening ceremonies, the wild cheering of 91,000 spectators, rippled the fabric of night. In a pocket of relative isolation, directly outside the massive stadium, near the epicenter of the festive atmosphere and yet removed from it, Price crouched with Captain Li's squad, gazing across the front hood of a green bus that bore the official markings of The Green Olympics.

The "green" Olympics was China's attempt to achieve an environmentally friendly Olympics. China had severe environmental problems. Its citizens lived under a permanent gray toxic cloud of smog, from what Price had seen during his two weeks of Olympics prep time spent here. Beijing had the most polluted air in the world; high nitrogen dioxide levels that many, worldwide, feared would be vitally dangerous to the health of the athletes, negatively affecting their performance during competition.

The passenger bus was parked just inside a ten-foot-high chain link fence that cordoned off one of the stadium's loading dock areas. With the opening ceremonies approaching their crescendo, busses and miscellaneous passenger vehicles were parked in every available place. On the loading dock, personnel hustled, worker ants under bright fluorescent lighting, unloading trucks and vans, pushing dollies, steering carts stacked high with boxes. The constant consumption and replenishment of the stadiums' concession stands, shops and restaurants was ongoing, an overheated process, especially tonight.

Price was a muscular man with a military haircut and dark, angular features. He had a lean, careful face. He wore black—T-shirt, denims, combat boots—with a silenced Glock 9mm nestled in a shoulder holster under his left arm and a photo tag pinned to his chest identifying him as an Incident Response Team security coordinator attached to the Olympics' Special Operations Command.

China had combined its military and police special forces elements to ensure the safety of the athletes and the Olympic venues. A single command authority, crossing all national and military region responsibilities, was deemed necessary for such a large-scale security effort, to enable the Chinese to deal with one security organization. This had resulted in formation of the SOC. The Beijing Olympics were inaugurating the "sleeping giant" of China onto the global stage. The 29th Olympiad would be the biggest sporting event ever to be held in China and the government was making certain that there was no room for embarrassment. The Olympic Games had increasingly served as the arena for debate about modern nationhood and international relations. The Tokyo Olympic Games in 1964 and the Seoul Olympic Games in 1988 had marked, respectively, the emergence of Japan and Korea as world powers. The Olympic Charter opposed any political abuse of sports and athletes, but the truth of the matter was, just as the original Olympics had their origins in the politics of the time, the modern Olympics had become the arena for wars, boycotts, protests, walkouts and terrorist attacks.

Price and the soldiers crouched in an area between the bus and the fence about ten feet wide, in the shadow cast by the bus. The young soldiers wore black, including knit caps, which could instantly become pullover masks. There were times when anonymity was preferable when enforcing the will of the state. This squad was from a Special Forces unit of the Peoples' Liberation Army's First Airborne Regiment, stationed in Xinjiang, deployed to the Olympics as one of China's many counter-terrorist measures. The soldiers carried silenced machine guns and were equipped with lightweight body armor.

At a gated checkpoint to the dock area, a step van, with colorful commercial markings, was being searched. The driver and a passenger, both Chinese in appearance, in their early twenties, wore matching uniforms featuring a corporate logo. They stood before one rifle-bearing sentry while another scrutinized their papers, communicating with his superiors via a lapel mic, verifying credentials and manifest. Three more commercial vehicles were lined up behind the van, waiting their turn. There was an air of perfunctory routine about the inspection. A sentry opened the rear doors of the van and briefly looked inside. Finally, the men were handed back their papers and they re-boarded the van. The officer in charge indicated that the gate be raised. The step van drove on through, onto the blacktop area that provided access to the dock. The van traveled within twenty feet of Price and the soldiers.

Captain Li, the team leader of this Special Forces unit, stood next to Price. Li was an intense, small-boned Cantonese man with sharp, dark eyes that missed nothing.

"The moment of truth, is it not?"

Price said, "Let's hope your intel is wrong."

"Our intelligence source is unimpeachable." Li spoke English, each word clipped and precise. He watched the van with tight eyes that revealed nothing. "But why would al Qaeda attempt an act of terrorism at our Olympics?"

"Why 9/11?" said Price. "It's a crazy world, Captain."

The tip had been developed by the Chinese, who could easily have circumvented the Special Operations Command except for their obsessive commitment to adhering strictly to the rules in everything large and small, so as not to compromise the integrity of the Green Olympics in the eyes of the world. And so this had come across Price's desk. Whatever "this" was, it was much too vague for his liking, originating as it supposedly did from a human intelligence source embedded by the Chinese inside a cell of the Islamic underground presence that survives in China, despite the country's brutal repression.

The step van angled away from the dock and came to a stop next to a row of parked vehicles. Its headlights and taillights were extinguished, and the engine was shut off.

China's internal threats included the "traditional" school of terrorism, such as the East Turkistan Islamic Movement, who advocated an "independent" Xinjiang Province, along with the extremists of the Tibetan separatist movement. Generally, though, the Muslims of the world looked upon China as a well-wisher because of its assistance to Pakistan in developing a military nuclear capability—the Islamic bomb—its assistance to Iran, and Libya in developing a nuclear missile capability, its opposition to the U.S. invasion and occupation of Iraq, and its support for Iran on the nuclear issue. Traditionally, al Qaeda had remained ambivalent toward China. But while they would have no motivation for targeting Chinese nationals, interests, and prestige during the Games, they would be strongly tempted not to miss such a spectacular occasion for mounting an act of terrorism directed at the participants from the United States, the United Kingdom, Australia and other countries forming part of the occupying forces in Iraq and Afghanistan.

There was a shift in the shadows to Price's right and Jody Simms materialized, advancing to crouch next to him. Jody wore dark clothes that melded her with the night. She held a 9mm Glock, identical to his, in a two-handed grip. She was twenty-seven years old. Her dark clothes could not conceal a nice figure. Shoulder-length chestnut hair framed a high-cheekboned face that was highlighted by intelligent brown eyes and a firm jaw.

The step van just sat where it had stopped. None of the workers on the dock appeared interested. A swell of wild cheering burst from inside the stadium, almost deafening.

Jody's eyes stayed on the van. "Looks like they're not making a delivery or a pickup."

Jody was Price's partner, not by his choice. She exuded professionalism, but he could remember a day when girls didn't play with guns. But the suits had decided she was his equal, and he had seen her on the firing range. She was good. Jody Simms had served in the military in Iraq, where she'd earned a Bronze Star, and had been plucked for this assignment from her civilian job as a detective with the Detroit Metro PD. She and Price got along, but he'd rather have been partnered with a man.

He scowled. "Why you pestering me, New Breed?" It was his nickname for her, not necessarily meant to be flattering, although she seemed like a nice enough kid. "You're supposed to be at the office with your ear to the ground to see what else might be out there we can move on."

"That's right, Old School. And that's why I'm here."

"You couldn't radio me? You couldn't wait until this was done?"

"I am waiting. What I think I've got, I don't want to broadcast, not even over our frequency."

The driver and his passenger emerged from the step van.

Price said, "Okay, tell me what's so important and tell me quick. Keep in mind that you're disobeying orders."

"It's big, Dan. Maybe the biggest take in history, about to go down right here at the Olympics. You want to know what else is out there, try this on for size. Paramilitary, if there's anything to the whisper I picked up."

"Paramilitary?"

"So far you're the only one I've told. You're my partner. You're the one I have to trust because I think when this comes down, it's coming from the inside."

"Do we have a name?"

14

She paused, catching his eye, silently indicating Captain Li, who remained engrossed in the step van.

She said, "We need to talk."

Li straightened. "What are they doing?"

The pair from the van had turned their backs to the bus behind which Price and the others waited. The two men prostrated themselves upon the blacktop, their foreheads touching the ground.

Jody said, "They're praying."

Li frowned. "But they're not Arabs."

She said, "They don't have to be. Islam is the second largest religion in the world."

Price nodded. "And those two are getting ready to enter paradise. Come on, let's *move!*"

He bolted from concealment and the others followed. The two by the van were startled beneath the sudden onslaught of uniforms and the soldiers' harsh commands in Chinese to raise their hands. Captain Li's men roughly threw them to the ground.

Another eruption of cheering rumbled from within the stadium and Price thought again of an ungodly, giant organism roaring at the heavens, gorged and rambunctious. He told himself to stop thinking like that. He now knew what he must do . . . even if he didn't like it. But he had no choice.

He and Jody hurried to the step van. Price ripped open the rear doors. The interior of the van seemed alive, crammed to capacity with inflated multicolored balloons. He and Jody leaped into the van and pawed through the balloons, only to find more balloons.

Jody said, "Are we sure about this?"

Price began searching the floor by touch. "I wasn't, but I am after watching those two face Mecca, just waiting to be delivered to their virgins in Paradise."

15

He pried open a strip of rubberized flooring. Throwing back a rectangular, latched trapdoor, he revealed an artfully concealed secret compartment obscured by the density of the cargo of joyous balloons. Inside was a metal box of approximately two-feet-by-five, reflecting the loading dock lights behind him like a shiny, new, oversized padlocked toolbox. Only, it wasn't a toolbox.

Price tried his ring of all-purpose passkeys on the lock, without success. His muscles cramped with a new concern that bordered on panic.

"Captain Li, search those men for keys!"

Li translated and his soldiers undertook a fast, thorough search of the prisoners, who remained passive while being manhandled, brusquely flip-flopped this way and that. Their expressionless faces and blank eyes could have been opiates or the bliss of imminent martyrdom.

Jody said, "The ignition." She dashed around to the front of the van.

Price's mind was racing. It couldn't end like this, before it even began! Were they all only heartbeats away from being vaporized at ground zero of the most cataclysmic terrorist act ever? *Hell, no!* He was here to prevent that.

He spoke calmly into his lapel mic, identifying himself and saying, "This is a Code Red." He stated their exact location. "I need a bomb squad like five minutes ago, and a complete lockdown of this sector."

In his earpiece he heard the female dispatcher's shellacked fingernails tapping across her keyboard before he'd finished speaking.

She said, "Bomb squad is enroute, ETA two minutes."

Price acknowledged that and returned to the lock, trying the small pick that was attached to his ring of passkeys. The padlock would not yield. He realized that he was sweating in the cool night air only when he found himself absently brushing the back of his sleeve across his face to wipe the drops from his eyes.

From where she had thrown herself into the driver's seat, Jody extended a hand back to him, offering a key ring.

"Try these."

He did so. The third key opened the lock. He flung open the lid.

It didn't look like much. A three-foot-long gadget of wires and parts, with a counter blinking off the seconds and it looked to Price like they were only seventy seconds from detonation. Price thought, *Oh, no . . .*

He said, "A goddamn suitcase bomb."

Jody stepped beside him. "Let me."

She held a small pair of pliers, which she glided straight to one of several color-coded wires. She snipped one of the wires.

The counter went blank. There was a peculiar mechanical sound as if the thing was sighing. And then . . . nothing; it was just a piece of fancy junk in a box.

Price eased back onto his haunches, expelling a long breath. "Nice work."

Jody grinned. "New Breed training," she said.

Price reminded himself of what he must do. He had ninety seconds before the bomb team arrived, maybe two minutes or two-and-a-half on the outside if the dispatcher was wildly optimistic in projecting an ETA. The passing mass of humanity beyond the dock area appeared wholly uninterested in this little scene in the shadows of the great stadium, but that would change once the bomb squad and the Chinese military backup arrived. This oasis of shadow would be overrun. The opening ceremonies were drawing to a climax. He had to move fast.

He nudged free of the balloons, leaving the van, and nodded at the prisoners.

"Let's question those two."

The prisoners sat with their hands cuffed behind them, staring up at the guns aimed at them.

When Price and Jody reached him, Captain Li stepped into their path, blocking their way.

He said, "I've radioed my superiors. These prisoners are in my custody, Mr. Price. As enemies of the state, they are under my jurisdiction. A squad has been dispatched to formally arrest them."

"Then that doesn't leave me much time, does it, Captain?"

Li's sharp eyes narrowed. "Sir?"

"Surely you understand. I've got to interrogate them too, however informally. My people don't want me to just let them slip out of our hands with nothing to show for it."

"This is an internal government matter," said Li briskly. "Your very presence here is but a courtesy extended by our government."

Price glanced at the prisoners. "Do they speak English?"

"They do not."

"Then you can translate. Let me talk to them while we're waiting for your people to get here. What harm can that do? You'll be present."

The sharp eyes bristled. "I would have it no other way."

"Great. Over behind the bus will do." Price clasped the upper arm of one handcuffed man and jerked him to his feet. "Come on, you."

Jody stepped forward. "Wait, Dan." She indicated the other prisoner. "What about him? Back in Detroit we'd separate them. I'll see what he knows."

"No," snapped Price. "I want you with me."

He placed his palm against the middle of the prisoner's back and shoved roughly. The man stumbled, struggling to keep his balance with his hands cuffed behind his back. Price followed him into the deeper shadows that were blocked from the others by the bus.

Captain Li hurried to catch up. "Mr. Price, wait—"

Advancing, Jody thought she heard the sounds of a scuffle. She followed Li around the front of the bus, only seconds behind him.

The prisoner was prone upon the ground and Dan Price, who had obviously surprised Captain Li by sidestepping to position himself behind the officer, had looped his left forearm across Captain Li's throat and was drawing Li forcibly back onto the blade of a knife, which Price rammed in savagely, to the hilt, twisting the handle to hasten death. Captain Li's body arched. He emitted a muffled, gurgling noise and was dead when Price flung him aside, swinging to face Jody, tracking around the submachine gun that he'd taken from Captain Li.

Jody stood her ground, starting to raise her pistol, her eyes widening in surprise and shock. "My God, Dan, what are you doing!?"

He stitched her with a short burst from the silenced machine gun. Jody shuddered and quaked on her feet as the bullets riddled her, spinning her about, tossing her facedown upon the ground, a rapidly widening pool of blood shining like spilled black ink on the blacktop beneath her.

From the other side of the bus came shouted queries and the stamping of combat boots, soldiers approaching on the run; they'd heard her shout even if they didn't understand English, and they were close enough to have heard the silenced chatter of the machine gun.

Price tossed the weapon to the ground, inches from the handcuffed prisoner who was staring up at him, stoic, implacable. Price thought, *he knows what's coming.* Price drew his pistol.

"Tell the virgins I said hello."

19

He shot the man once, between the eyes. With one of his master keys, he quickly uncuffed the wrists and placed the machine gun even closer to the dead man's hands.

A swell of music from the Stadium and the night sky exploded with multicolored fireworks. Explosions hammered the night. Weird, strobe-like illumination from high above limned everything in shimmering silver.

When the soldiers rushed around the front of the bus, they drew up short at the scene of carnage. Price stood in the center of a loose circle formed by the dead bodies. His pistol slipped from his fingers, dropping to the ground. There was a bewildered expression on his face.

CHAPTER 2

Until the moment her purse was stolen, this had been the second happiest night of Kelly Jackson's life, a night of sweet promise, anticipation and enthusiasm, shared with a capacity crowd and the more than ten thousand other athletes from around the world who had congregated in this great, magnificent stadium. She had never seen so much humanity compressed into one area before. Kelly hoped to attend art school whenever the time came for her to start living a normal life, and the Bohemian in her thought the stadium truly was a work of art. The ground vibrated beneath her feet. Fireworks rumbled, illuminating the skies overhead.

The Opening Ceremony had been a lengthy pageant of traditional Chinese culture and history, a colorful and noisy spectacle. Following the array of artistic performances, the parade of nations had entered the stadium, walking under the banners of more than two hundred countries. Based on audience reaction, the emotional high point of the parade was the entrance of the delegation from Afghanistan. The Iraqi delegation also stirred emotions.

The American teams were thunderously booed, although among so many spectators there was still considerable applause and some cheering as the Americans filed by the stands. Kelly concentrated on the cheering. Like her teammates, she raised her chin and strode with her head held high, a strange mixture of embarrassment and patriotism stirring within her.

She was twenty years old, a compact ninety-five pounds in a perfectly toned five-foot-one frame, her brown hair worn stylishly short. She had brown eyes that, people had told her ever since she was a child, always seemed to be smiling. She had been six years old, at a birthday party in a middle-class Milwaukee suburb, when a coach had noticed her doing cartwheels and roundoffs and mentioned to her mother that the child should start taking lessons, which she did soon afterward. By sixth grade, little Kelly Jackson was sleeping in her jersey on Friday nights in anticipation of Saturday morning gymnastics class. Her big break came when she was spotted by the famed coach Boris Temerov, who, during the Cold War, had defected to the United States from Bulgaria, where he had trained seven female Olympic gold gymnasts. Recognizing the makings of another winner in Kelly, Temerov had offered his services without charge if she would move to Atlanta and train at his facility. It had not been an easy decision for a girl of only fifteen, or for her parents, but her drive had won the day. Kelly had no intention of spending the remainder of her life knowing that she *could* have gone to the Olympics, always carrying with her the curse of *what if.* So her schooling was put on hold and she was packed off to Atlanta to study with the master.

Temerov was a stern, humorless, controversial taskmaster. The sports media and insiders who accused him of pushing "his girls" too far often decried his harsh Eastern European approach. Kelly knew better. Grueling, yes. It was boot camp hell, working with such a fierce trainer, plus she was only a kid. Temerov's regimen of eight hours per day and the ongoing pressure to succeed dominated her life. But he was a great motivator, and he instilled a confidence in her that she never would have found without him. She had blossomed into a world-class athlete under Boris's tutelage. The balance beam was her favorite event. At her debut at the American Cup in New York

City, she walked off with the all-around title, the first of three consecutive years she had done so. That same year, she became an American Classics champion. Under her mentor's guidance, she qualified for the Olympic team. She was going to be as big as Mary Lou Retton and Carly Patterson combined!

That was when her rising star sputtered and her luck ran out.

She'd injured her knee just six weeks before the 2004 Olympics in Athens. The injury had required surgery, and Kelly was told she would need at least three months of recovery before competing again. But she had no intention of putting her dreams on hold this time either. She had worked too hard, sacrificed so much—life with her family, a normal childhood of school and friends with varied interests, not to mention romance. She intended to return home with a case full of trophies. No one was about to put a limit on what Kelly Jackson could do. She'd had the operation, but was out of bed the next day. Within two days, she was delicately walking, and when the American women's gymnastics team arrived in sunny Athens that summer, the rising young star of women's gymnastics was on board and ready to go.

And that was *the* happiest night of Kelly's life, that glorious night four years ago when a spunky, self-assured 16-year-old had marched in *those* opening ceremonies. What a night that had been. The new thrill of it had coursed through her like electricity. She'd made it. She'd made it to the Olympics.

She gave her best. She thought so and her parents, who were her biggest fans, agreed. More importantly, so did Boris. But that year in sunny Athens brought a dark and disappointing truth. Dreams do not always come true. At least, not the first time around. Her knee had started acting up at the worst possible times, such as when she missed three landings on the floor exercise, finishing seventh overall.

The poor showing devastated her, but surprisingly it was

good enough for Boris, who had gruffly echoed her parents' sentiment that making it to the Olympics, out of all the contending athletes in America, was honor enough.

Athens became a stepping-stone, not a stumbling block. Champions do not give up. Nothing would ever match the thrill of that first time, but tonight in Beijing was a close second, making new memories and dreams that would be treasured for a lifetime. For months she had been training for more than thirty hours a week. The road from Athens to Beijing was long and demanding, but her commitment to performance and winning paid off under Boris Temerov's guiding hand. At the National Gymnastics Championships alone, she had earned the all-around silver medal. What happened in Athens only heightened her desire to win big in Beijing and she felt a deep and abiding gratitude—to her family, to Boris Temerov, and most of all, to God—for allowing her this second chance.

This time she *would* triumph.

Tonight's opening ceremony culminated in the lighting of the Olympic Cauldron, after which the stadium began to disgorge the one hundred thousand people in attendance; an orderly process for the most part, as far as Kelly could see. The athletes were treated like royalty, but with more than ten thousand of them, the main area, where transportation back to the Olympic Village awaited, was clogged with so many people that it could only be described as orderly chaos. An endless beeping of the horns of cars and busses enveloped the crowd, the laughter and camaraderie, the clothing and languages from every conceivable country. Handlers hustled their teams to this bus or that under a sky of exploding fireworks.

Her team's handlers guided Kelly and the other young women to a mini-bus that would take them to the American Women's Gymnast Team Dinner, to be held in their honor at the Olympic Village. Two of the team's bodyguards stood waiting at the doors, taking a headcount as the girls boarded, making certain everyone was accounted for.

The bodyguards could have been twins—beefy, oversized, muscular guys in their twenties with shaved skulls and permanent scowls. Some of the girls thought they were hot in a dangerous kind of way. The one difference distinguishing them was that one was white and the other was black.

Kelly found herself standing next to Tyrona Carey, a bright, sassy 16-year-old from Atlanta. Kelly could no longer contain her thoughts.

"Tyrona, do you think a person can have two favorite nights in their life?"

Tyrona grinned her sassy, street-wise grin. "Maybe more than two if they're lucky."

"Well, I feel lucky."

"Then maybe you'll *get* lucky tonight, girl, at this party they're throwing for us."

"Stop it. You know I'm not interested in anything like that. Boris doesn't leave me time for boy trouble. He told me it would cloud my focus."

"So they say. But girl, when it comes to what I'm talking about, everybody's interested, even a nice girl like you who's saving it for Mr. Right."

"Tyrona, please."

"I'm just saying maybe you'll meet Mr. Right tonight."

"I'll just settle for being around people we know instead of a hundred thousand people we don't!"

Tyrona's attention was drawn to an especially colorful and loud eruption of fireworks blazing in the sky. "Someone told me it was the Chinese who invented gunpowder. Count on folks like that to throw down a big party!"

And that's when it happened.

A breeze seemed to brush Kelly's left shoulder ever so faintly, where no breeze could have because of the density of the crowd, and a heartbeat later she realized the absence of the usual weight of her purse on her left forearm. Reaching down, she felt only dangling leather straps.

Tyrona sensed that something was wrong.

"Kel, what is it?"

"My purse. They used a razor on my purse." Kelly raised her voice. "Someone stole my purse!" She glanced in the direction that would have been downwind, had a breeze actually touched her, and there he was, a slim young man, no more than a teenager, wearing baggy slacks and a loud print shirt, darting through the tightly packed crowd, her purse clutched in his hand. She pointed after him. *"Stop him!"*

The two bodyguards responded automatically, racing after the thief, but they drew up short when a man in his mid-forties, trim and in shape in faded Levis, T-shirt and running shoes, emerged from the passing flow of people to intercept them. He flashed some sort of identification.

He told them, "Stay with the team. This could be a diversion. Get those young ladies home safely." He took off, running after the purse-snatcher and they both became lost to Kelly's sight, swallowed by the density of the crowd.

Kelly said, "But my purse—"

"You heard the man, miss. Sorry."

"Yeah," said his twin. "Onboard, ladies. You have a party to go to."

"But my purse—"

She couldn't lose her purse. Her life was in her purse. Her passport. Her papers. Credit cards. Driver's license. Everything. Her life was in her purse. *Her makeup was in her purse!*

One of the bodyguards said, "That guy who took over, he's from Olympic Security. He'll get your purse back, miss. He'll see that it gets returned to you. But please, we have to keep moving. Please get on the bus."

Tyrona sighed sympathetically and patted Kelly on the shoulder.

"Welcome to Beijing, girl. Let the games begin."

Using his elbow, and not being particularly polite about it, McCall was gaining on the kid when he raced into a lane of oncoming traffic, gaining the other side of the roadway amid screeching tires and the thump of a fender bender, followed by angry cursing in several languages. McCall sprinted across when he saw a break in the heavy traffic flow and resumed the chase, having lost valuable seconds. The kid was dashing into the stadium through an entrance that gave onto acres of shops, restaurants and arcades. The rapid slap-slapping of McCall's shoe leather on the sidewalk drew attention and cleared a way for him.

He thought, *Purse-snatchers.* It was a long way from guarding the Vice President of the United States.

He stormed through the entrance no more than fifteen seconds behind the kid, into the high domed, bright-as-day interior and for the first time, he lost sight of the perp. He hesitated, rooted firmly in the shuffling press of humanity surging about him, threatening to carry him away like driftwood on a fast current. He glanced about. He could radio for backup, but that would be overkill when all he was dealing with was a punk purse-snatcher.

Movement caught the corner of his eye.

Glimpsed through the thick, gold-tinted windows of an international restaurant, the kid in the baggy trousers and print shirt was a blur now, charging through an ornate dining room. McCall saw him collide with a waiter, sending the waiter toppling amid an airborne tray of food.

He had been trained to scan crowds, to detect slight

anomalies or unusual shifts in their composition; training courtesy of Uncle Sam's Secret Service, and they had trained him well—though not well enough to prepare him for that grand failure at Camp David two years ago when there hadn't even been a crowd. There had only been the Vice President, his family, and a security detail headed by Agent Taggart McCall. And, of course, there had been the assassination team that penetrated the outer defenses and made it so close to the house that the Vice President and his immediate family only barely escaped being shot. The would-be assassins—Russian ex-Spetnaz in the employ of someone never identified—were slain in a brutal firefight. Still, someone had to take the fall for such a total screwup. That someone was McCall. He found himself quietly, quickly and efficiently dropped from the government roles, unceremoniously booted into the street after an adult life spent in government service. No job. No friends. No history. No future, or so he'd thought at the time.

The following two years weren't easy. He did not take his fall from grace gracefully. Divorce. Annie took their fifteen-year-old daughter with her ("I won't have our child living with an alcoholic!") and moved back to California. The only way he could see Jen was to fly to the other side of the country for a court-approved visit. The fact that he was clean and sober and had been for six months thus far hadn't made a difference, although his lawyer in Maryland, where he maintained a residence, was working on it. But his daughter's mind and feelings had pretty well turned on him. He didn't blame Annie for poisoning Jen against him. They'd both seen him at his worst, a prideful, stupid, lost, abusive fool. He blamed himself for everything.

His resumé (glossing over the Camp David fiasco, naturally) had been enough to land him a job with a private U.S. security firm that had given him this assignment. So far, so good. Mc-

Call was a "floater," assigned to randomly stroll through the Olympic grounds, keeping his eyes open for trouble.

He angled through the crowd, toward the restaurant, struggling upstream against a tide of people leaving the stadium. It felt like fighting gravity.

And that's when the stabbing, white-hot pain jarred his heart, like being impaled with a hot poker, and for one terrible second, his every nerve end screamed nothing but agony . . . and then it was gone and the weird tingling, hollow sensation followed the constriction in his chest, and then it was as if nothing had happened.

The chest pains had started about three months ago, and at first he thought it was indigestion, but now he knew something was seriously wrong. During the past week, the attacks had become more frequent, there-and-gone jabs of pain, sometimes occurring twice a day where it used to happen only once a month. He kept putting off doing anything about it or telling anyone, as if keeping the secret would somehow make it go away. He would see a doctor about it as soon as he got back to the States.

He entered the restaurant's foyer, where people milled about, waiting to be admitted, mingling with those who were leaving. Beyond them, he saw the perp race through swinging doors leading to the kitchen. By the time McCall came running through the dining room in the kid's wake, the waiter had just picked himself up from the floor. McCall inadvertently bumped into him, knocking him over a second time as he charged past, muttering an apology over his shoulder that he wasn't sure the poor guy heard. Patrons scurried out of his way. He stormed into the kitchen at a dead run, an immaculate world of stainless steel and aged copper pots, the cleanliness nearly blinding. The clamor of a half-dozen cooks and their assistants at work had an industrious precision about it. The mingling scents of fried foods and spices filled the air.

The perp was on the far side of the large kitchen, having placed a cartful of dirty plates in his wake, just inside the swinging doors. McCall leaped over the obstacle without slackening his pace. Kitchen personnel were erupting into pandemonium around him, everyone trying to scramble out of harm's way. The perp kicked over a bucket of grease standing next to a grill, and the spill became a wicked slick. McCall briefly lost his footing and went pitching onto his backside, managing to twist about and recover his balance and continuing on up again, yanking his pistol from a concealed holster at the small of his back, under his T-shirt.

The kid was maybe ten yards ahead and moving fast toward where the narrow walkway intersected with a main thoroughfare. McCall gave chase, his longer, more powerful legs eating up the distance. He holstered his pistol. He would catch this rabbit before it got a chance to fade into the crowd. He wasn't about to take a human life over a stolen purse, no matter what the job or circumstance. And of course there was the danger of a bullet missing its mark and causing death or injury to innocent bystanders. When he was close enough, he propelled himself into a leap and took the young man down in a flying tackle.

The purse-snatcher emitted an *ooooff* as he hit the pavement. McCall had the perp's ankles with both arms and was about to roll the kid over and handcuff him, but he just laughed and started writhing like a snake shedding its skin. He slid out of the baggy trousers he was wearing, revealing a tighter-fitting pair of slacks worn underneath. Then he was up and running, leaving McCall holding the pair of empty pants.

McCall tossed the trousers aside and rose to his feet. This little brat was making it a real challenge. He had again lost sight of the kid.

That's when he heard the loud, unmistakable *thud* of a vehicle impacting a human body at a high rate of speed, drowned out under the squeal of tires and the dismayed cries of passersby. By the time he worked his way through the crowd to the curb, McCall saw at a glance, even in the artificial glow of the vapor lights and the fireworks overhead, that this perpetrator had snatched his last purse. The young man lay face down in the middle of the road, the lower half of his body twisted at an impossible angle from the upper half.

He radioed in the incident to the SOC dispatcher, Rose Campbell, a pleasant, good-looking gal his own age with a cigarettes-and-whiskey voice and a personality to match, although she, like him, would have to have been clean and sober to acquire her assignment. McCall and Rose had established a sort of ribald camaraderie over the tac net, but nothing had happened between them . . . yet.

She responded that an ambulance was being dispatched and would be arriving shortly.

"And when they get there," she added, "you high-tail it over to Loading Dock Seven. Something big's gone down over there."

"How big?"

"Don't know, Tag. Just get over there, okay? They're requesting all available personnel for crowd control."

An ambulance arrived in a flurry of flashing lights and ululating sirens.

In the confusion, McCall retrieved Kelly Jackson's purse and slipped it into his pocket. By the time he'd completed giving his statement to the Chinese police, her bus had delivered her team to the Olympic Village. He would get the girl's purse to her soon enough. But first, duty called.

He started walking in the direction of Dock Number Seven.

Purse-snatchers. Establishing crowd control. But it would look impressive on a resumé two weeks from now, he told himself, when the Olympics were over and done.

31

There was a funny, momentary clutching inside his chest, as if his heart murmured in agreement.

Two weeks. He could do that.

Sure, he could.

CHAPTER 3

The Chinese authorities had the crowd under control by the time he arrived at the Dock Seven gate, not that there were very many curiosity seekers. There was too much else going on, and whatever had happened here had been contained in an effective, low-key manner.

The police, who in China are uniformed officers of the Public Safety Bureau, made sure the vehicular traffic kept moving. There would be no gape spots to interrupt the orderly flow of people exiting the stadium grounds. The river of pedestrians passing a chain-link fence that bordered the dock area, paused to gather only near the gate, curious rubber-neckers drawn by the concentration of official vehicles bearing a wide array of government and Olympic authority markings. PSB officers did their best to dissuade pedestrians from gawking, urging people to keep moving, emphasized with an occasional poke with a baton.

The area was alive with the crackle of short-wave radios chattering in several languages and the flashing lights on official vehicles, an ambulance among them. Activity was at a standstill on the dock where workers stood idly watching. There was a heavy military presence. Soldiers blocked the gate, their silenced machine guns held at port arms. The guns were silenced to prevent panicking the crowd in case they were used. More soldiers formed a shoulder-to-shoulder line just inside the fence, holding up crowd-control shields to block the view from those outside of a narrow space between the fence and a passenger bus.

McCall raised Rose on his lapel mic. "Okay, I'm here. Now what? The local cops are in control."

Rose said into his ear, "Sid, Kawanda and Jeff should be circulating around there, too."

He saw Kawanda Brown off to his left, pretending not to notice him, playing the gawker from behind a Japanese family and some trendy Euro types. With those legs and the figure of a runway diva, Kawanda blended right in with the stylish Euros and a Hong Kong couple that happened along. Her eyes played over the moving crowd, watching.

McCall said, "Okay, I see Kawanda. So we're keeping an eye out for what, a perpetrator returning to the scene of a crime?"

Rose said, "I don't know if there's been a crime. It's still what they call breaking news. The Chinese have clamped down on it like a drum."

"So do we know anything?"

"Dan Price is involved."

"Okay, I just caught a glimpse of him too. Looks like he's in the middle of it."

Rose said, "Be safe, sugar. Something's coming in. Have to go," and she was no longer whispering in his ear.

Dan Price was inside the fenced-off area, standing toe-to-toe in earnest conversation with a uniformed PRC officer. More soldiers stood near them, their weapons not pointed at Price but not shoulder-slung either, aimed at the ground, a loose circle around Price and the officer he was conversing with near the front of the Green Olympics bus.

McCall could have been mistaken for just another gawker, which was his intention. He gravitated to a cluster of people on the far side of the gate from Kawanda. When a PSB officer nudged him along none too gently with a jab of his baton and a command in Cantonese, McCall strolled on, circling around and approaching the fence again, near where Kawanda had been standing. She had moved on, leaving him another opportunity to spy on Price and his predicament.

The Chinese officer was still doing most of the talking, but then Price spotted McCall over the man's shoulder. Price said something to the officer, who looked over his shoulder to stare straight at McCall.

Although there were several levels of bureaucracy between them, Price was essentially McCall's boss. McCall's paycheck was cut by Amberson, Inc., one of the private contract firms that had been cleared by the Chinese government to provide security for athletes as well and other services such as ground security in the form of people like McCall and Kawanda. Dan Price was Amberson's liaison with Special Operations Command, under whose aegis the security outfits operated.

The officer issued a command. Soldiers scurried to carry out that order and, less than a minute later, a PRC regular stood at McCall's either side, holding him in a vise-like grip just above the elbow and leading him through the gate, past the line of soldiers with their raised shields by the bus, toward where Price, the officer and his circle of rifle-bearing soldiers awaited him.

McCall fought the impulse to throw aside the two young soldiers escorting him. He had the size, strength and the training to do it, but they were just conscripted kids obeying orders, and this was as good a way as any to learn what had gone down. As they passed the bus, he saw what the line of soldiers was holding up their shields to prevent passersby from seeing.

The ambulance had backed up to the scene. Its rear doors yawned open. Three body bags were on the ground, approximately equidistant from each other, each being tagged by technicians prior to being transferred into the ambulance.

Dan Price's All-American/Navy SEAL–type build and rugged

good looks were frayed around the edges. He and McCall had never exchanged more than mundane pleasantries after SOC briefings. Price made a point of handshaking each person in the room to size them up as his personnel. McCall liked that.

Price said, "Tag, glad you're here. This is Major Yang, of the Internal Security Bureau."

Yang was unusually slight of build even for a Chinese, but the way he held himself, with his shoulders back, chin thrust out, not belligerently but combatively, and the direct, unblinking gaze from behind his steel-rimmed spectacles, combined to project authority and command. In his late-forties, he wore his smartly starched and pressed uniform like a second skin. He regarded McCall with eyes like flint.

"You will show me identification." He said with a sibilant Mandarin accent, the classic language of China, not the more common Cantonese.

McCall produced his wallet and extended his laminated Olympics ID for inspection. Yang snatched it from him and scrutinized the card, twice lifting flinty eyes from the photograph to compare it with McCall's features.

Price said, "Sorry to drag you into this, McCall. The Internal Security Bureau reports to the Ministry of State Security. They—"

Yang returned McCall's ID.

He said, as if he was not interrupting Price, "A most serious crime was narrowly avoided here tonight, but in the process, three people were killed. I am the ranking investigating officer. Mr. Price has suggested that you may have pertinent information."

McCall felt a sharpening of his every sense. Quite a bump up from trolling for pickpockets. "What information could I have? I don't even know what happened here."

"Suffice to say that degenerate reactionaries, enemies of

China, were foiled by a squad of our elite soldiers in the act of perpetrating what would have been a calamitous act. Mr. Price assisted the squad of soldiers."

Price cleared his throat. "Uh, please let me tell him the rest, Major. I'd feel better if you did."

Yang's eyes never seemed to blink behind the magnifying thickness of his glasses. "Feelings are hardly my concern, Mr. Price. Mr. McCall, two men were captured. Chinese nationals. One died, shot to death by Mr. Price."

Price muttered. "But not before the bastard killed their squad leader and one of our people."

McCall felt his throat go dry. A multiple homicide? He hadn't expected anything like this.

"Who did we lose?"

Price said, "Jody Simms. The son of a bitch had a blade on him that the soldiers missed and he used it to pick his handcuffs, don't ask me how." The words poured grimly forth, a surge of emotion. "He got the drop on Captain Li, then cut Jody down with Li's machine gun before I could put a bullet between his eyes. If only I'd been three seconds faster . . ." The words bleakly tapered off.

McCall had met Jody Simms, but that was about all. She and Rose had started palling around on their off-time and on two occasions Jody had joined Rose and McCall at their little table in the employees canteen. McCall pictured a bright-eyed, eminently competent, and likeable young woman who he would have never expected to lose so young, sparkling with the immortality of youth. *And now, forever young . . .*

He said, "I'll do anything I can to help."

Yang continued to scrutinize him. "You knew her?"

"We were co-workers, in a sense, though we didn't work together. She was a friend of a friend. If I knew more about what you're looking for—"

Price's craggy features were carved in stone, his emotions again held in check. "We don't know that ourselves. Jody wasn't even supposed to be here, that's what makes it worse. Yang's people had intel they were working and Captain Li was in charge. I was just along."

Price spoke with monotonic precision, like a cop at a crime scene. This time, Yang appeared satisfied with allowing him to speak. Yang listened, not missing a word or a nuance. McCall sensed a brain like a computer behind those flinty, bespeckled eyes. McCall hadn't seen any reason to initiate a personal background check on Dan Price, but he had the resources to do so, and he was certain that even a cursory search would yield a background in police procedure, military interrogation or both. A man drawing Price's honcho duties with the Special Operations Command made such a background mandatory, along with a squeaky clean professional and personal record.

McCall asked, "So why was Jody here if she wasn't supposed to be?"

Price said, "That's what we need to find out. Jody told me she said she had something and was secretive as hell and all caught up in it, but she never got the chance to tell me. What she had sounded vague. The bust went down and," he swallowed audibly, but his expression remained impassive. "Well, you know what happened."

"My conversations with her were strictly social," said McCall, "light and superficial."

Price said, "This mutual friend, Rose Campbell."

"That's right. Talk to Rose. She never said anything to me about Jody regarding anything sinister."

"Oh, we'll have a talk with Miss Campbell, you can count on that," said Price.

As if on cue, a small green van with SOC markings drew to a stop outside the gate. A side door slid open and a trio of men

38

emerged, their build and attire matching Price's, right down to shoulder-holstered pistols. They stood with their muscle-corded arms folded, scowling, emanating the impression, *Where's our man? We're not leaving without him.*

Price said, "Uh, will that be all, Major? I was hoping McCall here could furnish something but since he can't, well, uh, are we done for now? I want to get back to the office and try to pick up on whatever Jody came here to tell me about."

Yang considered this and nodded.

"I appreciate the service you have rendered our country tonight, Mr. Price. Captain Li's men in any case would have eliminated the treacherous dog who killed the Captain and your Miss Simms. But the fact of the matter is that you were here and you acted heroically. You avenged the death not only of Miss Simms, but also of a fine officer of the People's Republic of China. Necessary paperwork will be forwarded to your office in the morning. You will be expected to give a deposition at that time."

"Of course."

"Then for now you are free to go. On behalf of my country, I thank you, sir."

Price's stony features grew tight. His eyes were on the medics who were loading the body bags into the ambulance.

"Thanks, Major, but I feel more like condolences than appreciation. You're done with McCall too, right?"

Yang said, "For now," and he turned his back on them.

They walked to the gate.

McCall said, "That was a tough break. Jody seemed like a nice kid."

"Yeah. A nice kid. I called her New Breed." Price spoke brusquely, a growl more clipped than before. "Always underfoot. Always. She could be such a pain in the ass. Damn shame."

Personnel strode purposefully about, much of their attention centering on a step van parked midway between the bus and the loading dock. Radio chatter continued to pepper the air.

When they reached the SOC van at the gate, the trio of hard-cases—that was the only way McCall could think of them—stepped aside for Price to board. Each man wore the small laminated clip-on ID designating him as a member of the Special Operations Command.

McCall raised an eyebrow. "Enforcement arm of the SOC? Were they going to extract you if Major Yang came on too strong?"

The night was awash with the flash of multicolored lights from the official vehicles, creating here-and-gone shadows, making it impossible for McCall to read Price, even this close.

Price said, "I'm glad it didn't come to that. I'd offer you a ride back to the head shed but, uh, you're on duty, right?"

"Right. I'm a floater, so I guess I'll float along."

Price extended a hand. "Thanks for the help."

It was a firm, short handshake, the kind a man likes. Price boarded the van, the SOC guys clambering in behind him. The last one in closed the sliding door, and the van drove away.

Leaving McCall with things to think about. He angled away from the main gate and resumed mixing with the crowd. Thanks for your help. He hadn't contributed a damn thing back there and he knew it. Sure, he knew the dead woman slightly, but that was all he had and that was nothing. Or was Price just being polite?

And there was something else.

He hoped he was wrong. The flashing lights and the shadows and the movement notwithstanding, he could have sworn that, in his last glimpse of Dan Price in the interior of the van before the side door had slid shut, he'd seen Price speaking to one of the SOC men . . . and *smiling*.

CHAPTER 4

"Honey, are you feeling all right?"

"Guess I'm just worn out, Mom. It's been quite a day. And I wish someone would show up with my purse. I sure hope they got the guy who took it."

The roaring of the crowd, the music and the fireworks of the stadium ceremonies still seemed to ring in her ears.

Kelly normally would have been embarrassed by her mother publicly placing the back of her fingers to her daughter's forehead, to check Kelly's body temperature. But in this spacious, overcrowded, noisy dining room (did *everything* in China have to be larger than life?), her mother's touch softened the edge she had felt creeping over her. The party was seeming to drag on and on and strangely, right in the middle of all this celebration and socializing, she could feel the twinge of the nervous little child who slept in her jersey before weekend gymnastics, and who always counted on her mom.

"Yes, quite a day," her mom echoed with a chuckle. "For that matter, honey, it's been quite a four years getting here, and you're entitled to feel a little washed out." The back of her fingers left Kelly's forehead. "But you don't feel warm. You'll be fine. Just put on a happy smile. There are agency people here tonight, sweetie. Remember Mary Lou Retton? If we want to get you on millions of boxes of Wheaties, this is where it can happen." She patted Kelly's hand. "Now smile, honey. The show must go on!"

And that, thought Kelly, *could pretty much be her epitaph.* That was, if the day ever came when death managed to corral this sugarcoated dynamo. Candace Jackson, who even on an off day could be, and often was, mistaken for Kelly's older sister, was a young thirty-nine with a trim figure, a set of store-bought boobs to die for, and some plastic surgery, not enough to be obvious, around the chin and eyes to enhance a green-eyed, dazzling smile guaranteed to ignite any scene she chose to dominate. Her devotion to Kelly's career was either extremely supportive— Candace Jackson was in fact the official president of her daughter's online fan club, which had a registered membership in the thousands—or she was driven by that maniacal tunnel vision of countless show business moms before her. But she meant well.

Kelly's dad sipped from his glass of champagne.

"It's the pollution we're being forced to breathe every minute we're here. It's been playing hell with my sinuses since we landed."

Dad owned a car dealership in Brookfield, a suburb of Milwaukee, and had done all right for himself. Steve Jackson appeared in his own ads on local television. He was an amiable man of quiet strength, not particularly handsome, but with those middle-aged, steadfast good looks that men trusted and women felt comfortable with. A nice man. Theirs was a solid little family unit. Dad's success allowed them to regularly travel with her, and of course nothing would have kept them from Beijing, though her father had been griping about the infamously foul air even before they'd arrived.

Tyrona sipped her ginger ale. "Well, if we all want something to complain about, I'll complain about this here party. Borr-rring. There isn't a male here under the age of thirty!"

Candace said, "Well, Tyrona, it is a party for the *girls'* team."

"I'm down with that, Mrs. J. But that's why there should be

some boys, is all I'm saying." Like Kelly and their other team-mates at the party, Tyrona wore the uniform she'd marched in tonight, but somehow she still managed to look fresh and sparkling, even after the long day. "It's just that if it was up to me, there'd be a few fellas around who weren't old enough to have one foot in the grave. No offense, Mr. J."

Steve Jackson laughed a good-natured laugh. "None taken, Miss Thang." It was his pet name for Tyrona, whom they all adored.

Candace's attention shifted across the sea of socializing people. "It seems our Boris has his hands full in the romance department."

Boris Temerov was engaged in a close-in, personal conversation with a stunning brunette near the wet bar, which was getting heavy play from the adults.

Tyrona emitted a mock theatrical sigh. "I wish those two would just give it up." She nudged Kelly with an elbow. "My trainer and your trainer. What a match. The only time they see each other is when we get together for competition."

Kelly said, "Boris is an impressive man. He never remarried after his wife passed away all those years ago. I've seen women throw themselves at him. Women of all ages."

Her mother's smile grew brittle as she listened.

Temerov was nearing sixty, but had the lean musculature of an athlete thirty years younger. His coifed silvery hair indicated a streak of vanity, but his manner was one of poise and author-ity. Square jawed, with a trimmed salt-and-pepper beard, he was well turned out in tan slacks, open-necked shirt and a blue blazer. His eyes had been on Kelly across the room even as An-drea Cometti spoke to him, the exaggerated, purely Italian gesturing of her right hand jabbing in the air, becoming more emphatic. She caught herself and paused when she realized that Boris's attention was elsewhere.

43

Tyrona said, "Trouble in paradise."

Andrea was twenty years Boris's junior. Her figure was full, rounded in the hips and brazenly lush, front and back. By today's anorexic standards she might consider herself a trifle overweight, but to a man of Boris Temerov's age and background, she was voluptuous. She wore a strapless red gown, matching heels, purse and a necklace of carved jade.

She slapped Boris's face and stalked away, her head thrown back brazenly, midnight hair streaming with every determined stride away from Temerov, in the opposite direction of Kelly and those with her.

Boris stood for a moment and watched Andrea go. He seemed to Kelly like a solitary man even, or especially, in the center of all these happy people. He raised a palm to the side of his face where Andrea had delivered the slap. Those around Boris pretended not to have noticed, as if nothing had happened. The party went on, the conversations growing louder as a DJ kept the music volume notched up. Boris let his hand drop to his side and drew himself up straight with a deep breath, then started in their direction.

Tyrona said, in a stage whisper to Kelly and her parents, "I wonder how many of our trainers are, y'know, involved? Well, later," and she drifted away to mingle with some other girls on the team and the people with them.

Candace sighed. "Boris and Andrea certainly are a passionate pair. I suppose you have to be passionate to instill in others the desire to win." Kelly couldn't tell if her mother was disapproving or envious.

Her dad said, "Hush, now. It's Boris's business, not ours."

Kelly found herself nodding in agreement. "I wonder what else is going on around us right now that we don't even know about."

From behind her, a man's voice said, "Miss Jackson?"

CHAPTER 5

When Kelly Jackson turned to face him, McCall had an instantaneous reaction. A radiant spirit shone through a tired smile and intelligent eyes ready to meet and greet the world. She reminded McCall of Jennifer, and he assumed the adults with her to be her parents. He could see the family resemblance between mother and daughter. Jen wasn't into sports. Music was her thing, playing her guitar and writing songs like everyone from Jewel to Amy Winehouse. So they were different on the surface, but not at the core of a strong reserve of inner strength, call it resiliency. McCall wondered how his daughter was doing and his chest gave a tiny flutter inside, not painful, just a ripple to make him take a sharp breath and the thought crossed his mind, *Don't let me die in a foreign land without seeing my daughter again . . .*

"My purse!" Kelly's eyes popped wide and so did her smile. "You brought my purse!" She grabbed the diminutive handbag and clutched it like a mother reunited with a lost child. "Oh, I was so hoping you'd find it . . . and that you'd find me! Thank you so much, Mr.—"

It was difficult to suppress a smile in the face of this girlish enthusiasm, so he didn't try. "McCall. My pleasure."

"Mr. McCall, this is my father, Steve Jackson."

Jackson lifted his champagne glass in a cordial toast. "Well done. Do we owe you a reward?"

The blonde woman at his side stepped forward. Like her

husband, she appeared mildly buzzed on the champagne. She was undressing McCall with her eyes from head to heel.

"No, of course we don't tip him, Stephen."

"My mother," Kelly said to McCall by way of introduction.

"That would be an insult, like tipping a police officer, wouldn't it, Mr. McCall? Thank you so very much for performing your duties in such an exemplary manner."

She shifted her glass to her left hand and extended her right, and when her slim hand made contact with his flesh, a small electrical charge was generated when their palms pressed, as is usually reserved for a caress, not a handshake. Her eyes having finished sizing him up, were locked on his like twin laser beams.

McCall thought, *Uh-oh.*

He said, "Well, good night folks. Good luck at the Games, Miss Jackson. I'd better be getting back to my duties." He would have tipped his cap brim if he'd been wearing one—*just doing my job, ma'am*—but before he could disengage, a muscular, bearded guy, who McCall's mental database tabbed as Boris Temerov, joined them.

Temerov addressed Candace without preamble. "I saw you checking Kelly's body temperature."

Candace said, "Oh, she's fine. Aren't you, honey? Boris, are there people here tonight that you want us to meet?"

"No."

"No?"

"We must remember why we are here. Landing the big advertising contracts and so on can only come after the competition." Temerov's Eastern European accent had nearly disappeared after decades of life in America.

"Yes, I know, Boris," said Candace, "and I know that we've spoken about this before, but I was just thinking—"

He said, "My duty, my only concern, the sole reason for my and your daughter's presence in Beijing, is to *win*. That is all that matters and for that, Kelly must be well rested and focused at all times. I myself grow weary of this idle fraternization. Kelly, I will accompany you as far as your dorm if you'll permit me."

"Thanks, Boris. That would be great."

McCall couldn't help but note warmth and candid familiarity in the way she spoke that hadn't been there before Temerov had joined them.

Mrs. Jackson started to mouth a mild protest, but before she could speak, Steve Jackson said, "That would be fine, Boris." He gave his daughter a hug and a kiss on the forehead. "Good night, honey." He started to introduce McCall. "Boris, this is Mr.—"

"Another time," said Temerov. He whisked Kelly away, an arm solicitously about her shoulder, having successfully avoided eye contact with McCall. "Come then, child. It has been too long a day for the both of us, and tomorrow—" Their conversation was lost beneath the sounds of the party as they withdrew.

Candace watched them go. Her arms were folded before her. Her green eyes were steely points. "Sometimes that man is infuriating—"

Her husband put an arm around her waist.

"Now, lion, he's brought our little girl this far, hasn't he? She's at the Olympics, for crying out loud. If Boris says she needs to rest, then that's what she needs, especially if it's what Kelly wants. We trust our little girl, don't we?"

"Of course we do, but—"

McCall couldn't miss the wordless appeal in the look Steve Jackson sent him, and he was only too glad to take his cue.

"Good night, folks. Nice to have met you."

He left them feeling damn glad that he was not a part of their world, a compressed, self-contained world, and that included the daughter and her trainer, that pulsed with undercurrents

47

too deep for his concern or comfort. On the front steps of the building, he inhaled deeply, and even the heavy Beijing night air tasted fresh after the confines of the party.

He didn't blame Kelly for wanting out of there, nor Boris Temerov for that matter. He only wished he'd had the opportunity to read Boris eye-to-eye, up close. He would not tell Kelly that she reminded him of his daughter. That was too damn corny, and could be misconstrued by a mommy who was sending out signals of her own, or by a protective father. But Kelly Jackson did remind him of Jen, and it must have been for that reason that he felt a protective impulse toward Kelly that he wished he could act on. But that would only happen if she was in some sort of danger and, despite those undercurrents he'd picked up, he had to accept that Kelly was in good hands. Now that she'd been reunited with her purse, it was time to go on about his business.

The tree-lined walkways of the Olympic Village wended past well-tended meditation gardens that retained subtle, pleasant fragrances, even this late at night. More than one party was in progress in the Village, yet its residential atmosphere was a world away from the celebratory throngs that would still be filtering from the massive stadium.

McCall made his way toward a shuttle stop where he would catch a lift back to the stadium. The encounter at the party had momentarily distracted him from the sight of body bags being loaded onto an ambulance. Jody, poor Jody Simms. He wondered if Price's people had contacted Rose yet with the news, or would he be the one to tell her?

And he wondered about something else.

He wondered, back at the scene of whatever crime had gone down at that loading dock, why Dan Price had drawn him into it in the first place, as if McCall might have some important information that could make or break the case. That's the impression Price had been trying to make on Major Yang. Why? Something—some *thing*—wasn't right.

Let it go, he told himself. *Get back to work. Let it go.*

Dan Price pretended to be deeply moved by Jody Simms's ultimate sacrifice, but the truth of the matter was that he was damn glad to be rid of the snotty little know-it-all. His taste was for women, not grown-up tomboys who wanted to play with guns. Well, one bitch was done playing, for keeps.

An hour after the firefight, he stepped off by himself and, with no one paying attention, he thumbed autodial on his cell phone.

She answered on the first ring.

"You were never to call this number."

"I'm sorry. Something's happened." It was his plan, but he'd needed her to get General Chu set up and she had ended up setting up Chu and Dan Price in different ways. She had turned the tables on him and now he needed her for all kinds of things. He said, "There's been a problem, but I've taken care of it."

"Tell me, quickly."

This was a conversation beamed into outer space and back again via a satellite owned by Amberson, Inc.'s parent corporation, a signal impenetrable to even Federal eavesdropping.

"I've got to keep it short," said Price. "People are checking up on me. Remember Jody?"

"Of course. I detest women like her."

"Then you'll be happy to know that she is now among the dearly departed. I, uh, had to improvise, but it went down smooth. But before I took her out, she told me she'd come up with a name."

"Mine or yours?"

"Uh, I . . . I, uh, took her out before she could say."

"Idiot! You should have learned more and how she came by

her information."

"Uh, the point is, I'm calling to warn you. Be careful."

"I'm always careful, darling. General Chu is freshening my drink and waiting for me. Would you like to know what I'm wearing?"

"Yes, please."

She laughed softly. "Not now. I have the People's Liberation Army by the balls, literally in the next room. You command a squad of heavily armed and trained men loyal to you alone."

Price said, "Loyal to the cut they've been promised."

"Everything is in place, right where we want it."

"They'll be talking about this for the rest of the century."

She laughed softly again. "And that is how long it will take you to spend the money on me. Am I right?"

Price felt foolish, incompetent as always when she badgered him like this. And he felt again the white-hot throb of sexual hunger.

"Yes, ma'am."

"Now hang up the phone, slave. Mistress has work to do."

CHAPTER 6

The 29th Olympiad commenced under the clearest, cleanest skies that any previous visitor to Beijing could recall. Nothing mattered more to the Chinese than making a good impression on the nine million visitors besieging their city, and the satellite news media beaming live sights and sounds from Beijing to the world on an hourly basis. The government had ordered a complete, phased-in shutdown of all industry over the preceding months, weeks and days. It was hoped that the comfortable blue skies would remind the European, the Australian, or the visitor from Calgary, Alberta, of home, another subtle step toward globalization, the unification of east and west. China would benefit enormously through future investment and the economic bubble would only grow. Industry would kick back in to make up for time lost the moment the last Olympic visitor was on the last plane home.

Security was conspicuous, manned checkpoints at all entrances to the venues as well as walking patrols of soldiers, visible security for the athletes augmented by hundreds of cameras trained on practically every square foot of the Olympic Green. Additional plainclothes personnel circulated through the crowds.

Altogether, thirty-one venues were being used during the Olympics, most notably the National Stadium for athletics and football, the dazzling National Aquatics Center, which was hosting the swimming, diving, water polo and synchronized swimming competition, and the newly constructed National Indoor Stadium where the gymnastic, trampoline and handball competitions were held. Twenty-five hundred large-size buses and forty-five hundred minibuses were being operated by a total of eight thousand drivers to transport people to and from the various venues. Attendees were advised to allow three hours between events. There were the inevitable random delays due to language or cultural barriers, but these were quickly resolved and for the most part an air of civility, a classic sense of Mandarin grace rarely seen in the streets of Beijing, permeated opening day of the Olympics and was duly noted by most media commentators . . .

J. Bob Wiley had never seen so many damn foreigners. Back where J. Bob—or Joseph Robert, as his mother had always called him—hailed from, there wasn't hardly anybody but white folks. There were always some niggers around, of course, and lately beaners up from Mexico when the meager crops were ready for harvesting, but since he'd caught the Greyhound in front of Tucker's Store on the main drag and left home three days ago, J. Bob had been swept away in a world that sometimes felt like it was populated by nothing but what they called minorities.

One night, when he and Ma and Pa had been watching Comedy Central, some uppity comic had come on saying to a non-white audience that the only reason the minorities were flocking in to do the honest work was because inbred white folks were too damn lazy. The studio audience had still been whooping it up about that when Pa had picked up his shotgun and blew that TV to smithereens in disgust. Ma gave him holy hell of course, but there were three other TVs in the trailer, so it was okay.

When his Ma spoke to him in his dreams these days, she still called him Joseph Robert. And she kept telling him that he was doing the right thing, walking the righteous path, wanting to smite the people of those who had killed her and Pa on that pilgrimage to the Holy Land. Pastor Hemshaw had taken several families, including Ryman and Margaret Wiley. Five local families in all, including the pastor and his wife, gone ten days to see Jerusalem. And they never returned. A terrorist car bomb killed them all, along with sightseers from England, Japan and a half dozen European countries, during a visit to one of the ancient shopping bazaars.

J. Bob had started paying attention to the news on television then, to Fox News and CNN and the rest. The massacre was a big story, naturally. Whoever detonated the bomb had been vaporized in the blast that demolished the tourist bus, but the TV reported that it was traced to al Qaeda and that's where it started to get confusing. Politics and religion in the Mideast, and none of it made sense to J. Bob. What had his Ma and Pa ever done to make a bunch of ragheads want to blow them up? None of the talking heads on TV had an answer for that one.

J. Bob didn't need an answer. At twenty-seven, he still lived at home. He had gone to church with his Ma every Sunday. Vengeance is mine, sayeth the Lord. But Ma had taught him that he was an instrument of God's will. The way he figured, after watching enough news reports and burying Ma and Pa in a twin ceremony with closed caskets, them rotten Arab sons of bitches were no dang good and if no one else was going to avenge his flesh and blood, then J. Bob would see to it on his own.

The Greyhound had taken him as far as Texarkana, then another bus to Houston and he had flown out of Houston on this journey that had taken him to the other side of the world, where *he* was the minority, coming all the way to this cramped cheap seat in a huge auditorium, watching a wrestling match between the Afghan team and some European team.

Foreigners hemmed him in on every side, some of whom were cheering while others watched with rapt attention. It wasn't like the wrestling matches he'd gone to with Ma and Pa back home. One time they'd driven all the way to Jackson to see Baron von Blood knock the bejaspers out of his opponent, Captain Texas, using the referee as a human club. Of course everyone knew that sometime in the not too distant future, Captain Texas would take down the Baron and it wouldn't be pretty. Insults and aluminum cans, and not a few contraband bottles, had showered Baron von Blood that night in Jackson when the mousy, intimidated ref grudgingly hoisted his arm in victory. All the way home J. Bob and his folks had enthused about the dignity and restraint shown by Captain Texas who, regaining consciousness in the ring during announcement of the Baron's win, had to be held back at first from wanting to take the Baron apart right then and there, before choosing to concede gallantly, promising the Baron and the wild crowd that there would be another time, another battle between Captain Texas and Baron von Blood. Now *that* was wrestling! J. Bob found no such enthusiasm among this Olympic audience, which had to be nine or ten times the size of that crowd in Jackson. Even the cheering was polite whenever a wrestler scored points.

The outside of this massive venue was designed to evoke a folding fan, but inside to J. Bob it was nothing but overcrowded humanity, adding to the pressure that had started building behind his eyes, between his ears, when he first boarded that Greyhound back home and inhaled its stale air, like air that had been breathed too many times. The pressure was building because he saw Ma and Pa every time he closed his eyes, especially Ma, and he could hear her voice. He could hear her singing in church, standing beside him and Pa. And he remembered the Old Testament stories they told. An eye for an eye. A tooth for a tooth. *In this case, as many of these raghead ter-*

rorists as he could find a way to kill!

He wasn't sure yet how he was going to do it, and there was every chance that he wouldn't survive it, that he would lose his life wreaking the Lord's vengeance upon those that had stolen his parents from him. If so, let it be. He was ready. From Heaven, Ma and Pa were directing him.

But how would he do it? *How* would he kill? He was still working on that part. That's why he was sizing up as many games as he could with Arab teams, and getting as close to the Arab housing areas as their security patrols allowed. He would find a way. That's another thing Ma had taught him. *"Son, where there's a will, there's a way. You remember that. Always do what's got to be done."* Pa had just nodded in agreement and chewed his Skoal.

There was security all over, plain to see. Everywhere you looked, there was Chinese military, Beijing police, American and other personnel working security assignments. Cameras everywhere. And yes, guns everywhere.

Guns, now *that* was something he knew all about.

His eyes drifted back to the ring. A new match had begun, but he could not have cared less. Instead, he watched the armed security personnel positioned between the front rows of the audience and the competing athletes. He had been a bouncer back home at Tadpole's for a summer, and didn't mind roughing it up, even that time he'd taken sick leave because four GIs on leave didn't feel like quieting down and stop their bottle-busting, and they'd sent him to the ER with a busted nose, a cracked rib and two teeth missing. Within a week he'd tracked those guys down and paid them back with interest, when they didn't have each other to gang up on him. J. Bob Wiley didn't mind roughhousing and that's what it would take, he could see that now. He could charge one of those boys with a machine gun and wrestle it away and he'd blow away every Arab he saw and most likely end up in Heaven, reunited with Ma and Pa.

He had to do it, and he would. Not here. Not now. But when the time and place and circumstance were right, very soon now, he would strike. He would draw back the lid of Hell for those terrorist raghead sons of bitches. When he was sure that he could get the largest number of them in his sights, he would grab him one of those machine guns and open fire.

It would be easy.

CHAPTER 7

That night, McCall and Rose went out on a date they'd made days earlier. Neither one had an early shift scheduled for the following morning.

He greeted her with what had become their customary hug. "How are you doing, Rosie?"

"I'm glad you're taking me out to dinner."

"It's rough, what happened to Jody."

Pliant, full lips that on recent dates he'd taken to kissing good night, lips that could laugh with a merry bawdiness or merely smile with a warmth that always touched him inside, razored now into a severe line.

She took his arm. "Let's go exploring. I'm in the mood to see something new tonight."

The Chinese government had spent forty billion dollars on new streets and subway lines to improve the city's power grid and environment, making it an easy, fast trip on the metro to the Sanlitun district, the city's oldest and still most popular nightlife area.

They took in the sights, the sounds and excitement of Sanlitun Lu, a north–south strip of drinking establishments one long block east of Workers' Stadium. The bars along Sanlitun Lu were rowdy and raunchy, packed to overflowing with trendy, affluent young Chinese and the same international ethnic and cultural makeup as the Olympics. It was difficult to distinguish the many bars along what translated as Bar Street. Gaudy but tightly squeezed-in little hole-in-the-walls blaring neon in Chinese and English with names like the Side By Side and People Are Strange, with barkers out front shouting how good their bar was. "Just come in and take a seat!" There were a few flower sellers and DVD sellers, but more than seventy local laws and decrees had banished vagrants, beggars and people with mental illness from the city; a "special holiday," or forcible shutout, to make Beijing citizens stay at home during the Olympics.

McCall entwined his fingers with Rose's, and just like that they were holding hands and strolling along through the neon craziness like a couple of high school kids. When their eyes met, her smile was weak, sad, and he knew it would not be long now before they spoke of Jody. But not yet. It was too noisy along Sanlitun Lu to seriously discuss anything.

At the corner where the Phoenix Hotel rose into the night sky like a glittery beacon, they turned west and continued along the crowded sidewalks of the sprawling business district. Hotels and busy shopping malls, towering skyscrapers and an endless stream of traffic made the city seem much the same as any other. They chose a Western-style restaurant on one of the streets opposite Workers' Stadium, situated next to a disco and across from the stately City Hotel. There were more than a few such restaurants in Beijing, catering both to the locals and to homesick tourists. Well into the main course of roast duck, they chose by unspoken mutual consent to indulge in little more than small talk about the sights and sounds that had engulfed them since having left the subway station.

At last she said, with that smile he was coming to like more and more but with the sadness still in her eyes, "This is nice, Tag. Everybody expected the first day to be a bear, especially after last night, and no one was disappointed. I was dispatching like crazy. The nuttiest one had to be when the fans of the Iraqi soccer team got into a brawl with fans of the Lebanese team. Our people broke it up before the satellite news crowd could move in. They would have loved that one."

McCall had been waiting for the opportunity to speak what was on his mind. An idea had taken shape during the course of the day, which had been routine enough. Another purse snatching, although this one got away. Separate incidents involving holdup men who he just happened to stumble upon, making him wonder how many more such incidents were transpiring in the massed mob of humanity that was the Olympics. The holdups hadn't involved weapons, but threats of physical violence. McCall had taken down each man and summoned backup. And there had been the chore of hassling boy prostitutes who were trolling near the men's restroom facilities. The female sector of the world's oldest profession was mostly working off-street, assignations lined up via cell phone and credit card, but the gay hookers hadn't become that sophisticated or organized yet. And there had been more crowd control when some old German had decided to drop dead right in the main entrance of the Laoshan Velodrome after a cycling competition, and that had backed up traffic for thirty minutes. During it all, the events of last night kept returning to him, replaying in his mind. Routine kept it in check, and so had the exploring, the sights and sounds of Beijing at night. But now it was time to speak of what mattered.

He said, "Here's to Jody," and they clinked glasses.

"She did needlepoint, did you know that?"

"No. I didn't know anything about her, just those times when we ran into her."

"She was damn good at needlepoint. I always thought it was for little old ladies. Guess I was wrong. But it was funny to think about this competent, gun-toting woman living in a man's world, from the Detroit PD for crying out loud and, oh, Tag . . ."

"Did anything come through HQ today about it?"

"Not that I know of. Dan Price has closed the matter below his level, and that's well over my head."

"And you can bet the Chinese have shut it down from their side."

"Tag, I don't have a clue what happened at that loading dock last night, and I was at the dispatch console."

"That's why I want to talk about it," said McCall. "I know if anyone in the media went to the Chinese or the SOC, they wouldn't even get confirmation that anything happened. But Price has to walk past your station whenever he comes in or goes out."

"Supposedly."

"Last night when he broke the news to you about Jody, did he ask questions?"

"He wanted to know what we had been talking about over the past few days."

"And?"

Rose chuckled, a pleasing sound to his ears. He refilled her wine glass.

"Well, I guess we talked about nothing really, to be honest. I mean, you know, everyday stuff. Hair, shoes, men, the usual girl stuff. We talked about the crowds and how busy we were. Nothing ominous."

"I wonder why he wanted to know that?"

Rose frowned. "Why wouldn't he, if he was investigating Jody's death?"

"Because he knows who killed Jody. Supposedly it was a crazed prisoner with a knife. What do you think of him, Rosie?"

She blinked at the abrupt query. "He's been all business around me. He's never made a workplace pass at me. That always gets a man extra points."

He grinned. "Present company excluded?"

"Damn right and you know it, you big lug." They clinked glasses in a silent toast, then she asked, "So why all the curiosity about Dan?"

"Did he tell you that he pulled me off crowd and drew me into the on-site investigation?"

"No."

"It's been bugging me ever since, the *why* of it." He briefly told her what had happened at the loading dock, finishing with, "I had the feeling Price was improvising."

"How do you mean?"

"I'm not sure. A prisoner killed a PRA officer and Jody Simms, and then Price says he shot and killed the prisoner. That's an open and shut, clear-cut case."

"Was Major Yang suspicious of Dan?"

"No, and that's why Dan Price improvising is just a little too cute, and guys who play it too cute make me curious."

Rose drew back and there was new interest in her eyes. "That's a tone I haven't heard from you before."

He said, "I liked Jody. That's the only thing I know about her from the two times we met. I liked her. And now she's dead. I don't want whoever killed her to get away with it."

"And you think Dan Price . . ." She frowned at the thought. "Friendly fire? A cover-up?"

He shrugged. "My supervisor pulls me off crowd control and pitches me at the PRA Major. He threw me at Yang as a distraction, a diversion; extra hedging, just in case his story wasn't airtight enough."

"You could be wrong."

"I don't think so."

"You're a suspicious son of a bitch, did you know that, Mc-Call? You give a woman a lot to think about."

"So I've been told."

"I want to help. If you're right about Dan and there is

something going on . . . what can I do?"

"It would be nice if I knew who he called in the first half hour after his boys wheeled him away last night."

"I can do that."

"Don't get caught, Rosie. Don't take any risks."

She said, "You let me worry about that. Let's order dessert."

CHAPTER 8

The Tit For Tat Club was filled to capacity, and in Beijing that meant jam-packed. Most of the bars along Sanlitun Lu were small, and in China, people tend to stand and sit much closer together than in a Western club. Patrons were four deep at the American bar, which ran the length of the establishment. They stood, shouting orders. Everyone was smoking, the atmosphere so dense that the neon beer signs behind the bar were vague blurs of color beyond the wafting gray haze. The parties squeezed into the row of tables along the wall opposite the bar hardly had elbow room to raise their glasses. Traditional music was piped in from the speakers to either side of a curtained stage at the far end of the place.

Marv Helman would have chosen a higher class place, but as the CIA's officer in charge of the Beijing station, he had long ago adapted to local custom, or as much as any *gwai-lo* (foreign devil) could. He tipped a waiter two hundred RMB, which got him past a velvet rope to the warmly paneled and carpeted, dimly lit seating area with discreetly distanced booths and tables. A pretty waitress came over promptly and Helman ordered Coca-Colas for his three-drink minimum.

He allowed himself to relax in the padded booth. He lit a cigarette, grateful as always that he had yet to draw a stateside assignment where civil rights had been so perverted you were made to feel guilty for having a smoke. He had an unobstructed view of the stage beyond a sea of heads. He was sandy haired, thirty-six years old, average in appearance in every respect. This was by careful design. Helman's wallet held a Canadian passport identifying him as an employee of an electronics import firm that was secretly owned and operated by the Central Intelligence Agency. He had been in espionage for a long time. *Too long,* he sometimes thought.

The Chinese background music faded, replaced by American pop music with a strong, pumping bass line and backbeat. The curtain rose on a stage that was bare except for a dais. In syncopation to the beat, two dancers—one male, one female—approached the dais from opposite sides of the stage.

The man was muscular and taller than the average Chinese, with a well-developed physique clad only in a skimpy thong loincloth. The woman embodied the beauty of Chinese womanhood. Slim, with a muscular litheness to her tawny thighs and shoulders. Her black hair was stylishly short, framing a lovely face highlighted by lush lips and sensual eyes. She wore high heels and white nylons. Her curvy hips were encased in a bikini bottom and above that she wore only a smile and a shawl of Oriental pattern, bright and shimmering in the softened stage lighting.

Fog swirled in from an unseen smoke machine, licking the floor and walls, lending the artfully lighted dais a dream-like quality. The dancers faced each other, swaying. The woman's shoulders shimmied gently, gracefully, their feminine roundness accentuated by the artfully draped shawl. The dancers undulated, eyes closed. They moved into a steamy embrace, their lips meeting in an extended kiss. One of the man's hands slid beneath the shawl. She leaned her head back and mouthed a silent moan. The pulse of the music intensified.

A male voice pierced Helman's attention like a pin pricking a bubble.

"Helman-*xiānshēng,* it is most considerate of you to meet me in such a, uh, gaudy location."

The CIA officer drew his attention away from the stage. "That's all right, Chin. I'll go anywhere to pick up the General. That's how big this deal is."

Chin Qian was a slim man dressed in black, his hair a badly muffed attempt at a trendy spike style. He reminded Helman of a ferret. Chin had managed to stay alive on the fringes of the new Chinese underworld that had sprung up and become highly organized since the influx of Western money during the past decade. He had never spent a night in jail or worked an honest job, impressive achievements in authoritarian China, making him the ideal informant. Chin knew the bosses and he knew the fish peddlers. He seemed to know something about everyone and everything in Beijing that was not otherwise accessible to Helman, who had inherited Chin from his predecessor.

Chin said, "Come. I will take you to the General."

"He's here? Is he crazy?"

"Like a fox, is that not how the saying goes, Helman-*xiānshēng?*"

"Yeah, that's it. Okay, let's do it."

General Yu wanted to defect to the West with his family. Since the General had most of China's missile system information stored in his head, the powers that be had ordered Helman to facilitate this defection discreetly, under cover of the massive disruption to Chinese order that was the Olympics.

He followed Chin through a curtained archway at the rear of the private seating area into a passageway with a flight of stairs. Chin led the way upstairs. Helman's senses were on high alert, and he was glad for the comforting weight of the 9mm holstered at the small of his back. He trusted Chin as much as he trusted anyone, which meant not at all. In Helman's world it took only one screwup, one eyeblink that made you miss something vital, one wrong step, and you were dead.

There was no way the Western mind would ever understand the Eastern. He knew this. No way, and that worked both ways. But he was trusting Chin because the little ferret had made good money in the past and would continue to do so in the future as a hustler for Marv Helman and Uncle Sam. The potential of future earnings would keep Chin honest. But Helman stayed limber, just in case.

The second-floor landing opened to a hallway lined with doors to private rooms along either side. They passed men with women entering separate rooms. One man, an obese Mediterranean-type, had two girls with him. The prostitutes were Chinese, dressed pretty much alike in high heels that attractively jutted out the butt and breasts, shapely legs encased in colored thigh-high stockings, with tight waists and breasts encased in lace that accentuated deep cleavage. From behind most of the doors, exuberant lovemaking could be heard to the rocking of bedsprings. From behind one closed door came the sound of women making love. They reached a door at the far end of the corridor.

Chin knocked briskly with one knuckle. Not waiting for a response from within, he opened the door and stood aside, gesturing Helman in.

"General Yu," he announced.

The way his ferret eyes glittered with the hint of a sneer made Helman pause before stepping into the room. But he was too late, and his final thought was that *this* was *his* screwup, his eyeblink. The misstep that got him killed.

Major Yang stood by himself in the center of the bedroom. He and the inspector had never had reason to cross paths—why would an honest Canadian businessman have reason to concern the Internal Security Bureau?—but yes, he knew Major Yang well from the efficient bastard's CIA file.

Yang said, "Greetings, Mr. Helman, if that is your name."

His only chance would be to bluff this out. He said, "What is this? I'm just a good old boy and this here fella," he indicated Chin, "said I could buy me a nice piece of—"

Yang said, "Hello and farewell, spy."

Helman reached for his concealed pistol.

Chin swept in from behind, wrapping each end of a garrote in a fist and lowering it around Helman's throat. He began to strangle Helman, who danced a frantic jig, his fingers clawing at the garrote. He gasped wildly, vainly for air. After a few seconds, the harsh wheezing finally tapered off. The struggles weakened. When the tattoo of shoe heels upon the floor had ceased, Chin applied additional effort for another whole minute to make certain. Then he lowered Helman's corpse to the floor, unwinding the garrote from around the throat.

Major Yang said, "Very good. Summon your assistant. I want this piece of trash removed at once."

CHAPTER 9

Their return route led them along a street that ran parallel to the one that had brought them to the restaurant. Aged tenements with colorful ground-floor storefronts and market stalls lined the avenue. The sidewalks were clogged with pedestrians, with sightseers and locals going about their business. Two narrow lanes of vehicular traffic were clogged with vehicles of every description, from shiny white stretch limos to rattling old flatbed trucks stacked high with crates of squawking poultry. The cacophony of horns and the chattering in dozens of languages seasoned the night. They drew near Sanlitun Lu, intending to continue up the street of bars, past the local police station, to their subway stop.

As they passed the mouth of an alley, something, a shifting of the shadows, caught McCall's attention and once again the ex–Secret Service agent detected a quirky anomaly of movement.

Rose's arm was wrapped through his and she was making an observation about the peddler, a gnomish man, who had just accosted them, but while Rosie spoke, McCall's every sense was telescoping in on what appeared to be two men carrying the body of a third man down cement steps, leading from a doorway at the rear of a building, to a panel truck. The only illumination at that end of the alley was feeble light from the open doorway and refracted spillover from the street, but McCall discerned them clearly enough. They were carrying dead weight, one by the shoulders, the other scrabbling backward, holding the legs, almost to the truck.

Rose drew up beside him with a curious frown. "Tag, what—"

He said, "Stay here," and he ran into the alley, drawing his pistol from its concealed holster.

"Tag, wait!"

His approach and her instinctive cry made the two men glance up to find him crouched with his pistol aimed at them.

He said, "Freeze," sharply, figuring they'd get the idea even if they didn't speak English.

They dropped the dead weight cargo, which landed on alley pavement with a thump. He could not make out the features of the dead man, now that the body's form melded with utter darkness on the grimy alley pavement.

McCall said, "Rosie," over his shoulder, because he knew she would be standing nearby, "get the authorities on your cell phone."

Then Major Yang stepped into the lighted doorway and said, "That won't be necessary. The authorities are already here. I am Major Yang of the Internal Security Bureau. Lower your weapon."

McCall lowered his pistol. He tried not to show his surprise. "I know who you are, Major. These men are transporting what looks to be a dead body."

"And you just happened to be walking by and decided to become involved, Mr. . . . McCall, wasn't it?"

"That's right. Taggart McCall."

Yang emerged from the doorway. He stepped past the two men without giving them a glance and stood to face McCall.

"You were singled out by Mr. Dan Price last night at Dock Number Seven. Who is this?"

Rosie moved to stand beside him, her composure held in check, obviously unsure of what was going on here, but her back was straight and she stood shoulder to shoulder with him.

"My name is Rose Campbell." She stated her job description at SOC like a captured soldier volunteering name, rank and serial number.

Yang's alert eyes never left McCall. "Last night, Mr. Price suggested, McCall, that you might have vital information that would assist us."

McCall said, "Well, he was wrong. I knew the dead woman you were talking about but only slightly. Like I said last night, I barely knew her."

The two men remained in the shadows behind him, awaiting orders. Yang barked at them in Chinese, and they resumed lifting the body into the rear of the panel truck. McCall had a momentary déjà vu image of the bodies being loaded into an ambulance last night. At the mouth of the alley, pedestrians and vehicular traffic flowed by, unaware and unconcerned with this little drama.

Yang said, "I have it at my discretion to detain both of you."

"Under what charge?"

"Charge? This is China, Mr. McCall. If I wish, I could—" He paused and his demeanor softened as did his tone as he said, with a nod to Rose, "But fortunately for you both, I witnessed the whole thing. You were reacting admirably, but there is no need to distress or even concern yourself. This is government business."

Rosie said, "You're letting us go?"

The Major shifted his attention to her for the first time. "Yes, dear lady. You are innocent bystanders. Is that not the term used in your country?"

Rosie nodded her enthusiasm. "That's it, all right. Well, thank you kindly, Major. Come on, Tag, let's get a move on." McCall felt her tug at his sleeve.

The closing of the rear door of the panel truck echoed in the confines of the alley.

McCall said, "As you know, Major, I'm with SOC too." He indicated the truck. The men were behind it, no longer visible. "Any chance of me getting a hint about what's happening here?"

Rosie cleared her throat in a rather unladylike manner. "I don't think we need to press our luck, Tag."

Yang said, "The lady is quite right. You are dismissed, McCall." He bowed curtly in Rose's direction. "Miss Campbell, good evening."

McCall said, "All right, Major. See you around."

"Let us hope not, Mr. McCall."

Yang watched them walk away. Chin left the shadows of the truck and stood at his side without speaking until the Americans were out of earshot.

"Thank you, Major." He indicated the truck in which the body of Marvin Helman resided. "This could have been trouble for both of us, no?"

"Hardly, given my authority. Yet I do wish we had not been ordered to eliminate Helman. He would have led us to General Yu."

Yang did not care for any of it. His plan to simply kidnap the CIA man and wait for General Yu to meet Chin had fallen on deaf ears in the Ministry of State Security. By eliminating Helman, the logic was that the General would now be forced into the open, to contact someone at a lesser level of competence, a CIA contract worker, Chinese probably, who would be less dangerous than Helman, who had earned himself a justifiably formidable reputation. The General would trip some wire that would send Yang closing in to detain General Yu, preventing his defection and the loss of top secret data to the West. Yang understood their point of view, but they were wrong. The senile old men running the Ministry were outguessing themselves. The murder of a CIA field officer would only complicate everything.

McCall and the woman had reached the mouth of the alley.

They turned the corner and disappeared from sight.

Chin said, "What about him? Will he be trouble for us?"

"Mr. McCall would be trouble for anyone, if he chose to be. Now get to work. Dispose of Helman's body. As for Taggart McCall . . . he will bear watching."

CHAPTER 10

General Yu Bin was dreaming. He knew it was a dream, but somehow the awareness did nothing to ease the reality of the images that filled his mind.

It was lovely, at first. Some national holiday. The schools were closed. He was off-duty, and so he had taken his little family to the beach for the day.

The sand blazed almost as brightly as the sun itself, except beneath a beach umbrella where his wife, Ai Ti, lounged upon a blanket with his youngest daughter, Yuen, playing nearby. In his dream, he and his other daughter, Yim-fong, were swimming.

China's long-standing one-child-per-family law, meant to inhibit population growth, was as easily circumvented by his rank as it would have been for a civilian of his class, for the price of a well-placed bribe or two.

His oldest daughter had always been a fine swimmer. Still, when the water reached his shoulders, he instructed her to turn back, although he was no more than a dozen meters from the beach. But Yim-fong wanted to continue swimming with her father. She did not want to turn back. In his dream, she was only seven. A bright, precocious seven, respectful of her father, but very much with a mind of her own even at her tender age.

He had never been able to refuse either of his children anything they wanted, and he could not refuse Yim-fong now. They were safe enough, he reasoned. He was a good swimmer, as was Ai Ti, and there were other swimmers and sunbathers nearby. Treading water, surveying the scene, he felt consumed by a sense of well-being. Their family was strong and they were together. Nothing could be better. He gazed out to sea . . .

And something strange happened.

With an awesome, supernatural suddenness, gathering dark storm clouds coursed across the summer sky, devouring it, and the sea became cold and rough. Not understanding, he felt fright course through him. He fought the waves, trying to swim toward Yim-fong. He let out a sharp cry of terror at the sight of her disappearing beneath a cresting wave. Yim-fong swam as fast as she could, but the undertow slowed her, almost pulling her under. Everything had changed and grown dark. There were no swimmers. There were no sunbathers. The sand on the beach was an ominous gray.

Ai Ti and Yuen were nowhere in sight!

Yim-fong disappeared from his sight for a moment, then her head bobbed to the surface, her arms waving wildly about over her head. His legs scissored, his arms pumped with all of his might, but he seemed unable to make any progress toward his daughter, even though the distance was short enough for him to see vividly the horrible fright and terror upon the little girl's face. He had never felt more alone or helpless. He cried out when he saw Yim-fong's head disappear under another black wave, and this time his daughter's face did not reappear; the undertow caught Yim-fong and sucked her down into cold black nothingness.

Yu came awake with a start, awareness leaping back into his mind. He was bathed in clammy perspiration. He blinked against the harsh daylight pouring through a door that had just been opened.

It was only a dream, his awakening mind reminded him. As bad as his situation was, he would rather die than see any harm befall his family.

There were only three of them in reality. The one they had been going to name Ti had been a miscarriage. It had been

74

devastating. And then . . . they were blessed by Yim-fong, and had no doubt spoiled their little miracle beyond all bounds or common sense or tradition, which in no small measure accounted for the fact that, at seventeen, Yim-fong was a bright, precocious specimen of flowering Chinese womanhood who always managed to get her way thanks to a keen intellect and a probing mind. The General's only wish was that she could be more respectful at times. Yim-fong was in love with Western popular culture and technology.

She locked the hotel room door behind her. She held a newspaper in one hand and in the other, a white paper sack bearing the MacDonald's name and logo. She was dressed conservatively. It was only the promise of fleeing to the West that had convinced her to dress-down in a plain brown skirt and plain blouse and sensible shoes. Her banged hair was cut short and plain, although she would much rather have worn it spiked in the style of the punk rockers on the posters on the walls of the bedroom she had left behind.

Ai Ti removed three Styrofoam cups of steaming green tea from the MacDonald's sack along with wrapped breakfast sandwiches, and placed this upon the scarred-wood table next to the bathroom door of their shabby room. There was only enough space for two chairs, the table and bed and their suitcases, one each. Ai Ti's ashen features were drawn with the strain of the past twenty-four hours.

The General sat upon the edge of the bed and took the newspaper his daughter handed him.

He had dozed off, fully dressed. He reflected briefly on how these two women, his wife and his daughter had determined his future. His wife, because Ai Ti suffered from a cancer that could only be properly treated in Western hospitals, and his daughter . . . well, he hardly wanted to see Yim-fong become the singer in a punk rock band, but since infancy she had exhibited an extraordinary creative talent. Her impulsive crayon scribbling on their kitchen wall, when she had been a mere four-year-old, had been so precious as to remain untouched for years. He would see his daughter blossom into her full potential, just not in her homeland.

What would his father think of him, of his act of betrayal in defecting to the West? His grandfather had marched with Mao. His father had died a military man. He and his family were the elite, accorded extraordinary privilege. And he was abusing that trust and privilege "to the max," as Yim-fong would say. His wife would receive nothing but the best that his ample Swiss bank account could afford, and Yim-fong would flourish, freed of the yoke of an authoritarian regime that could only hobble her talent, inhibiting her creative soul.

And yes, *he* wanted out. He had been a good soldier, until now. But it had come to trouble him to be a cog in a repressive regime that could one day well plunge itself into a nuclear showdown of the type that should have gone forever with the end of the Cold War. China was increasingly possessed of an arrogance and pride in the false security of power touted by military hardliners whom he'd distrusted since his first days as a cadet. He no longer wanted any part of it. He loved to read. He was a man of letters. He loved world history. Perhaps he would own and operate one of those modest little secondhand bookshops in London or San Francisco.

But first, he had to get his family out of China, and that was proving far more difficult than Helman's original plan, which had seemed risky enough. They had traveled to Beijing from Guangxi, lost amid the throngs arriving for the Olympics. The risk was considerable. He was not just another soldier. That would have been bad enough. But General Yu Bin was a man who carried every detail of his country's missile system in his head. There would already be a bounty on his head and on his family. They would never permit him to leave China alive . . . if they could help it.

Less than twenty-four hours ago he had made telephone contact with Marv Helman, who had instructed them to register at a hotel that had been even seedier than this one. They were to wait for a man named Chin. They had checked in, but the General was no fool. He and his family "took an afternoon stroll," and had secretly watched the outside door of their hotel room. A man he assumed to be Chin did arrive, a brutish-looking civilian. Armed soldiers stood nearby and after Chin knocked on their door and there was no response, the soldiers had stormed in.

They had checked into this hotel, a small place near the Chang'an Avenue, where a disinterested desk clerk had not noticed or cared that this family of three was checking in without luggage, something the Internal Security Bureau details would surely have noted had conditions been normal. But every government agency, from the street police directing traffic right up to those determined to catch him, was undermanned and overworked because of the Olympics. Yim-fong had purchased them each a new set of clothes and they had spent the night here. The General had attempted to contact Helman by cell phone, but had only gotten the man's voice mail. He left no messages.

What he was looking for was buried on the bottom of page four of the newspaper, a brief article with no accompanying photograph yet it reached out from the page as if to grasp him by the throat. He read the article a second time, more slowly. Ai Ti noted the intensity of his eyes speed-reading across the page. She asked, "What is it? Has something gone wrong?"

Yim-fong licked the remnants of her sandwich from a finger. "I'll bet it's about Mr. Helman."

The General folded the newspaper, setting it aside.

"An American businessman named Marvin Helman was discovered early this morning in a park near the Summer Palace. It is reported as an act of random violence. He was strangled, the victim of a holdup, it seems, who paid the ultimate price for not cooperating."

Yim-fong said, "Chin was a double agent. They killed Helman after we eluded Chin and the soldiers." She sounded like a girl detective in a movie, trying to unravel a case. The General thought, *Perhaps she will be an actress.*

Ai Ti's gaze shifted, staring with melancholy eyes at a distant horizon neither the General nor his daughter could see. "But this is terrible news. You said Mr. Helman was the only round eyes you trusted." She clasped her bony fingers.

The General rose and crossed to the window, drawing aside the drape upon a gray morning, on a busy street scene below. There was no sign of a military presence, no indication of anyone keeping this room under surveillance.

He said, "It will take more than Mr. Helman's death to stop us. We will make contact with an American official." He let the curtain drop back into place. "But we can hardly go to the American embassy."

"It must be under surveillance." Yim-fong nodded. "We wouldn't get within a dozen meters."

Ai Ti closed her sad eyes and lowered her face. "We should never have left home. I miss my garden . . ."

The General rested his hands over hers. "We will plant a better garden, my love. I do this for you. But . . . are you well enough to travel?"

"Yes." With her hands clasped, she looked in prayer. "Forgive me. Of course, we must press on. But we know no one in Beijing. What can we do?"

"The Olympics," said the General.

Yim-fong nodded quick understanding. "Of course. It's how

we were able to get into Beijing, to come this far, lost in the influx of people attending the Games." She sparkled with the enthusiasm of youthful innocence. "And think of all the American officials who will be there. It will be difficult *not* to find someone who will take us in!"

The General stroked his chin in thought. "There will, of course, be a concentration of our government's security forces there as well. But the eyes of the world are on China and if we are careful . . . yes, it is our only chance. That is, if it's not too late to gain admission."

Yim-fong grinned. "You're forgetting the term computer geek. That's me! There are ways to get tickets if you know the Internet like I do. I saw a cyber café two blocks from here. I'll log online there and find where to get tickets."

Ai Ti's eyes remained closed, downcast, as if in prayer. "Is there no other way? Surely my child must not risk her life to gain my freedom."

Yim-fong embraced her mother. "Don't worry. I feel like a bird ready to be freed from its cage. I would risk anything for this. But there is no risk. I promise to be careful. No one will know that I am linked to Father when I get the tickets. I'll be fine, you'll see." She smiled at her father. "Of course, I will need some cash."

The General could not resist a chuckle.

"You already sound like a daughter of the West." He reached for his wallet. "But your mother is right. You must promise to be careful, to risk nothing, to return here safely even if without the tickets."

"I promise," said Yim-fong.

CHAPTER 11

"Dan, could you spare a moment, please?"

Rose had been waiting for this opportunity since showing up for work that morning. Dan Price passed the dispatcher's station usually only once or twice a day, if that. She worked with two other dispatchers on this busiest of the three shifts. To her left sat Toni, the glittery Italian urbanite who spoke three languages and, to her right, Dwayne, the gay guy from Indianapolis. Toni and Dwayne were both presently occupied, taking calls.

Dan Price paused in mid-stride to flash her his most cordial, apologetic smile, every inch the well mannered, likeable, All-American everyone knew him to be. Two men drew up behind him, a pair of his black T-shirted, shoulder-holstered SOC security officers. Price never went anywhere without at least two such hardcases at his side.

Private contractor paramilitary security firms, like those that had taken so much heat in Iraq, were a necessary evil of troubled modern times, especially at a world-class event like the Olympics. It wasn't the same, though, for those countries with known terrorist ties. With the demise of the Cold War, the Games had increasingly come to serve as an arena for debate about modern nationhood and international relations. And of course no one could forget the 1972 Munich Games, where a group of Islamic militants had slipped into the Olympic Village, killed two Israeli team members and took nine other members hostage. Later, in a botched rescue attempt, all nine hostages and the terrorists were killed in a shootout. Al-Qaeda would have no motivation for targeting Chinese nationals, interests and prestige before and during the Games. They would, however, be strongly tempted not to miss this spectacular occasion for mounting an act of terrorism directed at the participants from the United States, the United Kingdom, Australia and other countries forming part of the occupying forces in Iraq and Afghanistan. Tightened security measures made by the Chinese authorities had rendered it next to impossible for Al-Qaeda to infiltrate into the country before and during the Games. The danger was of terrorists infiltrating as members or office-bearers of the national teams from Iraq and Afghanistan participating in the Games.

The explosion in the cafeteria of the Iraqi Parliament, located inside the highly protected Green Zone of Baghdad, on April 12, 2007, had resulted from terrorists managing to get into the Zone under the garb of the security guard of one of the Members of Parliament. There had been large-scale infiltration of Iraqi security forces and other institutions by Al-Qaeda. It would be easy for them to infiltrate the national contingent from Iraq for the Games, for example. Therefore, each such national team had its own security team, but the security teams accompanying the national contingents had to be from State security agencies and not from private companies, since verification of the antecedents of private companies and their personnel were next to impossible. Strict verification of the antecedents of all participants—sportsmen or officials—had been given top priority.

In a job like Rose's, you were always prepared for *that* call, which happily hadn't come in yet and hopefully never would. But she felt the tension that in a noticeable way underpinned everything, and the presence of armed paramilitaries like those under Price's command could be reassuring.

He rested his elbows on the counter that enclosed the station, and Rose sensed a dangerous cool in his eyes that studied her with interest.

"I can spare a moment, but not much more."

"It's just that something's happened and I need to make a report. I'm not sure who I should make it out to."

"Report it to me. I'm supposed to be honchoing this madhouse. It will cross my desk eventually anyhow."

"Well, someone broke into my room last night."

"Really?"

"Yes. They did a good job of it. They used a passkey and they must have thought they left everything exactly the way they found it."

The suggestion of a smile crinkled the corners of his mouth. "But a woman knows better."

"This one does. A bookmark in the wrong page. The shoes in the closet not arranged just so. A perfume bottle turned a little different . . . anyway, while I was out last night, someone went through my belongings."

"Anything missing?"

"No, not that I could tell."

"I heard about you and McCall being out on the town last night. I got a phone call this morning from Major Yang."

"Then you know what happened. Have you had a chance to talk with Tag . . . with McCall?"

"I don't see any reason to. Tag's a big boy. Could what happened last night be connected to someone breaking into your room?"

She decided to dodge that one for the moment and asked, "What did Major Yang say?"

"That you and McCall briefly intruded on an undercover government assignment. Yang was the officer in charge."

"They were moving a body."

"The Major didn't say anything about that, and that's the way McCall will play it too. The Chinese authorities' problems aren't our problems, Rose. We're here to coordinate and provide security for the Games."

She said, "Just like with Jody Simms. Pretend it never happened."

"No one's doing that."

"After we left that incident, Tag and I came straight back here to the Green and said good night, and my room and belongings had already been gone through."

"What are you suggesting?"

"What happened to Jody . . . I think my break-in had something to do with that."

"How so?"

"Well, are there any loose ends in that investigation?"

"You know I can't discuss that. Major Yang—"

"I thought we didn't care about the Chinese, as long as we don't step on their toes."

Their eyes held in a subtle duel and she couldn't tell what it meant, if he was getting his back up just because an uppity woman was speaking her mind, or . . . she only knew that she did not like this man, and did not trust him.

"Talk straight, Rose. What are you saying?"

She gulped hard and forged on. "Is anything missing, that someone is looking for? I think maybe that someone, or a couple of someones, thinks Jody might have given that something to me, and that's why they searched my things."

"Her iPhone," he said, matter-of-factly. "There's a ton of leads in that if we find it. Jody was onto something. But she wasn't carrying it when she died and so far, it hasn't shown up. You wouldn't know anything about that, would you, Rose?"

"No, I wouldn't."

"Look, Rosie, much as I'm enjoying this, I do have places to go and people to see. Do you want me to assign someone to the break-in?"

"No, I just wanted to report it." She thought, *And I wanted you to know that I know, you smooth bastard.*

He drew back from the counter. "I'll be on my way then. Let me know if you find that iPhone. Have a nice day."

"You too, Dan. Thanks."

She watched him walk off with his pair of hardcase shadows. Jody's iPhone was in her purse, under the console. She had found it that morning in the hiding place Jody told her about.

Now Rose just hoped she had not overplayed her hand.

"On your knees, slave."

"Yes, Mistress."

"Kiss my boots. You know how."

"Yes, ma'am."

Dan Price reverently kissed the toes of the knee-high leather boots. He moaned with an exquisite sensation he was unable to get enough of. In everything else *he* was in control, he was the man in charge and everyone bowed to *him.* But not here . . .

"Have you been a good slave?"

"Yes."

"Tell me."

"Everything is ready. Everything we planned—"

"We? Tell me who planned this."

"You did, Mistress."

"Tell me what you have accomplished."

"I've selected two men from the SOC personnel roster. Tucker and Hanson. They're hungry and totally without morals, and . . . experienced. Everything is proceeding per schedule."

"And the Simms bitch?"

"Taken care of."

She chuckled lewdly from behind her leather mask.

"You want me, don't you, slave?"

"Yes, ma'am."

God, he would do anything for her, for the white-hot searing lust that only she and these sex games could stoke within him!

She said, "Beg."

CHAPTER 12

There are two Chinas.

There are two Beijings.

In her capacity as a field investigator for the Ministry of Internal Security, Mei Chen knew them both.

The development of the coastal cities to the exclusion of the hinterland, the gap between the registered citizens and the rural population, was severe and still widening, a split between the advanced, globalized part of the new China's economy and the vast labor force of self-employed farmers. Two decades of open door policy had triggered economic progress and consequent urban development of unprecedented speed and proportion. After emerging from near isolation, China was now the sixth largest economy in the world. Forty billion dollars had been spent on new roads and subway lines and efforts to improve Beijing's power grid for the Olympics, for instance. Yet while the most densely populated areas of the lower Yangzi River delta, the Pearl River delta and the Beijing-Tianjin-Bohai region, the three great "urban spheres," comprised five percent of China's total land area, twenty percent of its total national population and accounted for seventy percent of its total GDP, within an hour's drive of the outer reaches of any of these great metropolises, rice was still being cultivated much as it had been a thousand years ago.

Crimes against the state were committed in both of these starkly contrasting worlds, and thus Mei was familiar with both.

She was two months past her twenty-fourth birthday. Small-boned and slim-figured, she stayed in good physical condition through a vigorous regimen of daily exercise. She was not in uniform, attired instead in stylishly cut slacks and blouse that were conservative enough not to draw attention.

Mei sat in the front passenger seat of a government sedan parked at the curb across the street and a half-block down from a two-level brick structure, plain, aged and worn like the neighborhood itself. The building consisted of a vacant storefront at street level, with a second story designated as a private residence. The storefront was flanked on one side by a barber and on the other by a food stand that looked from this distance like an unclean rat hole populated by assorted riff-raff, the dregs of Beijing street life that had, for the most part, been banished from the tourist and Olympics areas.

Private ownership of vehicles in China was nowhere near that of the developed Western nations, but this side street was dense with local traffic beneath a sunny blue sky unsoiled by smog. The unmarked sedan went unnoticed except for the disinterested glance of the occasional passersby.

Mei was familiar with some areas of Beijing more than others, and this was one. She had been born and raised not far from this neighborhood. She knew these streets.

Women walked by dressed in the standard garb of drab cotton jackets and trousers, some with small children tied upon their backs while they made their rounds. Multicolored laundry hung from bamboo poles out of the windows of apartment houses. An old fortuneteller stood on the sidewalk, chanting, advertising her services. Bicyclists passed in both directions at high speed, magically darting and weaving in and out of each other's way.

Mei's driver was a wiry plainclothes detective who watched the passing street scene, alert for any indication of potential danger or trouble.

Mei concentrated on the storefront across the street. The flow of pedestrians along the sidewalks, the vehicular traffic and the customers patronizing the food counter and the barber combined to partially obstruct her view of a door directly next to the storefront, yet during the preceding twenty minutes she had observed a half-dozen people making their way through the doorway that led up to the second level, among them students, a nattily dressed Asian businessman and even an average, plainly dressed teenage girl. Quite an array. And every one of them had glanced about furtively upon arriving and leaving, as if well aware that they were participating in forbidden activity. If she took into account that she probably missed some of the people going in and out of that doorway because of all the activity on the street, it still added up to far more people than would be expected to visit any respectable private residence during such a short span of time. If one extrapolated the results of this short surveillance over a twenty-four-hour period . . . yes, the people in that "private residence" were doing a thriving business.

In a country awash with counterfeit clothes and DVDs, black marketeers were making a fortune selling counterfeit tickets to the Olympics and what the Americans called "scalped" tickets. It was big business. The most expensive tickets for the closing ceremony, for example, would cost over six hundred dollars. In order to ensure safety, prevent fraud and eliminate profit-oriented resale of tickets, state-of-the-art anti-counterfeit technologies had been adopted, including electronic chips in some tickets.

But old-fashioned police work was required, too.

She had been handed this assignment following the arrest of a highly placed Beijing government official who had taken large sums in bribes from foreign businessmen, then foolishly denied them the land he had promised. The foreigners complained to the Communist Party's Central Disciplinary Committee, the party's highest organ for investigating corruption, and the married husband and father was arrested in the company of prostitutes at a house in the outlying Beijing district of Huairou, an opulent residence equipped with a personal entertainment center replete with closed-circuit television cameras.

The official was rigorously interrogated and additionally confessed to Olympics profiteering in partnership with the Falun Gong, a Tibetan youth gang with strong links to the resistance movement opposing the Chinese occupation of Tibet. China was pouring hundreds of millions of dollars into road building and development projects in Tibet, boosting the economy while maintaining a large military presence and keeping close tabs on the locals via a vast security apparatus of cameras and informants, but the resistance was resilient both within Tibet and in the cities of China. The Falun Gong's aim was not to cause death, but to politically embarrass the Chinese government by staging acts of sabotage directed at the Games infrastructure. The Falun Gong had cyber disruption experts who had already caused problems, attempting to disrupt the information infrastructure set up for the Games. Other provocative acts included shouting slogans, demonstrations—and profiteering.

Mei spoke one word into her lapel mic: "Initiate."

A caravan of four official vehicles careened around a corner and onto the street with flashing lights and loud, discordant beeping sirens that sent pedestrians scurrying and vehicles drawing aside. Helmeted, armored, machine-gun-carrying officers poured from the vehicles even as they were screeching to a stop before the storefront and storming the stairwell doorway, establishing a perimeter around the building.

The popping of handguns, alternating with the stutter of machine guns, poured onto the street from inside the house, punctuated with indecipherable shouts.

Mei stepped from the vehicle, drawing her pistol, as did her driver. Witnesses who saw them stepped away.

She felt a restless urge to be doing something, but her role here was to command and to coordinate. Her investigation had confirmed and further developed the information supplied by the official. Her informants in the neighborhood had helped her pinpoint this base of operations. She scanned the adjacent buildings. For a second she thought it was only wishful thinking when something caught her attention, then she looked again beyond the line of vision of the policemen stationed around the house.

A window on the third floor had opened; someone leaned out to stretch a plank across the distance separating the buildings. First one figure, then others, scampered on all fours across the plank.

She again spoke into her lapel mic. "Cut around the back of the building next door." To her driver, she indicated the entrance of the apartment house. "Cover that door. Don't let anyone get through."

She raced into the building, taking the stairs three at a time until she pressed herself to the wall just below the first landing, her pistol up and ready. Frantic footfalls thundered down from above. Whether they headed out the front or the back, they would have to pass this landing on their way out.

Mei caught the first one across the mouth with a swipe of the pistol, breaking bone, popping the young man onto the floor, splattering droplets of blood across two of the four males, teenagers, crowding the steps on their way down. They were heavily armed with pistols and machine guns but they froze in complete surprise as she stepped onto the landing.

"Drop your weapons."

Their surprise yielded to arrogance and belligerence.

One, holding a machine gun, snarled. "You are a brave but foolish woman. There are four of us and one of you. Let's kill her," he said to the others, "and be gone."

She said, "You'll kill me. But I'll take two of you down with me, and the two who get past me won't make it beyond this building. Or you can drop your weapons. If you cooperate, things will go better for you. Right now the charge is only counterfeiting tickets for the Games. Don't add the murder of a government agent to it."

The tableau held like that for several more seconds. Then the clatter of weapons dropping to the floor, one by one, set time in motion again, and then the officers from below flooded in to take charge of the prisoners. Mei holstered her pistol and followed them down to the street.

CHAPTER 13

Kelly Jackson left the performance area. The cheers, the general hubbub of the capacity audience, rippled across the cavernous arena. A network television cameraman backpedaled furiously, blindly keeping apace with her so that her image at this instant could be beamed to millions of untold viewers worldwide. The camera never blinked, a famous news broadcaster had once proclaimed, and that had been drilled into her during her years of training. Always *look* like a winner. She returned to the sideline area where her parents waited with Boris Temerov.

She wanted to die. She no longer wanted to exist. If only she could simply evaporate, be gone somewhere else, away from here; anywhere, anything but this.

Her mother was keenly watching the big board where her tallied score would appear. Her father looked concerned. Boris stood with his arms crossed before his massive chest, his expression revealing nothing. The cameras were moving about, capturing not only her little drama but the crowd, the judges, the constant prattle from the stands, that expectant air before the score was announced.

Thus far at these Olympic Games, she had failed at her hopes of winning a single gold medal, and she had just completed her worst vault performance ever. The results that flashed upon the board verified it. For this vault she had performed a Yurchenko double twist and while she'd maintained a smooth body line, her crossed legs throughout the twist constituted a severe form break and she'd finished with a deduction for a far-from-solid landing.

Kelly averted her face from the cameras. She felt small, vulnerable.

Candace Jackson's vivacious green eyes and sparkling smile were frozen in place like a mask. She looked for all the world like a mother offering loving encouragement to her daughter. In reality she whispered in brittle anger into Kelly's ear, "Sweetheart, put on your happy face. Perk up, sweetie. Just keep thinking endorsement."

Steve Jackson cleared his throat, his normal good nature a little frayed around the edges. "Don't worry, Kel. You gave it your best."

Then they were flashing her score. She knew this because of her mother's disappointed sigh and because she could hear the crowd's polite applause that was wholly lacking in enthusiasm. Boris grumbled his displeasure in Russian.

She broke from her mother's embrace. "I need to be alone." She didn't exactly run away, but strode off purposefully, leaving them and the cameras and the crowd behind. Her mother called her name but she pretended not to hear. Her mother would be turning to her husband and Boris, keeping up the pretense of having an intelligent exchange with them, not wanting to make a scene. That was fine with Kelly.

Tyrona Carey and her trainer, Andrea Cometti, appeared, starting up the ramp that led into the arena. Tyrona was scheduled to perform her floor routine next. Her bright, sassy, sixteen-year-old attitude shown brightly. When she saw Kelly, she beamed a little brighter.

She called, "How'd you do, Kelly?"

"I don't know," said Kelly, hurrying past them. "Good luck!"

Tyrona hesitated. "Kelly, what's wrong?"

But Kelly was already past, head held high. *Act like you're a winner,* she kept telling herself.

Andrea was saying, "Come on, Tyrona. Now is not the time for girl talk. They're announcing you."

Then Kelly was alone in the relative seclusion of the locker room where she threw on a pair of slacks and a loose-fitting cotton shirt without bothering to shower or change from her leotards. Her heart was pounding. She heard the distant roar of the crowd cheering Tyrona's entrance. Her stomach muscles were cramping. Her breathing was shallow. *Am I having my first anxiety attack?* She had to get away, away from everyone and everything.

Boris was waiting for her when she stepped from the locker room. The corridor was strangely deserted. Echoes of the cheering crowd and the music from the arena merged into a low, steady rumble backdrop.

Kelly thought, *Plenty of enthusiasm for Tyrona . . .*

She looked around. "Where's Mom and Dad?"

Boris said, "They felt, as do I, that you and I should have a little heart-to-heart talk."

"I don't want to talk. I want to be alone."

He grasped her arm in a vise-like grip that was stern but not savage or rough, just firm. The nearness of him exuded male power, as always.

"Kelly, you must cease this behavior, do you hear me? This is not how I trained you."

"I know, Boris. I know. I was trained to win. But guess what? *I'm not winning!*"

"Your scores have been respectable. You're upset."

"Of course I'm upset. Why should I calm down? So the world won't think less of you, my wonderful trainer, the great Boris Temerov, who's finally managed to pick a loser?"

"Kelly, I forbid you to speak in this fashion."

Their eyes locked furiously.

"I'm old enough to face the truth, Boris. I came to Beijing for the Gold and so far I have one bronze medal, whoop de doo. Why shouldn't the world see what I'm feeling, what it's like to be a loser? What if giving your best and thinking positive thoughts and training, training, training, years of sacrifice . . . what if that's not enough? Maybe that's a message that needs to get out there too." She looked down at where he held her arm. "Now please take your hands off me."

His hand dropped away as if they'd received an electrical shock.

"Of course, my dear, of course. But where were you going? We need to go over the tapes of your routine, and this afternoon there's training—"

"I want some time alone."

She whirled about and stalked off and seconds later was gone from his sight.

A woman's voice spoke behind him. "I knew it, and now I've seen it with my own eyes."

Andrea Cometti stood there glaring at him, her hands on her hips balled into fists so tightly, the knuckles showed white.

He said, "Why aren't you out there watching Tyrona?"

"I'll get back to Tyrona. And she's shining, by the way. She's going for the gold and she may well get it, not like that little tramp of yours."

"What are you talking about?"

"I'm talking about you and sweet, innocent little Kelly. I see what's going on. That girl has done poorly because she's distracted by an older man taking advantage of her, and you're throwing *me* aside while you're at it!"

"It's obscene of you to suggest anything like that, and beneath you, frankly. My relationship with Kelly is strictly professional. I am her trainer, nothing more."

Andrea sneered. "I'm not losing you to another woman. I'm

losing you to a child."

A cheer swept through the arena, rumbling back to them.

"Please, Andrea, act mature about this."

Her demeanor and expression changed suddenly. The emotion left her and she was the cool, competent trainer the gymnastic world knew and respected.

"Very well, Boris. As long as you know that *I* know about you and that girl. Quite soon, others will know. The whole world will know and you, you bastard, and her too, the little witch, will deserve everything you get."

Chapter 14

That morning in the shower, McCall's heart kicked his ass.

One moment he was standing there, thirty minutes before reporting for his shift, enjoying the hot, fine spray from the shower nozzle needling his chest, opening his pores prior to his standard procedure of finishing up with a bracing thirty seconds of the water turned on ice cold.

Then the assault on his chest from within was like a sharp, direct blow from a rifle butt that knocked the wind from his lungs and slammed him against the tile of the shower cubicle, where there was nothing to grab for support and the best he could do was brace against one of the clouded-glass walls. His knees bent, then he was sliding down, the hot water pounding him but more than that, an invisible pressure squeezing him, squeezing the life from him but slowly, with a tightening pain that was worse than any of the other times before, like the thumb of a cruel child slowing squashing the life out of a bug.

He had just completed his strenuous regimen of daily exercise—part yoga, part standard calisthenics—that kept him limber. His abs and general musculature were nothing to be ashamed of, although he wasn't the type to show off. He just felt and functioned better with a properly toned body . . .

The pressure felt like it was crushing his chest, making him gasp for air on the floor of the shower, gulping like a beached fish. The excruciating pain, the needling shower water, the *knowing* that he was dying merged into a kaleidoscope of fleeting, fragmentary images from these past days.

Day had followed day. With so many faces from so many races and nationalities thrown together in mighty crowds against such a vast, vibrant setting as the Olympics, the word "routine" could never have applied to McCall's daily rounds of drifting through those crowds, keeping his eyes open, paying attention, busting pickpockets and purse snatchers and con artists. If it wasn't exactly routine, a rhythm had settled in after about Day Five, not only for him as a security officer but also for the Olympics in general. The initial excitement, the building-up and immediate aftermath of the opening night ceremonies, had yielded to the inherent drama of the Games themselves.

And through it all, his heart had behaved like a good heart should to the point that he had played with the idea of not bothering with a doctor after he returned stateside. He'd pretend the chest pains never happened and get on with his life.

The explosion of chest pain and the kaleidoscope of these past days seemed to go on for an eternity, but it could only have been a minute or less before the pain started abruptly to recede from stabbing white-hot to becoming again that terrible squeezing sensation. The kaleidoscope images blurred and disappeared and he was sitting on the floor of the shower with the water needling down at him.

He turned off the faucet and made his way from the steamy bathroom, into the comparative coolness of his one-room apartment. It was a small box—single bed, nightstand, TV, writing desk, and bathroom—the walls bare. His vision remained bleary, the only remnant of his ordeal. He stretched out atop the made bed and thought, *Oh, my God. My heart. Dear God, my heart . . .*

Staring at the ceiling, his vision cleared. His breathing returned to normal. The pain was gone for now. Everything seemed normal—the murmur of conversation from people passing outside his door; a bus accelerating away from the bus stop near his window. The hum of the air conditioner.

He had two choices. He could remain scared out of his wits with the knowledge that he could well be living the last days— perhaps the final hours—of his life. He did not want to die. He'd ridden out some tough breaks, but life was getting good again. His daughter, he wanted to see Jennifer become a grown woman. And there was Rose. And a job he was doing well. His life was back on track. No, he did not want to die. He could think about that, or he could throw himself into his work.

A climactic undercurrent was beginning to build across the Olympics. He'd started noticing it yesterday with the approach of the Closing Ceremonies. His work here was a world unto itself that embraced him from outside, occupying him with activity amid the vast backdrop of this once-in-a-lifetime historic event. He would embrace his work, not his fear.

Today he would be wearing tan slacks, brown loafers and a loud print shirt, just another American come to see the Games . . . except of course for the concealed pistol holstered at the small of his back. He climbed into his clothes and allowed himself enough time to walk over to check in at the SOC HQ. It was the sort of warm but pleasant, blue-sky day that the Chinese had desperately hoped would bless their Olympics. McCall was surprised at how good he felt. He didn't feel like he was sick at all.

Rose sent him a wink and small smile from her dispatch station. She and her co-workers looked like they were presently swamped. He returned the smile with a wink of his own.

Nothing in that shared glance would indicate that in the past week, they had become lovers—twice, in fact, and he had to admit that was something he found himself thinking about more than he'd expected and more than he was at first comfortable with. But what the hell? He hadn't been with another woman since Ann. When the so-called "freedom" of divorce set him free amid a world of single women . . . well, he hadn't been on a date yet. He'd met some interesting women, but either the good ones were always taken, that old saying was true, or the timing wasn't right.

And then, Rosie.

Easy on the eyes, easy to talk with and she had a good heart. The death of her friend, Jody, and the incident when she and McCall were together in the alley with Major Yang had somehow bonded two people who had been hurt before but who might, just might be ready for another try at the romance thing. They spoke of their past lives before having met each other. He didn't spare her any of the truths about himself and hoped that she would not judge him too harshly, and was relieved when she seemed not to judge him at all. She had a teenage son, a college freshman, and she talked about him proudly. She had raised him alone after divorcing his father for cheating on her seven years ago. Since then, she'd let work and raising a child consume her every waking hour, leaving little room for even thoughts of love.

They didn't only unload personal histories on each other. They spoke of places they knew, movies and music and before long their pleasurable flow of conversation, the effortless ease of communication, had led to what the kids used to call necking, and it wasn't any different from a couple of shyly awkward high school kids on a first date. After a second such necking session, nature had taken its course.

McCall was learning one important truth about himself. He could not have a casual sexual affair. He couldn't get sweet Rosie Campbell out of his mind. He hoped he was not a delusional fool. Were they just "fuck buddies," ships passing in the night who would never see each other again once the Olympics were over and finished? He didn't think so. She had kind ways, a gentle touch and a droll but sassy wit that never stung because it also came packaged with the goodness that was her essence. Their lovemaking the first time was tentative but gentle. They were compatible. The second time, well, McCall smiled at the memory of last night.

Behind that sweet smile, beneath modest nature and invisible walls she had built up to protect her emotions from ever being hurt again, lurked unleashed passion, a lust for love and loving. They were great together in bed.

There was only one thing he held back on. He didn't tell her about the chest pains. He promised that he would, and soon. Before they left Beijing . . .

Hopes of uncovering anything new on the death of Jody Simms had dead-ended from the beginning. Jody's iPhone had proven to be of such little use, McCall almost wished that they had left it for Dan Price and his men to find. Rose had been able to verify every number Jody called since coming to the Olympics. All of the calls had been routine. Personnel background checks, SOC communication. A few calls to the States proved to be to a now-distraught fiancée. The dead-end meant that in all likelihood, there had been nothing more to Jody's death beyond Killed in Action in performance of her duties. Zigging when she should have zagged. Catching a bullet for that fatal error. If anything had been orchestrated, if Jody had been killed for a reason, then there appeared to be no clues pointing in that direction, at least not in her iPhone or in anything Rose could recall of her conversations with Jody and what she knew of her friend's life.

Rose was still not ready to dismiss Jody's death as it appeared. There had been Dan Price's manner and little things like his pointed interest in the iPhone. Rose didn't like Dan Price, even though she had to work for him and be nice to him on a daily basis. She was willing to admit their suspicions regarding him at this point amounted to her intuition alone.

McCall clocked in, and then went out and about his rounds. He was walking the sixth-level concourse of the National Stadium when he saw Kelly Jackson, from a distance, emerging from an elevator.

This level was comprised of the high money seats. People strolling along the concourse, chatting, taking pictures, eating or having a drink at one of the concessions, or browsing through the gift shops; fat prey for pickpockets who, in this age of identity theft, had become particularly adept at their profession. The Chinese authorities had provided SOC with access to a database, including mug shots, of every known pickpocket likely to be working the Games. Several had already been picked up. And a whole new slew of international pros had descended on Beijing for these two weeks in August.

He watched Kelly after she left the elevator as if she'd been ejected from it. She headed off up the concourse away from him. She wore a shirt thrown over her performance outfit, which was unusual. She held the same little handbag that he had retrieved and returned to her almost two weeks ago. He would have expected her to be in street clothes, however casual. He'd sized her mother up that way. Candace Jackson would never allow her Kelly to be seen dressed like this in public, but in this cosmopolitan setting, no one looked twice.

But something wasn't right.

He followed her at a discreet distance, not that she would have noticed had he been walking alongside her. She had that brisk tunnel-vision stride of someone in a hurry, preoccupied. He lost sight of her where a crowd had gathered around a German beer garden. Noisy revelry was in progress, much beer and laughter. A drunk got in his way and after he worked his way through, Kelly had rounded a corner.

When he rounded that corner, she was gone.

A pang of panic rippled through him. His eyes swept the

people, the shops, settling on a stairway that led up to the next level. He crossed to the stairway. A wide white ribbon was stretched across it from knee to mid-chest level and upon it was printed, in red, KEEP OUT, ENTRANCE IS STRICTLY FORDBIDDEN in five languages.

The stairs led to the seventh, highest level of the stadium, the domain of the elite within the Chinese government. The fact that no sentry now stood at the foot of those stairs indicated that there was no one of importance at this hour. The Premier's box was on Level 7, but the absolute elite were only attending the opening and closing ceremonies. At the closing ceremony, security would be infinitely tighter.

Stooping under the ribbon barrier, McCall hurried up the stairs. At the next landing was a spectacular view of Tiananmen Square. To his right, a heavily carpeted, oak paneled, warmly lit hallway was lined with doors. To his left, a gray metal door with a glass rectangular window led to an outdoor balcony overlooking another view of the Square. The balcony was encased in twelve-foot-high wire mesh fencing.

Kelly stood, staring out across the city. One of her ankles was bent around the other and her arms were extended over her head, the fingers of each hand curled through the wire mesh of the fence as if she was ready to spring up and start climbing. The sun was warmer this high up. A brisk breeze played with strands of her hair.

At first she was not aware of his presence when he eased the door open and stepped onto the balcony behind her. He cleared his throat. She whirled away from the fence, releasing her hold on it and facing him with a deer-in-the-headlights panic in her eyes, her compact body crouching, ready to flee.

"Who are you? What are you doing here?"

He produced his wallet and extended his laminated ID for

her to read. "My name is McCall. I'm a security officer with the SOC."

She relaxed, but only somewhat. Her eyes narrowed. "I know you. We've met before."

"I'm the sprinter who got your purse back on opening night."

Now she did relax. She even gave him a little grin, cute as hell.

"That's right." She patted her purse. "As you can see, I've been holding onto it." There was a quaver in her voice.

"What are you doing up here, Kelly? This area is off limits, even to athletes. You saw the sign. You shouldn't be up here."

"I know. I just wanted to be alone. There was no one guarding the stairs, so I came up. Why are you here? Are you following me? Did my mother send you?"

"No one sent me. I just happened to see you downstairs. You looked like someone who could be in trouble. So here I am. I'm that kind of guy."

"I was just in a hurry to get away from everyone." She resumed her pose, arms reaching up, fingers curled through the wire mesh, ankles entwined. She looked out across Beijing. "Jesus H., isn't there anywhere on the planet I can just be alone?"

"You're not thinking of climbing that fence and jumping, are you?"

She maintained the pose but swung her eyes on him with an exaggerated show of indulgence. "I'm depressed. I'm a loser and I hate Beijing and the Olympics and my mother and most of all myself. I am hormonal. But don't worry, I'm not suicidal. Not yet." She added, precisely spacing and enunciating each word for emphasis, "I just want to be alone."

"That could be difficult, you being a star American gymnast and this being the Olympics and all."

She gave him a little smile. "Hardly a star. You're nice. It was nice, to care and to follow me up here the way you did." She regarded him differently then, with the appraising, speculative look of a woman assessing a man *as* a man. "You've been around, haven't you, Mr. McCall?"

"Heck, I've been to a few places twice."

"Well then, maybe you can tell me. In all of this traveling and living, have you ever had the rug pulled right out from under you and I mean big time? Did you ever put years into something, investing everything you had and know and are, only to have it turn to dust right before your eyes and slip right through your fingers, and there was nothing you could do to stop it?"

"Kelly, that happens to more people than you might think, sometimes to the same person more than once."

"Has it ever happened to you?"

He thought about his marriage, about the Camp David fiasco; a rising star of a career, shot down in flames.

"It's happened to me a couple of times."

"So what should I do?"

"Put one foot in front of the other. Keep pushing, one day at a time."

"Yeah? And then what? When does it start getting easier?"

"It will, for you. You're young. Do you have another competition?"

"One more."

"So give it your best. You don't look like a quitter."

"I'm not."

"You can be alone after you've completed your mission. You're here to compete. You're only really a loser if you don't show, if you're not there for your team."

"Thanks, McCall."

"But whatever you do, do it somewhere else, okay? This level is off limits."

"Okay," she said. "I'll behave," and before he knew it or could react, Kelly stood on her tiptoes and planted a chaste kiss on his left cheek, then turned gracefully from him and was gone.

He gave her a minute head start to get lost in the flow of people on the concourse. He looked out over the city. A flock of white-winged doves scattered from their nest somewhere below, wings snow white as they banked in formation against the blue sky. He thought about what had just happened. He couldn't do any more than put in his two cents, which he had, and now Kelly Jackson's life was her own again and he was no longer any part of it. But the warm, moist impression from the touch of her lips against his cheek remained . . .

Turning to leave, he was visibly startled, something he instantly regretted.

Hanson and Tucker stood there, having come up on him silently; he hadn't a hint they were there. Dan Price's twin hardcases wore their customary black. Each man rested a hand on his holstered sidearm.

Hanson said, "What are you doing up here, McCall?"

Tucker snickered. "Sending little girls home to their mamas is what it looks like. And we saw that kiss, McCall. You score yourself some of that young stuff."

Hanson said, "Shut the fuck up, you idiot." To McCall he repeated, "What are you doing up here?"

"Pretty much what your buddy said. The kid was having a personal meltdown and I helped straighten her out, I hope."

Tucker snickered some more. "Uh-*huh*."

This was the most McCall had ever spoken to these two. Their paths never crossed because they were always Dan Price's shadows and McCall's work amid the crowds did not intersect with Price's activities.

Hanson said, "So now that you've sent the little brat on her way, what are you doing up here?"

"I'm leaving. I'm going back to work." McCall kept his eyes

106

dueling with Hanson's and his voice steady. "I would like to know one thing. What are you guys doing up here?"

Tucker said, "Security for the Premier. You know, Closing Ceremonies."

"Come on. The Chinese are handling that."

Hanson growled, "Don't push it, McCall. Get gone."

McCall said, "Right. See you boys around."

CHAPTER 15

J. Bob Wiley stood behind the massive National Indoor Stadium, where the Iranian team was expected to do well in an upcoming handball competition. The sun was baking a crowd of onlookers and well-wishers, and he stood at the front of it, close to the barrier of concertina wire surrounding an asphalt area where an Olympics bus was just now arriving with the Iranian team. Four Chinese soldiers, armed with machine guns, were posted at equidistant intervals, facing outward, each scanning the crowd steadily from left to right and back again.

The bus eased to a stop, its air brakes huffing and whistling. The taste and smell of burnt diesel fumes irritated his nostrils and made J. Bob want to sneeze, but he pinched his nostrils to avoid doing so. He didn't want to draw any attention to himself. At least, not quite yet. Then the bus driver was opening the door, and staff members of the Iranian team emerged while the team players could be seen rising to their feet inside and starting toward the door.

J. Bob had waited almost two weeks before making his move. It wasn't that he was chicken. In fact, it was damn frustrating to keep *planning* and not *doing*. J. Bob had whupped some serious ass back home just the week before last after a football game. He'd put three good old boys in the hospital that time. So it sure wasn't lack of guts, his not rushing some guard, grabbing his weapon at some event and going to work mowing down ragheads before now. It had been more difficult than he'd thought, getting close to the Arab teams so he could plan and carry out his vengeance.

Two weeks of being shuffled about in these crowds, of then going back to his crummy little hotel room on one of the off-streets south of Tiananmen Square. He hated the food here. He missed his country music. He hated the way all these damn chinks looked alike, same as the niggers back home. And most of all, what really got him peeved was being treated like he was a minority. Maybe he was surrounded by slant-eyes, but at least every damn one of them knew it was white folks who ran the world, who kicked butt in the name of God and glory when called upon to do so.

He had done his homework while sitting up nights in that grimy, shabby hotel room, staring at the English-speaking channels on the TV, paying the most attention to the sidebar items that they used to season the around-the-clock Games coverage.

Iran was the bad guys!

He'd settled on the Iranians mainly because they had, comparatively, the sloppiest security. The Syrians, for instance, weren't even letting people get within an eighth of a mile of their team in transit from their lodgings to the individual events, and their beefed-up security was worthy of a head of state. The Iranians, on the other hand, seemed too proud or too lazy or both to be so extreme. These different Arab nationalities all seemed like a bunch of four-flushing rattlesnakes, and J. Bob wouldn't have minded taking out a whole slew of them. But he had to stay realistic and within reason.

This was the third time he'd stood here in the past four days, watching the green busses unload teams for the competitions, all as a dry run for today. A forty-foot paved walkway extended from the bus to double iron doors through which the team would enter the stadium. Within the building, the seats would already have begun filling up. But even with the Iranian team's personal bodyguards, their security augmented by the Chinese military, there remained an opportunity for a person with enough grit and determination to breach that security and deliver a serious ass-whupping.

J. Bob intended to be that person. He would take whoever was closest to him—in this case, a late-middle-aged Japanese man who stood to his left, accompanied by an attractive young wife who appeared to be half the man's age. Or maybe she wasn't his wife. Anyway, he was twice the little Jap's size. He would hurl the Jap runt across the concertina wire, dash over the guy like a human bridge, grinding the dude's face into hamburger when he mashed it against the razor-sharp edge, and J. Bob would take down the nearest chink soldier by surprise and appropriate his weapon.

The first members of the Iranian team stepped from the bus, then the next, then the next, and before long this bunch of representatives of their axis of evil were strutting like they were proud or something, and the nearest soldier was presently glancing up range in his scanning of this crowd.

J. Bob drew back a couple of steps so he could forcefully charge the little Jap and pummel him with unexpected momentum onto the concertina wire. But instead, he bumped into a woman standing directly behind him with enough force to knock her to the ground. In his enthusiasm, he'd neglected to look around first.

The woman he'd knocked to the ground looked to be about nine months pregnant! She was as well turned-out as could be expected, given her condition, with a group of well-dressed Europeans who were erupting with concern. Her husband and their young children and some of the ladies of the group rushed to attend to her while some of the men turned angry looks in his direction and spoke rudely in a language he didn't understand, though he guessed it was French.

He gestured with his hands. "Gosh, I'm sorry, I didn't see—"
Then he decided to shut up.

The pregnant woman was being helped to her feet and seemed to be okay. Her husband had his arm around her and her lady friends were fussing over her while the children looked on. But between them and J. Bob stood the men who did not appear satisfied with an apology and the fact that the mother-to-be was uninjured. There were clenching fists and puffed-out chests.

J. Bob chose what seemed a prudent course of action and hightailed it out of there. His whole plan had gone to hell. The chink soldiers were looking straight at him. The element of surprise was completely lost. Those soldiers would cut him down before he even got a chance to negotiate the concertina wire, much less wrestle a weapon from one of them to open fire with on the athletes. And when the chink soldiers did open fire, some of their bullets might hit that poor pregnant French lady. He didn't want that to happen. Some things are sacred, and motherhood was one of them.

Now what?

He wasn't about to give up. He had come to Beijing to kill him some Arabs in atonement for losing his Ma and Pa, and by God that's what he would do. He would find another way, another time, another place.

But time was running out. He would have to work fast.

Luckily, he had coordinated several alternative plans . . .

Dan Price's office at SOC Headquarters was soundproofed, as were the offices of other section chiefs who needed to discuss matters related to national security. Tonight's visit by the American ambassador, who, along with dignitaries from several other countries, would be a guest of the Chinese Premier at the closing ceremonies, was just one such matter.

Stephen Mertz

After he heard Hanson and Tucker report, Price was damn glad of the soundproofing. He slammed his desktop with a clenched fist.

"So you let him just walk away?"

Tucker gulped loudly. "Uh sir, what were we supposed to do? It was sort of uncomfortable all around."

Price's eyes narrowed. "Uncomfortable?"

The temperature in the room seemed to drop several degrees. Overhead fluorescents lighted the windowless office. The walls were bare except for maps. The paperwork on Price's desk was neatly organized.

Hanson said, "I thought it best not to arouse suspicion."

"You should have detained him and contacted me. With Major Yang's help, I could have buried McCall in the Chinese jail system. He's the sort of man with the training and instinct to get suspicious just from seeing you two up there. Who was it he was talking to?"

Hanson referred to a small notepad. "We checked her picture on the database. It was a kid on the gymnastics team. Kelly Jackson."

"And they were just talking to each other, that's all?"

"That's right."

"It didn't look like a lover's quarrel or anything like that?"

Tucker chimed in with, "Naw, I don't think he's doing her, Mr. Price. I sort of razzed him along them lines and McCall didn't care much for it."

"That doesn't mean a thing," said Price. "I'd love to have something like that for leverage over the guy." He was thinking, *I never should have drawn McCall in to muddy the waters with Yang in the first place.* But there was no reason to voice this to Hanson and Tucker, or anybody else.

"We'll keep a close eye on him between now and showtime."

Tucker nodded. "Him and that sexy old broad he's running

112

with, that gal out front at the dispatch station, Rose."

Price let his eyes drift thoughtfully into space, gazing out the window in the direction of the garden outside his office. But he was seeing nothing but his thoughts.

"Rose Campbell having been friends with Jody Simms and involved with McCall could lead to something we'll need to take care of."

Tucker frowned. "What are you suggesting, sir? That we kill them both?"

Hanson sighed and said to Tucker, "You're such an idiot."

Price growled, "Can it. I don't need dissension in the ranks."

Tucker laughed. "Aw, Mr. Price, Hanson here, he always likes to tug on my chain when we're working together. He knows I carry my weight."

Hanson gave a begrudging grunt. "You're half decent once the shooting starts. It sure would be nice to know what that Simms bitch had stumbled on to."

Price sat forward, placing his elbows on the desk, the fingertips on one hand absently tugging at his left earlobe. "She told me she hadn't told anyone else and she trusted me, so I believe her. We were going into a firefight situation, and the method of containment seemed obvious. I took advantage of an opportunity. I believe she was telling the truth because no shit has hit the fan."

Tucker said, "What about that Campbell broad getting slick about the iPhone? You think she handed it over to McCall?"

"I'm sure she did or we would have found it," said Price. "I don't think McCall and the woman actually *know* a damn thing; they're just damn suspicious. But two SOC people buying the farm right before we initiate could draw too much attention. If they start getting too close to the truth, only then do we neutralize them."

Hanson said, "The computer at the arsenal has been

programmed to authorize us checking out all of the firepower we'll need. We're ready to initiate on your command."

Price said, "The Premier's people have confirmed that they're running on schedule. The Premier's party, including his guests, will be ensconced in the VIP box at 1900 hours. We'll hit them at 1930, after they're settled in and comfortable. After that, it's our show. Nothing Taggart McCall can do will matter worth a damn then."

CHAPTER 16

Candace Jackson didn't care for Mei Chen from the start.

Kelly's mother did not think of herself as a particularly attractive woman. In fact, after a shower, alone in her bathroom and wiping the steam from the mirror, she would scrutinize her face daily and see nothing but the lines, the need for a nip here and a tuck there. She hated the way she looked, and always had. And yet the world thought she was a beautiful, photogenic woman and she knew why. It was style, makeup and a cheery, outward disposition that made people *think* she was lovely. Naturally enough, she preferred those qualities in others.

Mei Chen was the first responder to Steve Jackson's call to Olympics security reporting their daughter as unaccounted for.

In a normal situation back in the States, the authorities would wait a period of time before considering someone missing, especially a strong-willed twenty-year-old. But this was hardly a normal situation. Participating in the Olympics was everything Kelly had strived for, and her schedule today especially was so filled, that it was inconceivable that she would just walk away and disappear without letting anyone know where she was going, especially her mother who had encouraged, been supportive, and yes, pushed her daughter since Kelly was a preteen.

They had walked to one of the rooms where the girls' team was quartered in the Athletes Village. Steve was his usual stolid, steadfast self and after ninety minutes had elapsed, had finally relented and made the call.

Candace, continuing to relentlessly thumb the redial on her cell phone every few minutes, hoping for some, any, contact with Kelly, exercised her utmost self-control. The vibrant blonde became a chilly ice queen in order to conceal the tumult of emotions within her, approaching panic. *Kelly's just in a mood,* she kept telling herself. *I wonder where Boris is?*

After twenty minutes of grumbling about Kelly being an irresponsible, spoiled child, Boris had left them and Candace was glad to be rid of that overbearing man who had so come to monopolize her and Steve's life since the start of their daughter's journey to the Olympics.

Her relief that someone would at least be responding to help was dashed when that someone turned out to be Mei Chen, who had attitude, all right, or rather an absence of it. She could have been a beauty if she'd do something with her hair, tried some makeup and a more alluring demeanor. There was about her no style, no makeup, no jewelry except for a ruby ring worn on her right hand and no cheery, outward disposition, only a remote sort of professionalism that bordered on aloofness and disdain for Candace and her husband as soon as she entered the room and introduced herself.

The first thing out of Candace's mouth was, "I thought they would send . . . one of our people."

"The SOC will have dispatched someone by now and they should arrive here shortly," said Mei Chen. "The Ministry of Internal Security monitors incoming calls to their switchboard. I was assigned to meet with you while the SOC was still deciding on the validity of your husband's call and who to dispatch. It is my responsibility to determine if your daughter's disappearance could in any way be connected, however remotely, with the activities of enemies of the state."

"Oh, I, I see."

Steve said, "Honey, I'm sure it will be fine."

"When did you last see your daughter?"

Steve replied, "Right after she finished her routine. She, uh, left without saying much."

Candace watched her husband addressing the woman and she wondered, *Does he see how beautiful she could be if that firm young body were to be partially clad in silk and lace that revealed yet concealed?* Of course he could see that. He was a man. And she liked Mei Chen even less.

"And your daughter said nothing to indicate where she was going or when she would be back? Has she been upset or showed any indication of unusual behavior?"

Candace said, "Kelly hasn't done as well in Beijing as . . . we'd hoped, but my daughter is a professional athlete. She can handle defeat, can't she, Steve?"

"Well now, honey, Kelly has been feeling stressed."

"Nonsense. Kelly would tell me about anything. I'm her mother. I've done everything for her."

"Sometimes," said Mei Chen, "the people we think we know the best are those we know the least."

And Candace heard herself snapping, "What, is that something Confucius would say? Are you going to pretend to be a little Charlie Chan for us, or are you going to find our daughter? And where are *our* people, for God sakes?"

A man said, from the doorway, "Here I am. Hello, everyone. Sorry for breaking up the party,"

She recognized him at once, the man who had returned Kelly's purse at that opening night party. She'd been a little tipsy then, not just from the champagne but also from that whole exciting day, and had brazenly tried to convey something sexy to him with her eyes when they had briefly pressed their flesh together in a customary handshake. Yes, she remembered . . . and he was still pleasing to her eyes as he strode in to join them.

She said, "At last, someone to help us."

Mei and McCall did not shake hands in the Western fashion, nor did they bow slightly as was the Asian custom; rather, there was only the slightest nod from each. Their eyes did most of the talking. As McCall identified himself, and Mei in turn told him who she was, each sized the other up in a way that made Candace feel a flicker of jealousy; this was more than clinical, professional interest she saw mirrored in their eyes.

Then when the moment passed and there followed a joint interrogation of the Jacksons, Candace could think of it as nothing else. Mei Chen and McCall took turns asking pointed questions like a relay team. Their questions concerned Kelly's state of mind and Steve, damn him, actually elaborated on how Kelly had become moody as the Games began winding down. Candace tried to soft pedal what Steve told them, but could plainly see that they believed him more than they believed her. They asked what Kelly was last seen wearing. Candace's description included the cotton shirt Boris had mentioned having last seen her in. They asked about Kelly's friends, and she supplied Tyrona's name. Was Kelly on medication? Had she ever done anything like this before, or threatened to? McCall was nowhere near as aggressive or assertive as Candace would have liked. He was downright deferential to Mei Chen, who never lost her cool veneer of professionalism, revealing nothing in tone of voice or demeanor, yet managing to convey disdain for Candace and her husband.

It was nothing she could put her finger on, but Candace had radar for that sort of thing and had never been wrong yet about a person. She would have died to know what McCall and the woman thought of each other. Had McCall received the come-on Candace had sent him at that party? *What must he think of me now? And why am I thinking like this at a time like this?*

118

With the interrogation completed, McCall and Mei Chen each left a card with Steve and thanked the Jacksons for their time. They left together.

When they were alone, Steve exhaled explosively. "Are you crazy? Are you out of your mind?"

"Regarding what, darling?"

"Regarding the way you treat people! That woman was sent to help us find Kelly. What in the world gets into you?"

"I saw the way you were looking at her. Don't deny it."

"Oh, for crying out loud."

Candace looked away and took a deep breath, exhaling slowly. She must control these emotions. She made a placating gesture.

"You're right. Let's not quarrel. The only thing that matters right now is getting our little darling back."

"That's more like it."

But she couldn't help herself.

"And when we do, I'm going to strangle the ungrateful little brat. After everything I've done for that little . . . *thing,* to pull a stunt like this! If even the whisper of this gets to the networks or the tabloids, or even only to the business reps, what chance do you think we'll have then of landing an endorsement deal, hmm?"

"Stop it. That's the sort of talk that drove our little girl away."

"And that's the problem, Steve. She's a world-class athlete. You still see her as your little girl."

"So did you, once upon a time. Now you treat her like she's a product, not a person. What happened, Candace? Let's turn this around. You've lost your way."

"The only thing lost right now," she said, "is one scatterbrained young woman. But I'm not worried and you shouldn't be either, darling. This will turn out all right. I don't know how, but it will. I may not think much of your sweet little Charlie Chan impersonator, but I can tell Mr. McCall has what it takes to find Kelly and bring her back."

"I know," said Steve quietly. "I saw the way you were looking at him."

General Yu Bin stood with his wife and daughter on the subway platform, watching the train slide efficiently and almost sound-lessly from high speed to a complete stop before them. The side doors whooshed open. The General made eye contact with Ai Ti and Yim-fong and nodded and, as a small unit, they merged with passengers jostling their way into the overcrowded car. The cramped discomfort was immediate. Additional passengers stepped aboard behind them. The compressed nearness of so many strangers precluded any notion of personal space.

This was the last underground stop before the shiny new train traveled on to shoot above ground for the final approach to the Olympic Green station, which was the end of the line.

The General had never traveled beyond China's borders, but from his reading he understood that, even taking into account the crowded urban conditions of Paris, London or New York, subway riding in Asia, regardless of country or city but especially in China, was considered far more primitive to the point of barbaric. Chivalry in the confines of these sardine cans on wheels, for instance, was not only dead but also long forgotten, as if it had never existed. That applied to manners and civility in general. Things were not made better just because these fellow passengers were moneyed tourists.

The General scanned the surrounding faces, seeing nothing to alarm him. He watched the two Beijing police officers on the platform that appeared extremely bored, watching the mass of humanity flowing past them.

This was exactly what he was hoping for. He was adapting a strategy from his tactics class in military school. The best time to attack was in the hours before dawn, when the anticipation of the coming dawn preoccupies and dulls a soldier's senses, as does the lethargy born of another long night passed without incident. That is when security is most lax. He was applying this principle by bringing his family to the final day of the Olympics.

Today was the day he would defect. Today he and his family—his ailing but stoic wife and his headstrong daughter—would make their bid for freedom. It had been an eventful two weeks at the Olympics. The televisions in the rooms they'd been staying in had vividly broadcast the non-athletic human dramas as much as the games. After two such intense weeks, he was hoping that security would be softening.

The time had not passed easily. They moved every night from cut-rate hotel to cut-rate hotel, using cash to bribe compliant desk clerks into foregoing the standard sign-in procedure. Given their unremitting close proximity to each other, the daily moving about, a building undercurrent of apprehension about this day had simmered. His wife and daughter had even taken to quarreling on three occasions, something heretofore unheard of. Yim-fong, while continuing to dress down so as to conceal her embracing of Western culture, had gone out on occasion. She came home safely each time, but it worried her parents.

During the previous two days, he had attended games with the tickets Yim-fong had acquired, once with his daughter and once alone. From his previous visits to the Olympic Green, he had a few ideas.

He listened to the amiable chattering in so many different languages around them in the subway car and a thrill coursed through him. This closeness of people who would soon be leaving China to return to their lands of freedom . . . he and his family would soon be among them.

The General put one arm around the shoulders of each of his two women and drew Ai-Ti and Yim-fong to him. His wife's features were stoic as ever as of late, as if carved in stone. Ai-Ti appeared strong enough but was quieter than he'd ever seen her and when his wife did speak, it was most often to wonder about the flowers she'd left behind in their garden. Who would tend them now? His daughter's eyes were wide with the excited anticipation of youth, worrying not about their danger, but enthralled by the promise of freedom instead.

Everything in his life, it seemed, had been building up to now, today . . . to *this*. He was about to do it. He was about to commit the ultimate act of betrayal. Defection to the other side. There would be a degree of improvisation in what was about to happen. He would look for the best, safest opportunity, and then they would do it.

The doors whooshed shut. The train jolted into rapidly accelerating motion.

CHAPTER 17

Mei Chen suggested they have a cup of tea and so, less than ten minutes after leaving Candace and Steve Jackson, McCall found himself at a small sidewalk café, one of the countless concessions dotting the Olympic Green, sharing a cup of green tea and conversation with an intelligent, well-put-together young Asian woman.

The flow of pedestrian traffic was steady and dense. McCall, who had been monitoring the moods and rhythms of these Olympics crowds for the past two weeks, could markedly sense a downshifting in the energy level of the passing crowd now that the end of these Olympic Games was approaching. Some had that glassy-eyed look of a Las Vegas visitor who dresses up for a night at the casino with a million bucks in credit and shambles back to his room stone broke. And yet there was a steady influx of new blood to the Games; many visitors only booked in for a weekend, or a block of days but not the entire two weeks. This steady turnover of enthusiastic new arrivals replacing those drained fans heading home, and the excitement of athletic competition of the games themselves and the attendant human drama, kept the atmosphere buoyant, though diminished from the first days.

McCall had drawn a few conclusions about Mei Chen during the short time spent in her company. She was lovely, as anyone could plainly see even within the social context of women who did not noticeably use makeup or accentuate their charms and appearance, the way a Western woman would. Mei was intelligent. That too was obvious in every word she spoke, and she only spoke when she had something to say. She was competent. This was evident from her participation in the interrogation of the Jacksons. And she was ruthless. She would have needed to be in order to rise to the level of field investigator for the Ministry of Internal Security in a historically, relentlessly male-dominated society; she would have needed more, much more, than mere competence and looks alone to reach her present position. Investigator Mei Chen was proud, strong and self-contained. And to McCall, she was unreadable.

When they were seated at a small, round glass table, each took a polite sip of the delicate tea, McCall waiting for her to start the conversation, since this was at her suggestion . . . not that he minded in the least. His chest pains of that morning, the fright that he was about to have a massive heart attack and die, seemed like another, half-forgotten reality out here in a world bustling with people, with a lovely woman seated across from him.

Mei said, "I thought we should compare notes. That is the colloquialism, is it not?"

"That's it." He gave her a tight grin. "But I'm afraid I don't have much to compare."

"Mrs. Jackson said during the interrogation that you'd met her daughter once before, when you returned her stolen purse. Surely you must have formed an opinion of her."

"Of Mrs. Jackson or her daughter?"

"The daughter, of course. Why would I be interested in the mother?"

"She wasn't very nice to you."

"She's American. What can one expect?"

"I'm American."

"Please stay with the conversation, Mr. McCall. The missing

girl. Did you form an impression of her?"

"A nice kid. So you don't like Americans?"

"I did not care for your Mrs. Jackson."

He chuckled. "In the interest of international diplomacy, let's get it right from the start. She's not *my* Mrs. Jackson."

"She is in the sense that she represents the culture that you represent."

Intelligent, McCall thought again. *And sharp as a new razor.*

He said, "Let's not be too harsh. I know she was rotten to you, but she does have a missing daughter. We're professionals, right? We shouldn't let emotions cloud our investigation."

"I never would. But you asked me what I thought of Americans, and she represents what I think. Mrs. Jackson is the spoiled mother of a spoiled daughter, and the telling thing of it is that they are spoiled by a man they have emasculated."

"You paint with a broad brush. Those are strong conclusions to draw from such a brief encounter."

"I am a trained interrogator. I draw conclusions from my questions and observations. Yours is a shallow, empty-headed culture. You Westerners are loutish, crude barbarians who would tear down ancient civilizations in the Mideast and in Asia that were flourishing while your ancestors were living in caves and beating each other to death with clubs. My people were cultivating an ancient society of tradition and strength and grace that has endured. Is there not even a fad in your culture for Eastern philosophies?"

"You must have broken a few ancient traditions when you were promoted as a field investigator."

She sipped her tea, eyeing him over the rim of her cup. "You would engage me in debate?"

"Why not? Can't reasonable minds disagree?"

"Very well. Some traditions evolve. The influence of woman

can no longer be restricted to the roles of motherhood and concubine."

"It's called feminism," said McCall, chiding but ever so gently. "It caught hold in my culture about fifty years ago."

She set her cup down with an audible clink. "Let us be frank, then."

"I, uh, thought you were plenty of that." He softened the remark with another chuckle.

She said, "I have not risen that far, you know. With such great social and political upheaval as China is undergoing today, sometimes one new face is considered sufficient window dressing by the old men in power. They wish to impress the outside world that they are permitting cultural change without really having to change anything. Everyone in my department, all of them male, has more prestige and receives better pay and promotions than I. They have me investigating the occasional crimes of passion, I believe they're called, and burglaries or disappearances where there might be even a remote possibility of anti-government activity."

"That must be the case here, I mean with Kelly Jackson."

"I suppose. One can never be sure, of course, which is why I was assigned to investigate. There is the possibility of a kidnapping. A hostage situation. Demands to be met. No demands have been made, but then the disappearance has only just been reported."

McCall said, "As a matter of fact, I spoke with Kelly shortly after the Jacksons last saw her. I wouldn't call her spoiled. She has the discipline of a trained athlete. You'd like her, or at least respect her."

"Indeed. And how disciplined did this trained athlete seem to you today when you saw her? What did you talk about?"

"Not much. She was feeling restless."

She considered this during another sip of tea. "I must speak with this Boris Temerov. One more routine job unless there is the whiff of criminal activity, whereupon you can rest assured the affair will be taken out of our hands and turned over to a higher echelon response unit."

"You sound bitter."

"I'm not. As you point out, my promotion was unusual enough and thus sufficient to satisfy me. But what about you, McCall?"

He blinked. Her cool directness was mildly unsettling.

"What about me?"

"I remember you."

"We've met?"

"No. But on the second day of my assignment to his unit, Major Yang passed around your file. I have a photographic memory, you see. It has been to no small extent responsible for my success."

"I crossed paths with your Major twice in twenty-four hours."

"We were told to pay particular attention to you should you cross our path." She registered a fleeting smile. "The Major, it seems, is not wholly satisfied with an equal working relationship with the SOC and Daniel Price's men."

"Dan Price is my superior. I wouldn't call myself one of his men."

"And what would you call yourself, Mr. McCall?"

The query caught him off guard.

His shrug was genuinely self-deprecating. "A guy of some experience."

"Major Yang was concerned in that you were directly involved in two separate investigations."

"Inadvertent bad timing."

"The first was the death of the American agent, Jody Simms."

"I knew her very slightly. That's what I told Major Yang and I thought that was the end of it."

"The Major is under the impression that you have a continuing interest in the Simms death. Have you?"

"She was a friend of a friend. Your Major seems to know quite a bit about me."

"Have you learned anything on your own about the woman's death, I mean beyond the fact that she was shot to death by a terrorist?"

"If I did, would I be likely to tell an agent of the Ministry of Internal Security?"

She liked that. Another smile, not quite so fleeting as the first, not quite so aloof; a glimmer of good humor behind the mask of professionalism.

"We are interrogators interrogating each other."

He nodded. He said, "Let's track down Boris Temerov. I'd like to talk to him too."

As they rose from the table, his cell phone sounded.

It was Rose. "I need you, Tag. We may have a hot one."

He glanced at Mei, who was eyeing him keenly. He turned his back on her. He spoke into the phone, quietly, "I'm not alone. Let's hear it."

"The Aquatics Center, west side. Some sort of scuffle. The call just came in and we're sending uniformed backup but you're closest. The caller reported seeing someone flashing a gun. Could be a hoax, could be a mistake, but we've got to respond and fast."

He turned back to Mei, maintaining as bland an expression as possible. *A weapon flashed by a civilian at the Olympics? That would be a first in the time he'd been here.*

He said, in a voice that he hoped matched his bored sigh, "Damn office politics. Okay, tell his majesty I'll be in to kowtow appropriately." He thumbed the disconnect button.

Mei's interrogator eyes were on him like laser beams. "You sound bitter." The tone was mildly chiding.

He said, "We'll have to resume our investigation later. I need to tend to office politics. My bureaucratic skills have always been found lacking."

"Is it Dan Price you were speaking of?"

"It's nothing important, but it is necessary and it might take awhile."

She handed him her card. "Then I shall proceed in my investigation without you."

He gave her a parting nod, which she did not acknowledge. He felt those steady laser beams on his back as he walked away. He caught her reflection in a line of windows.

She was walking away unhurriedly in another direction, speaking into her cell phone.

The moment she vanished into the heavy flow of people, Mc-Call broke into a run.

CHAPTER 18

The National Aquatics Center was another prominent show-piece of Olympic Green, covering more than sixteen acres with a capacity of 17,000.

McCall raced up the wide steps in a professional, sideways run, easing through the crowd at a dead heat, in and out of clusters of attendees who ambled about with no reason to hurry, passing them before they even knew he'd gone by. As he reached the mall at the top of the steps in the shadow of the looming Aquatics Center, the unmistakable *pop! pop! pop!* of a handgun thumped dully in the sunny, open air, the gunshots sounding hollow as they echoed.

The shots were followed by shrieks and alarmed cries.

He was nearly knocked off his feet as the crowd on the mall began scattering madly. He held his ground, not yet ready to draw his pistol from its concealed holster. That would attract attention and at this point, he did not want to draw any notice to himself.

A man was running through the crowd, coming in his direction; a thin, bespectacled, in-shape guy wearing the standard drab white shirt and khaki of the Chinese citizen, dashing pell-mell through the crowd, nearly stumbling more than once because he kept throwing glances over his shoulder. McCall saw desperation in the man's eyes.

Behind him, two men in similar attire were giving chase, their pistols high, waving off anyone in their path. The gunmen were closing in, but enough people continued to gawk or stood immobilized by fear, so the gunmen could not get a clear shot.

McCall took a step forward and intercepted the running man, who collided with him with enough force to take them both down except that McCall was prepared for the impact and pivoted on one leg to accommodate so both men remained standing, McCall's arm around the other's shoulders, steadying him.

The gunmen had drawn up a few yards away. Even previously immobilized bystanders were now darting for cover.

The man did not try to escape from McCall, who had no intention of committing himself to a specific course of action until he knew the players and the name of the game. For all McCall knew, he was a thief or a rapist or maybe even a murderer on the run.

The man was winded. "I am General Yu Bin. I wish to defect. Those men are trying to kill me. They are agents of my government."

McCall spoke sharply. "Down."

He pushed the General to the pavement, flattening himself next to him as two handguns began blasting, the reports magnified by the buildings facing the Aquatic Center. Bleats of pain and horror and shock as bullets kicked bystanders off their feet. Tumbling bodies. Blood splattered across the pavement.

"Please," the General rasped. *"Help me!"*

McCall said, "Let's go."

He didn't have a clue. The man could be lying. But innocent people were being massacred. Staying as low as possible to the ground, not only to keep out of the line of fire but also out of sight of the gunmen, he led the General by the wrist, hustling him away from there in a crouching withdrawal as fast as they could move.

The mall was deserted now except for the fallen: a wounded,

131

crying child; a middle-aged woman jackknifed and trembling and coughing blood; an old man with the top of his head blown off. A pair of Chinese parents knelt over the downed child, wailing for help, but as yet no one was brave enough to come forward.

The gunmen stood there, not concerned in the least with anything except searching through the melee for their quarry. One of the men shouted and pointed. The second gunman saw what his partner was pointing at. They both opened fire.

McCall muttered, "Damn!"

Bullets whistled, ricocheting off the sidewalk and building fronts.

Rage and frustration pulsed through him. They were practically in the open! Most bystanders had sought cover inside doorways or behind whatever cover there was—light poles, trash cans, overturned tables at the concessions. He wanted to draw his pistol and return fire, but the danger was too great that he would cause additional collateral damage, that more innocents would stop more stray bullets. The only responsible thing he could do for any onlookers in the line of fire was to draw the fight away from here.

The General was only slightly winded. "We cannot outrun their bullets. Perhaps I shoulder surrender. My family is nearby, my wife and daughter, but they're safe." There was desperation in his eyes, but up close McCall also discerned the stony determination of a trained soldier.

Ten feet away was a narrow walkway that cut behind two of the structures opposite the Aquatics Center. The walkway was closed off with a padlocked chain-link fence affixed with a sign reading *Staff Personnel Only.*

McCall said, "That fence. Can you make it? Can you climb it?"

"Of course."

"Then let's do it. Good luck, General."

"And to you, sir," said the General. "And thank you!"

They dashed toward the fence. A peculiar hush had fallen like a heavy blanket across the mall in the aftermath of the blasting violence, as if this tiny corner of the world was holding its collective breath, waiting to see what would happen, who would die next. In that hush, the slap of shoe leather on the pavement seemed magnified, both the running feet of McCall and the man who ran alongside him shoulder to shoulder, and of their pursuers.

They would have to be Chinese agents sent to stop the General's defection at any cost, if there was merit to the man's story, and McCall was willing to believe the man had told him the truth, considering his composure under fire and military conditioning. The sight of those cut down—*a child, a woman, an elderly man . . . good God!*—was seared into McCall's mind, and he knew he'd have a fifty-fifty chance of taking down one or both of those sons of bitches that did it even if one of them got lucky and he bought the farm. But the other side of that coin remained: the more bullets fired, the better the chance of another kid, another old man, maybe a young pregnant mother, catching a stray round. And if these two bastards were so kill-happy as to stop the General's defection by any means possible, that meant the General was, or was carrying, something really valuable. McCall's first priority therefore would be getting him to safety.

They reached the fence.

McCall said, "You first."

He provided a step-up by cupping his hands. The running man planted one foot in the cupped hands and propelled himself at the fence, scrabbling up and over. McCall reeled to face their pursuers.

One man fired a round on the run that whistled by McCall's

left ear close enough for him to feel the heat. The second agent was raising his pistol as they closed in fast.

Aw, the hell with it, McCall decided.

He drew his pistol and fired two rounds into the air. The pursuers drew up short, suddenly more cautious. McCall spun back to the fence, reholstering his pistol and utilizing the sparse window of opportunity to clamber up and over the fence. The General was waiting for him.

The pursuers were up and racing toward the gate. They both opened fire. Saffron flame barked from their weapons. More ricochets, the sizzling of more near misses.

McCall took point. He and the General hurried down the walkway that led to a T where a wider alley in either direction was lined with dumpsters. McCall paused to glance along their backtrack. The first of the gunmen was scaling the fence without effort, about to drop to the other side to continue in hot pursuit, his partner behind him, starting up the fence.

To McCall's right, beyond the first couple of dumpsters, was a low overhang above a rear door, closed now, through which deliveries were made or the trash taken out. Beyond the overhang, more dumpsters. To the left the bare walls of the alley extending beyond the T. No one was in sight.

McCall said, "This way," and sprinted right.

Another gunshot.

The General said, *"Ugh!"* and lurched sideways, his head snapping back as if he'd taken a punch. But he remained on his feet and ran beside McCall, continuing to maintain a shoulder-to-shoulder pace. There was a long, thin red line along the General's left cheek, oozing droplets of blood. He caught McCall's sideways glance of concern.

"It's nothing. I am all right."

"I'll say you are," said McCall, having definitely made up his mind about the guy. "You're some tough stuff, General. And you ran into the right man. Grab cover behind that dumpster over there."

The General frowned and slowed his pace. "You will not fight alone on my behalf. It is not my nature to hide."

"You came to me," McCall reminded him. "Let me handle this. We don't have much time."

Picking up his own pace, he placed a flattened palm to the middle of the General's back and gave the shorter man a forceful shove that sent the General forward to brace himself against the dumpster.

"Very well. You're right, of course."

Bending his knees, frowning at the undignified behavior to which he was being subjected, the General lowered himself from sight in the space behind the dumpster, between it and the wall beneath the tin overhang.

McCall bounded atop the closed dumpster with enough forward momentum to send him right on up onto the tin overhang. He pressed himself flat. The tin was warm from the reflected sunlight, not too hot to touch but hot enough to make sweat beads pop out along his hairline. He inched his way across the overhang so he could peer with one eye over the edge at the T of the alley. His heart was hammering against his rib cage like a drum solo.

The two gunmen appeared, assuming a professional back-to-back stance, simultaneously sweeping the alley in different directions with alert eyes and pistols held ready. To a manhunter in an urban environment, an empty alley is far more treacherous than one with visible adversaries. They snapped a curt exchange and split up, warily treading off in opposite directions from the T.

The one coming toward McCall's place of concealment was raising his line of vision toward the tin overhang.

It was now or never.

McCall sprang as if launched from a catapult, intending to come down on the gunman in a full body slam that would have taken them both down with McCall on top, whereupon he had intended to disarm the man, cuff him and make a run for it before his partner could make it to this end of the alley. But the guy turned unexpectedly, apparently to call over to his partner, resulting in McCall coming down at a slightly off angle that sent both men sprawling to the ground, the gun spinning from the man's grasp, but it was no body slam. The man rolled into a somersault and was back on his feet in no time, retrieving his pistol and tracking on McCall with death in his eyes while Mc-Call was still reaching a sweaty palm back to draw his own weapon, and he knew suddenly, with crystal clarity, as if this were happening in slow motion, that a bullet was about to end his life before a heart attack ever got a chance.

General Yu exploded from behind the dumpster, swooping in on the gunman from his blind side. He took hold of the man's shirt collar and his belt, catching him by complete surprise. The General shifted his weight and struck the top of the man's head against the corner of the dumpster. The blow was of such force that the dumpster shimmied. The gun dropped from the stunned man's hand again and he made no move to retrieve it this time. He started to wobble before the General smashed the man's head into the side of the dumpster again . . . and again, and again.

McCall shifted his attention to the second gunman, who had witnessed the ambush and was running toward them, firing his pistol. The gunfire pummeled McCall's eardrums within the confines of the alley. He brought his pistol up into a two-handed target acquisition and squeezed off a round intended for the man's legs, to take him down. But his aim was off. The bullet snicked away part of the gunman's skull, dropping him into a death stumble.

McCall turned to see the General releasing his hold on the other man. The man collapsed to the pavement like discarded rubbish. He did not move. The corner of the green dumpster glistened with oozing splashes of pulpy pink brain matter and the white chips of skull fragments.

The General dusted off his hands, then dusted himself off. "We seem to make a formidable team."

McCall sighed. "It would have been better if we hadn't killed these two, not that they didn't deserve what they got."

Faces were peering from windows. A few brave souls stared at them from doorways along the alley.

General Yu said, "And what now, Mr. . . ."

"McCall. Taggart McCall. Well, I'd say a good start would be to leave these two—" he indicated the bodies, "—for whoever wants them, and for you and me to initiate a damn speedy withdrawal."

CHAPTER 19

J. Bob gingerly picked himself up off the pavement. Those around him were beginning to stir. Like him, they had dropped to the pavement when it became apparent something terrible was occurring in their midst.

He'd been walking in the direction of the Beijing National Stadium and had just passed the Aquatics Center when he heard the gunfire, sounding at first like fireworks. (If there was one thing you could say about chinks, they sure loved their fireworks.) But the notion that it was some frivolous celebration over some team winning one of the Games was quickly shattered, panic rippling through the crowd in the mall like a wave across the bay down at Galveston.

The crowd parted like the Red Sea for the two men—an American, from the look of him, racing side by side with a chink—while behind them two more Chinamen fired off rounds that were finding human targets but missing the fleeing men.

With bullets flying about and seeming to be ricocheting everywhere amid the mad melee of scurrying to get out of the line of fire, J. Bob had done like those around him and merely dropped to the ground, making himself as flat a target as possible. He craned his neck as far as he could from that position. He saw the empty plaza, the fallen bodies and the gunmen continuing to fire and give chase. He saw the American assist the Chinaman over a chain-link fence, then following him but not before firing a couple rounds in the air from a concealed weapon.

The Chinese gunmen went over the chain-link fence and soon the four of them were gone from sight.

That's when folks started picking themselves up and brushing themselves off, warily at first. Frightened eyes. Whispered mutterings from the dazed, the confused, the frightened. Wails of anguish from where the innocents had been hit. Sirens could be heard approaching from every direction.

Across the mall, SWAT-suited Chinese soldiers were pouring in to secure the area, machine guns held at port arms, followed by police and Olympics security, including a medical team that established a quick perimeter around the wounded and dead.

J. Bob dusted himself off and resumed walking in the direction of the National Stadium. The "bird's nest" towered, majestic as ever, like an enormous jewel sparkling beneath the summer sun.

He walked with his hands in his pockets, aware that his lumbering, T-shirted form was intimidating to many of the smaller-boned, better-dressed Asians and Europeans around him. They stepped aside. The soldiers hadn't reached his side of the mall yet. No one tried to stop him. He had no time or interest in being detained by authorities who might want to question witnesses.

He'd established a new goal for himself before this violence had erupted, and he must pursue it to conclusion with absolute single-mindedness. The hell with just waltzing in and greasing a bunch of rag heads, he had decided. Maybe it was his second failed attempt—he had waited for hours after a match, with a posted soldier all marked as the one he would take the weapon from to open fire with when the team showed; he had been ready to pounce, only to learn that the team had slipped out a secret exit after their match ninety minutes earlier. He'd stewed about that until it came to him that he was about to risk everything but he would only be nailing the small fry, the athletes sent to compete and the fans supporting them. Worthy targets but, shoot yeah, real small fish. He realized how small when he saw the update on TV about the raghead representatives, big shots in their governments, who would be attending the closing ceremony. In addition to the Chinese Premier and his select dignitary group of diplomats, there were other VIP boxes and one of them would be host to ambassadors from Iran, Syria, and Saudi Arabia. . . . Shoot! Why not take the snake off right at the neck, something Ma and Pa would be damn proud of when he rode his thunderbolt to join them in Heaven. He would have left his mark on the pages of world history, damn straight. That's what he was fixing to do. He would sly his way up to that raghead VIP box and deal them some serious retribution for what they had done to his Ma and Pa.

And nothing was going to stop him.

Kelly regained consciousness with a scream that stayed trapped in her throat because electrical tape had been pasted across her mouth. The scream almost choked her; it was so strong, born of the pain racing through her, and the panic that came with being unable to see. *She was blindfolded!*

She was instantly alert, aware of her situation. Her pain emanated from a spot behind her right ear that pulsated as if on fire and every pulse sent pain jolting through her. She was bound to a low-backed chair, her ankles lashed to the front chair legs. Her wrists were tied behind its back with what felt like rubberized clothesline. It was not comfortable. She thought, *Thank God my muscles are conditioned to physical endurance. And Thank God I'm still wearing my clothes!*

She couldn't see, but she could feel and hear. She felt closeness. She was in a small room. The air was warm. She detected her own scent and she was glad she was wearing perfume. And close by . . . *someone was breathing,* a shallow, normal, steady breathing, not excited or lascivious, but constant and nerve-wracking.

It took a few moments for her to summon the final events before she'd lost consciousness, like awakening and trying to recall your final thoughts before you fell asleep the night before. Then she recalled her conversation with Taggart McCall and what happened afterward, returning to her like the trickle of a stream that became a flowing river and carried her from Mc-Call, following his instructions and leaving the off-limits area, returning to the main concourse.

She had decided to return to the floor to see how Tyrona had done in her competition. Somehow, talking with McCall had renewed her. The competent, rock-solid *maleness* of him had been reassuring as well as making something quiver deep down within her *femaleness,* where she experienced an attraction to him despite the gap in their ages and his obvious worldliness. There didn't seem to be many men around like Taggart McCall anymore. She wished her father was more like McCall, instead of the affable but weak-willed man dominated by her mother. But she was one to talk! Her mother had controlled her life since enrollment in her first gymnastics class as a child.

Within minutes after leaving McCall, she had been accosted by the slight, middle-aged Chinese man who, soft-spoken and humble, had requested that she accompany him, please, to where his wife was waiting with their eleven-year-old daughter, who was living life in a wheelchair. The daughter was a huge fan of Miss Jackson's and it would mean the world to her if Miss Jackson could kindly spare only a moment, please, to go with him to briefly meet the little girl, to autograph her Olympics Game program. Could anyone have said no to *that?* Her ego had been flattered, of course, and had reawakened the knowledge that, beyond her vanity, this was as much what her job here was about as winning or losing. She was in Beijing to be a role model, an ideal and an inspiration as she was to this man's little girl. And that was a job worth doing right.

But there had been no little girl in a wheelchair, no nice mother waiting with more profuse gratitude. There had been a turn through a double iron doorway that the man held open for her, and she barely noted the door latching shut behind her because she was still bubbling along, full of the milk of human kindness and her big fat ego. When she stopped in her tracks, realizing that the man had led her into a stony, long and narrow service corridor without doors or windows, leading only God knew where, she should have felt alarm more quickly, she realized now. She might have been able to resist. She was a trained gymnast, for crying out loud! She knew nothing about physical combat, but she knew the strengths and weaknesses of the human body and where defensive force could be applied if only—

Stop it, she told herself, taking in long draws of air through her nostrils, twitching her mouth beneath the duct tape, realizing she was totally, effectively gagged. All of the hassles that had troubled her—her mom and dad, the harshness of Boris and, mostly, her own crappy performance in competition— seemed so trivial, so insignificant now, tied to a chair God knows where, blindfolded, being studied by someone who was sitting there content with nothing more for the moment than breathing and silence.

She had started to turn, started to say something, but she never got the chance. The man held what she identified as a leather sap, and he popped her behind the right ear before she could even half-turn to face him, and that was her last memory before falling into dead-to-the-world unconsciousness. She had been transported here and she was certain that the person breathing in this little room with her was the solicitous, beseeching, humble Chinese man with the invalid daughter.

How ironic that such a short time ago she had been surrounded by a sea of people and had wanted only to be alone. Right now she would have given anything for someone to come to her aid. But she had to wonder if anyone cared. Had anyone missed Kelly Jackson yet and initiated a search?

She wished Tag McCall knew of her predicament.

What in the world would happen next?

CHAPTER 20

McCall and the General paused at the far end of the alley and pressed themselves against the wall as a military SWAT team hustled past in the direction of the mall and the shootings. They waited for a ten count after the soldiers had passed, then negotiated the chain-link fence barring the alley and seamlessly merged with the streaming crowd along the southern side of the Aquatics Center, where the endless parade of chattering Olympics attendees indicated they were unaware of the commotion that McCall and the General were leaving further behind with every step they took. Eventually they slowed their pace to a normal stride, angling away from the Center. McCall raised SOC headquarters on his cell phone.

Rose Campbell caught the call at the dispatch station and her caller ID told her who was calling.

"Hello, Tag." He could see that Irish smile of hers in the warmth of her voice. "Business or pleasure?"

"A little of both," he said, "but this isn't about us. I'm coming in with a friend. I need to see Dan Price."

"I think he just slipped out the back way a little while ago with his two shadows, Tucker and Hanson."

"I need to see Dan Price. Immediately."

"Care to give me a hint? It might help me get him in."

"Major Yang and his people are monitoring this and all of the calls and communications coming into SOC."

"That's it? We sort of suspected that, didn't we?"

"It's why I'm not saying anything. I need Dan in his office right now. I'm five minutes out."

"I'll see what I can do."

"Have him there, Rosie," said McCall, and he thumbed off the connection.

Price was waiting in the doorway of his office when McCall and the General walked in, past the dispatch station.

Rose caught McCall's eye with a smile. "Anything else?"

"Thanks, Rosie."

Then he and the General were seated across from Price, who clipped, "All right, McCall. What's this all about? Who is this man?"

"This is General Yu Bin. He's defecting. He came to me. He's seeking political asylum for himself and his family."

The General added, "My wife and teenage daughter. They are safe. I asked them to remain standing nearby and was about to accost one of the officials of the American team at the Aquatics Center, when I was seen by two officers of Internal Security."

Dan Price said, "Oh, shit." He nailed McCall with a steely stare. "That trouble over there just awhile ago . . . that was you?"

McCall said, "The General ran up to me. The bastards were shooting people down, Dan. So I got him out of there."

"And killed two Chinese National agents in the process. Holy shit."

The General said, "I killed one of those men."

"I see," said Price. He was quiet for several heartbeats, as if silently counting to ten but he only made it to five. He rose from behind his desk. "General, I need to have a few words with Mr. McCall in private. Will you wait outside my office, please?"

"But . . . why?" The General asked, his voice troubled. He gave no indication of rising.

Price used his right hand to unhitch a cell phone from his belt and snapped it open with a flick of his wrist. With his left hand he held the General by the arm.

The General did not forcibly resist being guided to his feet.

McCall said, "What up, Dan?"

Price said, "I'll get to you in a minute." Into the phone he said, without preamble, "Hanson, you and Tucker meet me in front of my office—*now.*" He terminated the connection and guided the General across his office, to the door.

The General said, "Please understand, Mr. Price. I am at your mercy. There are people sent to kill me. I have come to you for help."

"I appreciate that." Price opened the door and firmly guided the General through. "We will help you, and your family."

The General stepped into the corridor with one last look over his shoulder, beseeching McCall with his eyes to help him; a man used to issuing commands and having his orders obeyed, yet here he was on uncertain ground, he and his family in mortal danger and he had come to McCall for help.

McCall tasted bile at the back of his throat. A sudden, white-hot jab of pain ice-picked his chest, kicking the wind from his lungs. Then it was past. He brought himself to his feet.

"Hold on, Dan. I told the General—"

Price closed the door on General Yu Bin. He turned to face McCall.

"You hold on. You heard my call to Tucker and Hanson. They'll be here any second. The General will be safe enough and his family will be too. But you've put me in a hell of a position. Who the hell authorized you to take a hand in something like this?"

"I didn't have much choice. He picked me, not the other way around."

"And why the hell should he pick you?"

146

"Hell if I know. I'm dressed like an American. He wants to defect to the West. Those two Chinese agents after him were killing everything in their sight to get to him."

"That's their prerogative, McCall. This is their country."

"They were shooting down women and children. No one has that prerogative. Not while I'm around."

"McCall, you're not being realistic. China is putting on its best face to the world because they want to lure us in and devour us in a world economy that they can rig. They don't need missiles and armies to take over the world. All they need is their slave labor and they grow fat and powerful. And in their country, they do whatever the hell they want. What the hell were you thinking? You do remember Major Yang, don't you? Who do you think is in charge of the manhunt to capture the General and prevent his defection? That's right, the same Bureau that Mei Chen works for. You see how complicated things can get?"

"Doesn't seem complicated to me at all. I'm clean on those kills in the alley unless they've got security camera footage and if they did, they would have already sent it to you with an order for my head. So we're clean there."

"Dammit, McCall, you're dicking with my mission. Big time."

"Yeah, I was wondering about all this personal concern. What mission would that be, Dan?"

"Don't play it cagey, pal. You're not up to it. You're a burnout and that's why you're picking up nowhere change walking through crowds looking for purse-snatchers. I'm your boss, Mc-Call, and my mission is to keep this SOC unit functioning effectively, which I've done since we arrived. Now, with less than twenty-four hours to go, one of my people is responsible for the death of two host government agents and the defection of one of their military officers. And another thing. What were you doing up on the off-limits level with that Kelly Jackson girl? Tucker and Hanson told me about that."

"Knew they would. I was wondering how long it would take for you to get around to that. That's why you had me assigned once her parents reported her missing. You like tightly wrapped packages, don't you, Dan? I was going to ask what your two hardcase boys were doing up there myself."

"I don't like your manner, McCall."

"That's all right, it's not for sale. Like you said, I'm earning my chump change rounding up purse-snatchers."

Something close to a sneer curled the corner of Price's mouth.

"Yeah, and that's what you're going back to. I'm turning the Kelly Jackson situation over to someone more experienced. I'll find someone. And I'll take care of the General."

"After what happened to Jody Simms," said McCall, "that's not real reassuring, is it?"

Price's eyes narrowed. "What are you saying? General Yu's defection has nothing to do with that, and I had nothing to do with Jody Simms's death except to take down the terrorist son of a bitch who capped her. Now get out of my sight, burnout. You're back to pounding the beat as of right now. I don't want anything from you but strict routine for the duration."

McCall decided he'd said enough.

"You're the boss, Dan." He opened the office door. "I'll say goodbye to the General on my way out."

The General was gone.

The corridor was busy. The SOC lobby was a hub of activity.

Price said, "Where is he?"

"Maybe he stepped away to use the restroom."

The General was not in the restroom.

When they returned to the lobby, Rose had just finished fielding a call.

Price asked her, "What happened to the man who came in with McCall? He was standing outside my office."

"He walked off as soon as you closed your door. Sorry, I didn't know you wanted an eye kept on him. You showed him out of the office and the minute you closed the door, he walked away."

Hanson and Tucker walked up, their eyes on McCall, cautious.

Hanson said, "Sorry, sir, we would've gotten here sooner except for that mess over at the Aquatics Center."

Tucker added, "And the damn crowds are getting really heavy for the final games. Got here as fast as we could."

McCall said, "You didn't happen to pass a Chinese gentleman on his way out?"

Tucker snickered. "Saw a couple thousand chinks walking around out there."

"Uh-huh. The one I'm talking about was supposed to be waiting for you outside Dan's office."

Hanson said, "Nope, we didn't see any chinks once we got inside. What's up?"

McCall eyed Price. "That's what I was going to ask. Why couldn't the General wait inside your office with us until your two goons showed up?"

Tucker thrust out his blunt chin. "Hey, who you calling goons?"

Hanson glowered, his hand resting on the grip of his holstered sidearm. "Yeah, and who's this General you're talking about?"

"I'm thinking that maybe you boys already know that. It wouldn't be like you to intercept the man on his way out, would it?"

Tucker scratched the back of his red, sunburned neck and turned to Price. "Sir, what the hell is this man talking about?"

Price was staring daggers. "Yeah, McCall, what the hell *are* you talking about? You've been slinging enough innuendo around to fall just short of accusing me of something."

Tucker said, "Huh?"

Hanson told Tucker, "Shut up, idiot."

Price said, "First you talk about Jody Simms and now this. Talk straight, McCall. What have you got? What are you saying?"

Maybe, McCall decided, *he had not said quite enough.*

"I don't know, Dan. I don't have the proof to accuse anybody of anything. As for the innuendo . . . well, why couldn't the General wait in your office an extra five minutes until these two showed up? The way you gave him the heave-ho, it's like you wanted him to walk off, or set him up to be taken off. That was a temporary lapse in judgment, letting you pull that off. Maybe I am a burnout but dammit, I'm a persistent burnout."

"Maybe I did want him to walk off," said Price. "Have you thought about that, burnout? He knew he was cornered. He saw his out and he took it. Yeah, like I expected him to."

"Care to tell me why?" asked McCall.

"I already did. The General never came to you, okay? You never brought him to my office, got it? This unit has kept a clean nose so far with the Chinese authorities and it's going to stay that way as long as it's on my watch. That's why it's personal. Now get out there and get back to trolling for purse-snatchers."

McCall said, "After lunch." He tossed a grin at Rose Campbell as if none of this happened. "What do you say, Rosie?"

That dimpled smile of hers came up at full wattage. "I'd say you're talking to a hungry girl, mister."

She removed her headset after a nod from each of her co-workers, who could not help but overhear, and grabbed her purse.

McCall nodded at Dan Price and Hanson and Tucker.

"Gentlemen."

They watched McCall and Rose walk off across the busy lobby.

Tucker said, "I'd like to kill that son of a bitch and take my time doing it." He spoke low so that only Price and Hanson could hear him.

"Sir," said Hanson, "do you want us to—"

Price stopped him with a gesture. "No. Too much is going down and we're almost at zero hour. You heard what I said about keeping this unit clean. We can't put ourselves under scrutiny now, for Chrissake. If this unit became involved in the defection of a high-ranking Chinese general, the Chinese would be all over us and we'd have to scrub our mission. So, no. We don't kill McCall. Not yet. Not with everything that's at stake."

Tucker stared after where McCall and Rose had disappeared into the passing crowd outside.

"I'd like to kill them both. And I'd take my time with the bitch, too. She'd scream to die a long time before I killed her. It'll be sweet."

Hanson glanced about to make sure that no one could overhear them.

"Shut the hell up, you crazy bastard. There will be killing soon enough."

Price said, "Get lost, both of you. You know the countdown numbers. And don't worry, Tucker. You'll get your chance. McCall and that lady friend of his, they're walking dead. They just don't know it. But they will, soon enough."

CHAPTER 21

McCall sat with Rose in one of the employees' cafeterias, at the same table where Rose had introduced him to Jody Simms. This time they shared the table with Mei Chen, who had contacted McCall on his cell phone just after he and Rose left the SOC HQ.

Mei informed McCall that she had completed her interview with Boris Temerov. Was McCall free to rejoin the investigation?

McCall told her, "Dan Price pulled me off that."

"When did this happen?"

"A few minutes ago."

"Where will you be for the next thirty minutes?"

He told her, adding, "I'm with a friend."

"Ask the friend to expect me," she said coolly, and she broke the connection.

McCall and Rose had continued walking along. "Sorry. I hope you don't mind."

"Mind? Why should I mind?" Rosie kept it light with that pretty smile in place, but McCall had come to know her well enough and he heard the truth of her feelings in her voice.

He said, "I was looking forward to some time alone with you too, but this comes under the heading of work."

That brought an arched eyebrow. "How so?"

"Damned if I know. The lady's tied in with Major Yang, and he's tied in with Dan Price and . . . hell, the whole thing's just too balled up right now for me to figure, to tell you the truth. Maybe Mei Chen will change some of that."

Mei arrived minutes after they did and declined anything but bottled water while McCall and Rose each had a rice bowl.

Having acknowledged to himself long ago that he would never be politically correct, McCall could not help but mentally catalogue and compare the two women seated across from him.

They were both lovely. Mei, all slim and muscular efficiency of manner, even if her style and demeanor muted, but did not conceal, an embodiment of the exotic essence of the Asian woman. And Rose Campbell, who could not have been more in contrast. Rosie's earthy good nature and sharpness of mind was combined with scant shyness in expressing her every opinion as it occurred to her, always in a witty and appealing way.

Mei joined them just as they were starting on their meals. Rose was polite, but she eyed Mei Chen with the universal look of any woman sharing a table with a man she's sleeping with and a woman of his acquaintance whom she's just met.

Mei said, "I have spoken with Dan Price. I persuaded him to keep you on the Kelly Jackson assignment until it is resolved."

Rose smiled. "You must have used considerable charm. I've never known anyone to change Dan's mind about anything."

If Mei discerned anything catty in that remark, it did not penetrate her demeanor of professional cool bordering on aloofness.

"Charm was unnecessary in this case. It is one of the feminine traits I have yet to cultivate. I reminded Mr. Price that it was necessary to have an SOC agent involved, as stated in the Olympic charter. And you, McCall, are particularly suited to such an assignment since you have already had two encounters with Miss Jackson."

McCall said, "As a matter of fact, I was the last one to see her before she disappeared."

"I additionally informed Mr. Price that I specifically wanted to work with you."

Rose studied McCall with a Mona Lisa smile. An edgy Mona Lisa smile.

"Yes, he really is something, isn't he?"

McCall wanted to say, *Ease up, Rose, there's nothing to be jealous about.* But he kept his mouth shut on that subject, the way a wise man would.

He said, "Thanks, Mei. However you pulled that trick off, thank you. You're right; I am the man for the job. Kelly Jackson reminds me of someone very close to me, my own daughter, but that's a bonus point. She's a good kid, I like her from the two short times we met, and I want to be the one who finds out what happened to her and then get her back in the game."

Mei said, "I've spoken with Boris Temerov. A typical Russian. Surly, uncommunicative, arrogant."

"Arrogance," Rose mused quietly, as if speaking to her rice bowl. "Wouldn't want any of that going around."

This time McCall said, "Rosie . . ."

Mei feigned obliviousness to that exchange. "Temerov claims to have no idea where she could be. He suggested that we speak to one of Kelly's teammates, Tyrona Carey. Apparently the two are best friends."

Rose sighed and said, in a different tone than she'd been using before, "You know, I think I like you, Mei Chen."

Mei regarded Rose solely, as if for the first time. "Indeed?"

Rose nodded. "Indeed. You're obviously a more than competent investigator, and whether it was your good looks or your brains, you turned Dan Price. That trumps my pettiness. I'm sorry, hon."

Mei blinked at being called *hon.* "The two of you don't like Dan Price. Why is that so? Does it concern the death of Jody Simms?"

Now it was Rose's turn to blink. She said, "We have our suspicions."

"I will delve into Dan Price's file in our records, if you think that would help," said Mei. "What do you suspect him of, and why?"

McCall decided it was time to redirect the conversation. Mei Chen was working for Major Yang. That meant she would love to apprehend General Yu Bin, or kill him on sight. McCall wanted to find Kelly Jackson, which meant working with Mei. But he wanted to help the General and his family too. There was a good chance he would see the General again. Having taken fire together, the General could well make an effort to approach him. But Mei would be at his side until Kelly Jackson was found or heard from. Time was of the essence in a tangled web, and adhering to a need-to-know policy was his best bet.

He finished the last of his rice bowl and set aside the chopsticks.

"Let's concentrate on the matter at hand, okay? The women's gymnastics team has a match coming up, so right now Tyrona Carey will either be having a meal or training."

Rose said, "I should be getting back to work too."

Rose caught his eye and for an instant they communicated in that nonverbal way copacetic lovers have, which Mei did not see. Rose got what he was doing and she was okay with it. They had been unlucky thus far in their quest for a hook into anything suspicious about Jody Simms's death, but they were also lucky in that their probing had gone undetected by Dan Price so far. They didn't know what, if anything, he was up to, but by the same token he didn't know that they were snooping. The more people drawn into the inquiry, the faster Price would learn of their endeavors, whereupon he would check and double-check to make sure his back trail was clean, and they would not have advanced, but would effectively be stymied.

Mei said, "Very well. Let us find this silly Kelly Jackson girl, then. Let us interrogate the Carey girl."

"You interrogate her," said McCall. "I'll interview her. She's an American gymnast, Mei, not a criminal—or a Chinese citizen."

Mei conceded this with a short nod. "As you say."

When they were halfway to the main entrance, Rose said, "Mei, I'd like to speak with Tag alone for just a moment, please."

Mei's eyes clouded. "Tag?" Then she understood. "Oh. Short for Taggart. Of course. Yes, I will wait outside."

When she was beyond earshot, Rose said, "Hon, I want to apologize for acting like a jealous wife just now."

He chuckled. "Hey, it was good for my ego. Don't sweat it."

"Maybe we should let her help us."

"She'll look into Price on her own if she hasn't already, just out of curiosity."

"God, I hate it when I act like a bitch. It won't happen often, I promise."

"Rosie, go back to work. It's professional mind games Mei Chen and me are playing. Cop games. How much to tell the other to get everything the other one knows without really giving up a damn thing."

"I had a dream about Jody again last night."

"Don't worry, I won't forget Jody. And that's another reason I want to work with Mei Chin. If she finds a clue linking Dan Price to anything suspicious, we can follow that lead. Something is going on, and my guess is that Jody stumbled onto it. She found the one clue that linked whatever it is to Dan Price and that's what got her killed. I'm going to find that clue if I have to shake Dan Price's house down. But first, I've got a missing gymnast to find. Watch your back, Rosie."

"You too, hon," and she kissed him lightly on the cheek.

CHAPTER 22

Major's Yang's office was on the fourteenth floor of the Great Hall of the People, overlooking Tiananmen Square. It was an austere office, the walls adorned only with a Chinese flag, citations, a map of Beijing, and another map of the Olympic Green.

He had invited Colonel Po to view security camera footage that had been delivered to Yang's office ten minutes earlier. The television screen in one corner of the office pulsated with grainy gray images of men fleeing through a crowd.

Colonel Po frowned when the screen showed civilians toppling before the unheard gunfire. He leaned forward in his chair at the images of two men breaking from the crowd. At the far right of the screen, they climbed a chain-link fence before disappearing into an alley, beyond the camera's range . . . but not before one of the men drew his concealed weapon and fired.

Yang thumbed the stop function on his video remote and the TV screen went dark.

"Our technical people at this moment are working to refine and improve the imagery. Then we will know with complete certainty, but it appears to me that one of those fleeing men is General Yu Bin."

Po continued frowning. "It is good that so much of the area is covered by camera surveillance, but bad that those bystanders were shot down." He spoke Mandarin and looked the part, a vigorous, compactly built man with a well-groomed moustache and a precise military bearing. "This will not look good on the

Internet or the satellite news stations. The Politburo would be most displeased with the both of us."

"I've seen to that," Yang assured him. "There's a seven-second transmission delay."

The delay was protected by dual firewalls and intrusion-detection system probes at every edge and location. In fact, the network itself was closed to the outside world except for links to MSNBC and some news agencies for sending results and other information. The Internet connection was separate too.

Major Po relaxed in his chair and his frown dissolved. "Then your plan is working, Major."

Yang tried not to visibly display his pleasure at receiving the compliment. He said, "If the American agent, Helman, had made contact with Yu Bin, we would most likely never have seen the General again after his defection was accomplished, except from those news satellite stations you speak of. By neutralizing Helman, we have forced the General into the open, into the most camera-saturated place on earth. My agents reported a positive identification of the General when they first initiated the foot chase."

"And those agents are dead?"

"Yes, sir. They followed the General and his accomplice into that alley where, sadly, there are no cameras. They killed the two agents who were chasing them, then escaped."

"The man with the General, who fired his weapon before he negotiated that chain-link fence as if it wasn't there . . . who is he?"

"The footage is too grainy to be certain at this point, but I have made a few deductions. I believe the man is Taggart Mc-Call, and he works for the Special Operations Command. I've already encountered him twice. There's just something about the way the man is reacting, and initiating action . . . peculiarly American, yes; aggressive, straightforward. I may be wrong, but

I don't think so. It's McCall."

"We should go after him."

"I knew you would suggest that, sir, and I've thought about it. I would suggest an alternative to that course of action. McCall is with the SOC. Another camera, only a short time ago, captured General Yu Bin leaving the SOC headquarters via a side entrance."

"Where is he now?"

Yang lowered his eyes to a pencil he toyed with on his desk. "Sadly, the cameras again lost track of him. But we know he is in the Olympic Green, and that he has a sickly wife and a teenage daughter with him."

"I did not see them in the film footage."

"No, sir. He would have had them waiting nearby. What I believe happened is that the General approached McCall, most likely spontaneously, and McCall took the General to SOC headquarters after affecting their escape from my agents. But something happened there that prompted the General to leave."

"Has the SOC contacted us regarding this?"

"No, sir, and I'm giving that my attention, particularly a man there named Dan Price, about whom I have my suspicions. But he's clever and, well, I'm keeping an eye on him."

"What do you think this Price is involved in?"

Yang set the pencil aside and resumed eye contact with his superior. "I wish I knew. But I will know, and soon."

Po's features grew stern. "We must contain this, Major. There must not be a whiff of this matter revealed to the world. Is that understood?"

"Of course, Colonel, of course."

"And if that was Taggart McCall on that surveillance video, why is he so important that we should not detain him at once? Those bystanders shot down on the mall can easily be attributed to him, with the footage of him waving a pistol about and firing.

Yes, that will work nicely."

Yang leaned forward earnestly, an elbow on the desk, again making direct eye contact with Po. "Sir, I believe we can make more effective use of Taggart McCall. I believe that since he assisted the General so efficiently, the General will contact him again."

"But you said Yu Bin had evaded them once they got into the SOC."

"I suspect that had more to do with Dan Price than with McCall and as I say, I have my eye on Price and his unit. But as for the General, we've narrowed his options severely and the best one he'll think he has remaining is McCall. It benefits us to allow him to remain free for now."

Colonel Po rose from his chair and stepped to the window. He gazed out upon the vast Square.

"I see what you mean. It does make sense, as you explain it. A good plan, Major."

"I am gratified that you approve, sir. McCall is free, yes, but he remains under constant surveillance, his every move reported to me. I almost know what he's thinking."

Po turned from the window, admiration in his eyes as Yang knew there would be.

"Very impressive indeed, Major. And how have you accomplished that?"

Yang said, "Her name is Mei Chen."

In one of the small parks that dot the Olympic Green, the General sat with his wife and daughter on a shaded bench.

The small park was a landscaped oasis, the bustling world beyond its perimeter only a softly thrumming drone in this realm of cool lawn bordered by flowers, where couples walked hand-in-hand along a pathway sheltered from the world by a natural barrier of shrubbery and willow trees.

He had instructed Ai-Ti and Yim-Fong to meet him here because the shrubbery and trees also created a sanctuary from the ubiquitous surveillance cameras that watched most of the venues and thoroughfares. He had never been more thankful for his rigorous regimen of daily exercise that allowed him the stamina to climb a chain-link fence to avoid being shot. Had those gunmen randomly spotted him in the crowd, or had a sharp-eyed monitor identified him and radioed in his location? The gunmen most certainly had been Major Yang's men.

After he had recounted his misadventure, Ai-Ti asked, "But why did you leave the Americans? Why did you not send them for us?" Her voice ached with discouragement.

His arms were around her, there on the bench, holding to him this sad, forlorn, ill woman he loved so. "I implore you to continue to trust me," he told his wife and daughter. "Trust my perceptions. When I was with the Americans, I sensed betrayal. I saw it in the eyes of a man named Dan Price. He was considering turning me over to the Chinese."

Yim-Fong said, "But father, why wouldn't they help?"

"They pretended to. I cannot explain, I can only say that I felt it. Something did not feel right. I saw an opportunity to withdraw, and so I took advantage of it."

Ai-Ti said, "We will not leave here alive. That is what I feel."

"No, mother, please," said Yim-Fong. "Father will find a way out of this predicament, and he is not alone. I will help, just as I helped by acquiring our tickets. What will we do next, Father?"

The General said, "The American I first accosted, his name is Taggart McCall. I believe he would have stood up for me, but that might not have been enough. But if I could reconnect with him, he would get us to the people we need to reach."

Yim-Fong asked, "As when he took you to this man, Dan Price?"

"He was following protocol. I believe he will break protocol if

I give him the chance. Major Yang and his devils will be watching all the more closely now that they know we're here. I must find a way to make contact with this McCall. He is our one hope."

CHAPTER 23

Tyrona Carey was aware that her focus wasn't where it should be. She tried not to think about Kelly's disappearance. She had learned early in her gymnast career that the most important thing during competition was focus. Whether in a training room, working the parallel bars as she was now, or performing in front of an audience of thousands, the focus must always remain the same, on her performance, commanding her body to do the amazing things that made gymnasts among the most impressive of the Olympic competitors. The adulation of the crowd that came afterward, if you performed well, was something to be savored. But when you were working through your routine, it was only you and the bars or the beam and the focus to excel. But . . . where was Kelly?

She was working out alone except for her trainer, in a private workout room. She began with a jump to handstand mount before performing a front stradler, then proceeded to perform nearly every release move with not quite the precise amplitude and control for which she was known. She finished with a dismount that rose above the bar.

Andrea Cometti attached her magnetic pen to its clipboard and reviewed what she had written, frowning. She was stylish in black capris, low heels and a red blouse with just a hint of cleavage.

"Not good," she said. "Not good at all. You will have to do much better than that in competition, Tyrona. You started the whole routine off with trouble."

"I know. I'm sorry."

Andrea's mouth was a tight line. "And that full pirouette at the end was positively ghastly. Really, Tyrona, if you perform this poorly in competition, you may as well go into hiding with your friend Kelly."

Tyrona flinched. Andrea Cometti may have been a lovely, lush woman who was still flirtatious and attractive with most of the men she met, but she was every bit the slave-driving taskmaster that Kelly Jackson was complaining her Boris Temerov was. Yes, that was the sort of harsh discipline, the setting of impossibly high standards and then the applying relentless pressure to adhere to or surpass those standards, that was required, but that didn't mean the athlete had to like it. Tyrona respected her trainer, but they had never been friends. Kelly was Tyrona's friend, and anger now surged through her.

"Andrea, that's no way to talk. Kelly could be in trouble. Something bad may have happened to Kelly."

"We will not discuss that," said Andrea. "You will stay focused. I want you to perform that routine again, and keep those arms straight!"

A man's cough from their blind side startled them both. They had been so engrossed in each other that she and Andrea had both failed to realize they were no longer alone.

An American man and a Chinese woman had let themselves into the training room. They stood patiently, just inside the steel door. They were not a couple, Tyrona could see from the way they stood side-by-side, as if barely acknowledging each other. The woman was in her twenties and would have been attractive if she'd used some makeup and done something with her hair. It was a moment before she recognized the man. It was the guy who had retrieved Kelly's purse on the first night of the opening ceremonies.

164

Andrea did not like being interrupted, or startled.

"Yes, what is it?"

The man and woman each extended a palm holding a leather packet that contained a laminated identification card.

"I'm Taggart McCall. This is Mei Chen. She represents the Chinese authorities. We're investigating the disappearance of Kelly Jackson."

Andrea chortled, not pleasantly. "I'd hardly call it a disappearance. A self-absorbed little twit wanders off and everyone goes into a panic. She is twenty years old. She's an adult, and apparently a moody and selfish one at that."

McCall said, "She's a young adult. Why the name-calling? Aren't things going well on the women's gymnastics team?"

"They're not going well for the team," said Andrea, "and that in no small measure is the fault of Kelly Jackson and her abysmal showings. Tyrona here will at least be going home with silver, and we're not done yet. It would be just selfish enough of Kelly to sabotage everyone else's chances. I for one am not amused, nor am I indulgent of such behavior."

McCall said, "I see your point, but her parents have reported her missing, and we're trying to piece together what happened so we can locate her. We're not asking for your indulgence. We're asking for cooperation."

A heartbeat. Andrea drew a deep breath and exhaled it slowly.

"Of course. Forgive me. How can I help?"

Mei Chen ignored her. She was studying Tyrona, to whom she said, "You and Kelly Jackson are friends?"

Tyrona nodded with relief at getting the subject back on track.

"We're best friends and the funny thing is, about the only time me and Kelly see each other is at competitions in the States and sometimes overseas. But we lead a pretty strange life, people like me and Kelly and all the girls who made the team.

You don't get to meet many people you can get tight with, you want the truth." Tyrona cast a glance at Andrea to make sure the bitch knew who she was talking about. "Kelly's good people. I'm a long way from my home in the projects. Kelly treated me like I grew up right next door to her in some fly white suburb. I love Kelly." Again the sideways glance at Andrea for emphasis. "Me and Kelly, we cover each other's back."

Mei said, "And that is why we have come to speak with you. Boris Temerov suggested that we do so."

Andrea sniffed. "There's the person you want to talk to."

McCall arched an eyebrow. "What do you mean?"

Another jolt of anger flashed through Tyrona.

She heard herself snapping at Andrea before she could stop the words from spitting out. "You don't be talking trash now. Kelly always told me how tough Boris was on her, but she had nothing but the highest regard for him. It ain't Boris's fault that Kelly ain't doing better here, it's cause she ain't measuring up, and she knows it's her own fault. Andrea, you just trying to make trouble for Boris cause he done put you down. Why don't you tell these people about that?"

Then Tyrona was biting her lip to keep from saying more, knowing that she'd already said more than enough! The bad grammar of her upbringing always surfaced when she flew off the handle.

Andrea cleared her throat politely and said, in a smooth, controlled voice, "Please forgive Tyrona." Her eyes narrowed, looking directly at Tyrona, "The pressure of competition at this level can be a terrible thing."

Mei Chen regarded them with distaste.

"We do not have time to listen to emotional hysteria unless this has something to do with determining the whereabouts of Kelly Jackson. Can you help us?"

Tyrona said, "I don't know where she is, if that's what you mean."

Andrea cleared her throat again. "As a matter of fact, I do have information that may help and it does involve Boris Temerov."

Tyrona said, "Andrea, where you going with this? You better not be trying to say that Kelly and that old man—"

Andrea said, "You may leave us now, Tyrona."

"Hell if I will."

McCall said, "We'll do the dismissing as long as this interview is in progress. Ma'am, what do you have to tell us?"

"Simply this. The last time I saw Kelly, she was with Boris. They were having some sort of personal, intense conversation. It seemed to me like an argument."

Mei Chen said, "Where was this?"

"Outside the locker rooms. It was—well, I hate to discuss this in front of Tyrona."

Tyrona said, "Oh I'm just dying to hear what you're fixing to throw down."

Another deep breath from Andrea. This time, a fast exhalation.

"Very well. Boris had a hold of Kelly by the arm. She did not appear to want to be held. I couldn't hear what they were saying, but it did look like . . . like a lover's quarrel."

"That's a lie!" said Tyrona. "Kelly would have said something to me if she'd been sleeping with that old . . . well, that's just crazy talk and you know it. Kelly would never do that! She would've told me if she had."

Andrea said, "I know what I saw. Are you calling me a liar, Tyrona? If you are, then perhaps you had better find a new trainer and I'll catch the next flight home."

"Enough," Mei Chen said sharply. "I told you, I have no patience for this. You are silly American women, both of you.

You will not distract me with this nonsense."

Tyrona blinked, taken aback, her anger short-circuited.

McCall eyed Andrea. "Are you suggesting that Boris Temerov is involved in the disappearance of Kelly Jackson?"

Tyrona glared at Andrea. "She better not be saying that."

Andrea said, "I have no idea what happened to that young woman. I'm only telling you what I saw."

"Maybe," said McCall, "you saw a heated confrontation between an overbearing trainer and a high-strung young athlete who just wanted some time alone to regroup."

Tyrona raised a clenched fist to shoulder level and said with a sassy grin, "Now you're talking. You're seeing it right."

Andrea said, "Again, I am only reporting what I saw and offering you my interpretation. You are free, of course, to draw your own conclusions, although you weren't there and you are a man. Men tend to stick together in matters of this sort."

"Let's talk about you for a minute," said McCall, "and why you're offering up your interpretation."

Tyrona said, "Double-wham, mister man."

"Are you and Boris Temerov an, uh, item," he pressed, "or, were you an item?"

Andrea lifted her chin. "I don't see what that has to do with anything. I—" a pause as she searched for the right word, "—admire Boris. He is a fine personal trainer. Why should my background pertain to anything about this?"

"I'm just trying to get a reading on how honest you're being with your interpretation. You have some catty things to say about a kid I kind of like. I'm wondering why."

Mei Chen's unblinking scrutiny had settled on Andrea.

Mei said, "If Boris Temerov is involved in her disappearance, would it be against her will?"

Tyrona looked to McCall for sympathy. "Here we go again! Anything like that just ain't happening."

"In answer to your question," said Andrea, "no, I have no ideas along those lines. Like I said—"

McCall interrupted her. "You're only telling us what you saw. Y'know, I've got an idea. Why don't we cool down this conversation?"

Mei Chen glared at him. She had not been consulted.

"And why should we do that?"

"Because we've learned all these ladies have to tell us," said McCall, "or all they want to tell us."

Andrea said, "I resent that," but her tone had softened.

McCall rested a hand on Tyrona's shoulder, "And this girl has another shot at the gold. I say she deserves to be at her best and should get back to her training."

Tyrona spoke in her best practiced—she liked to think, cultured—voice. "Thank you, Mr. McCall. And if there's anything wrong with Kelly, you'll find her and you'll fix it, won't you? She likes you."

Mei said, "We will find her," and indicated that the interview was over by striding off so abruptly, it caught McCall by surprise. He hurried to rejoin her after he gave Tyrona's shoulder a gentle but firm squeeze of encouragement.

When they were alone again, Andrea referred to her clipboard as if nothing had happened. "Very well, then." She nodded to the parallel bars. "Let us continue. I want you to concentrate, Tyrona. You must keep those arms *straight*."

CHAPTER 24

McCall said, "I want to apologize for letting that woman get under my skin."

He and Mei Chen were walking toward the subway station where one of the commuter express trains, which left every fifteen minutes, would have them at Tiananmen Square within minutes. She said she had an apartment—she called it a flat—a short walk from where the subway would stop.

Mei walked through the crowd with her standard aggressive stride. " 'Under my skin,' " she repeated. "It is a colloquialism I have not heard before." She permitted the briefest upward twitch at the corners of her lips. "Yes, she irked me as well. You and I at least have that much in common. And you were correct in terminating the interview as you did, McCall. Your concern for what was important to that girl—Tyrona, what a strange name; it does not sound American. I've never seen a Chinese man treat a girl that age with such respect, not even my own father. I commend you."

"So I'm not all bad anymore?"

"We shall see," she said with a straight face. "When we reach my flat, I will access the Ministry files on my laptop."

"I'm glad you want to keep this low key and not drag me into your office. I don't think Major Yang would be overly enthused to see me."

Another deadpan glance. "You will not be prowling about my home, either. The Major knows that we are working on this together but yes, I agree that there is no need to stir up personal animosity between you. But a search through the Ministry database on my laptop may yield something on Boris Temerov."

He said, "Andrea could be casting aspersions because she's a woman scorned. But back where I come from, seems like male teachers are always running off with underage schoolgirls. The girls think they're in love and, well, it happens often enough, so something like this wouldn't be a first."

"But if that were the case here, surely they would wait to— elope, is that the word?—until the Olympics were over."

"Depends on how grand one of them wants their romantic gesture to be. If we follow Andrea Cometti's salacious line of speculation, Boris is either shacked up right now with Kelly. Or he's engineered some sort of nefarious abduction against her will."

"Shacked up? What does that mean?"

"Uh, sorry. Use your imagination."

"But I don't understand."

They had reached the station. There were not many people standing on the platform at this time of day, waiting to leave the Olympic Green.

McCall said, "After we check on Boris, what say we run a search on my boss?"

"Dan Price? Don't you trust him?"

He gave a noncommittal shrug. "I'd just like to see what, if anything, the Ministry of State Security files might have on him."

"And what about Kelly Jackson?"

"After we finish at your place, we'll return to the Green and hold a meeting with Boris and Andrea, and Kelly's parents. It could be helpful to bring those four face-to-face and see what comes of it."

A sudden commotion brought them around.

McCall was unprepared for what he saw.

Lying upon the wooden platform, her knees drawn up and legs spread wide, was a very pregnant young woman staring up at them, eyes wide with fright and other emotions. She was in the advanced stages of labor. A man dressed in the European fashion, as was she—apparently her husband—seemed beside himself, near panic as he knelt next to her, holding one of her hands in both of his. The other people on the platform stood watching this with jaws agape.

McCall dropped to one knee beside the young woman. She looked at him with glazed, imploring eyes.

Mei reached for her cell phone. "I will summon medical assistance."

"No time for that," said McCall. He looked at the young man. "Mister, if I'm any judge of the female condition, you're about to become a daddy." He smiled down at the woman as reassuringly as he could and said over his shoulder, to Mei, "I'm going to need your help."

When no prompt response was forthcoming, he glanced back to see her frozen in place. Her aloof professionalism had dissolved.

"But I know nothing about childbirth—"

"Well, you're about to learn . . . and so am I, for that matter."

"But an ambulance can be here within minutes."

Several onlookers were chattering into their cell phones.

He told her, "Someone is calling this in right now but I don't think we have that much time."

Mei gulped hard and thrust her shoulders back and she again embodied sternness and discipline, betrayed only by the uncertainty in her eyes.

"Very well. What—" a catch in her voice, "—what should I do?"

"You and the husband take her hands, steady her."

He had never been more grateful for having been present in the delivery room when his daughter was born, but that had been two decades ago. He tried to remember. It was a natural process though, and if you approached it using common sense . . . who was he kidding? His heart clumped with a dull lurch inside his chest, but he hardly noticed.

The husband and Mei Chen crouched to either side of the woman, each holding one of her arms. She was bathed in sweat, her flitting eyes wild. Amid this, a subway train glided to a stop. The doors opened to disgorge new arrivals. It was quite an audience. Mei and the woman's husband were repeating soothing phrases, trying to get her to relax. That was the important thing, that she be relaxed.

McCall placed a palm upon her enormous belly. He could feel her tension easing. Then a spasm rocked her. The baby was close, real close. The woman let out a short, throaty scream, her breathing harsh and rapid now, and her contractions more intense, almost on top of one another.

McCall moved between her open thighs and crouched there. He calmly mumbled half-words, half-sounds soothingly to her.

"That's it," he said quietly. "That's real good. Just keep doing what you're doing."

She was huffing and puffing, her body writhing and slamming against the wooden platform as Mei and the husband steadied her. Her fingers were scratching against the wood. She screamed again.

McCall leaned forward, trying not to be awkward, and the immediacy of the moment washing away any sense of embarrassment. He saw something. The baby's head. Hands that could wield a gun or a knife with silent, deadly efficiency, that had been trained to strangle the life out of an enemy, now reached down and grasped the baby's head with the utmost care and

173

tenderness, easing a new life into the world.

"Come on!" he whispered to the woman.

And then the baby was out and McCall was holding it aloft and swatting its butt to start it crying and breathing. Its thin little wail of life was practically buried beneath the commotion around them. An ambulance was approaching, sirens blaring.

He felt the feeble kicking of newborn muscles, and emotion surged through him. He gently cleared the newborn's nose and mouth, and then massaged the mother's abdomen. At his slow tug on the umbilical cord, the placenta separated. He was pinching his thumb and index finger together to temporarily clamp the little boy's belly button when the running paramedics reached them.

Mei Chen lived in one of the newer large housing blocks within the city center. Such twelve-story structures, not unlike the housing projects of American inner cities, are home to the majority of Beijing residents. Many of the older house blocks were not built to acceptable standards and looked it, drab and dirty from the outside.

McCall's first impression of the interior of Mei's building was not positive. The sparse lobby and elevator area were dusty and trash strewn. But that wasn't unusual in China, he'd come to learn. A cultural oddity over here was that people did not seem to pay much attention to the cleanliness of common public areas. And there was the onslaught of dust, pollution and the dry windy weather that beats down on Beijing on a daily basis. It was as if the citizenry chose not to notice the dust and grime.

Mei's apartment was a cocoon of cleanliness, as he suspected were most of the individual apartments in the building. The furniture was spartan, the walls decorated with only a few landscape prints, yet there was no bright overhead lighting. The apartment, or flat, was not dimly lit, but the lighting was tastefully indirect, creating a comfortable ambiance somewhat at odds with the austere personae of its tenant. An alcove off the bedroom had been converted into a workspace, with a bookshelf of what looked like manuals and reference works—all of them in Chinese, of course—a filing cabinet and a small desk, upon which rested her laptop computer.

McCall was mildly surprised when she lighted a stick of incense extending from a holder to the side of her desk, although he avoided registering any reaction. He was in observation mode, noting and mentally cataloguing everything he saw, a habit from his bodyguarding days in the Secret Service when, if you were preceding a possible target into a room, every detail of that room was gauged automatically. A thin white stream of smoke snaked up from the incense to waft delicately between them, caressing his nostrils with the trace of musk.

After the birthing on the subway platform, McCall had withdrawn to a men's room and thoroughly washed up. The husband, a German in his early twenties who didn't speak English and certainly didn't know Chinese, had been nonetheless profuse in expressing his fervent gratitude. The mother was placed on a gurney and wheeled away, gratitude glazing her goodbye look too. The husband scurried off alongside the gurney, bending to embrace his wife and his new son.

Mei had been reserved on the subway ride from the Olympic Green. Few words were spoken by either of them. She maintained her stern, cool demeanor, but the aloofness was gone and the sternness was not quite so brittle. They walked in silence the block-and-a-half from the subway stop to her building. She did not elbow through the crowded sidewalks of central Beijing with her usual aggressive stride. It would be difficult for a woman—or any man, for that matter—to not be affected by what had occurred. How could witnessing such an event—or as in Mei's case, participating in it—*not* cause ripples at some level of a person's psyche? Her expression had remained impassive, yet he caught something new in her eyes when their eyes did meet.

She visibly relaxed once they entered her apartment. In the few seconds it took for her laptop computer to boot up, she touched an index finger to a button on a diminutive CD player next to the incense holder. Soft, soothing traditional Chinese music—flutes and obscure string instruments—wafted through the apartment like the wispy trails of incense.

She said, "Let us research Mr. Temerov first."

She sat with her back ramrod straight. Her expression was a mask of concentration as her fingertips, the nails worn sensibly short, flew across the keyboard with speed and precision, her attention riveted on the screen.

He drew up a chair beside hers. "It would be nice to know what we're looking for. Anything that stands out will do."

Within seconds she had accessed the highly classified database of the Ministry of Internal Security.

The Chinese characters flowing across the screen told him nothing.

She said, "I cannot have this translated to English without arousing questions and possible suspicion from Major Yang. Do you trust me to interpret?"

"Do I have a choice?"

He softened the barb with a tight grin, but she wasn't paying attention to him. It was a rhetorical question. She clicked through different pages on the site.

"I'm quite sure there is nothing here that is not already in Temerov's SOC file, as this seems to all be drawn from public record. His defection in the early 1980s. The training of gold medal Olympic athletes and other high-profile achievements in the world of competitive gymnastics. He is a respected man."

"Kind of what we expected, isn't it? Okay, how about Dan Price?"

She paused and turned a quizzical glance on him. "When I asked before, you were vague about why you're interested in your superior. So I ask again: what am I looking for?"

"That's just it," said McCall. "I'm damned if I know. But I'll know it when I hear it and if I'm lucky, so will you when you read it . . . I don't know, any sort of anomaly in his files."

"Does this have to do with the death of the woman, Jody Simms?"

"I'd rather not say."

Another moment lapsed, and then another during which she scrutinized him. He returned her gaze without blinking, expecting resistance or an argument. But she surprised him.

She said, almost meekly, "I will see what I can find."

A new document appeared on the screen. She scrolled down, again reading aloud what she considered the pertinent facts. But he already knew about Dan Price's military career as an Army Ranger and his subsequent security work.

When she reached the end of the document he said, "In other words, a dead end. Right where I was before."

"Is there anyone else who might know something about whatever it is you suspect? Have you and Rose Campbell shared your suspicions with anyone? I could check their files."

"Nothing there," he told her. "With nothing but suspicions to go on, Rosie and I have kept this to ourselves. But wait, you've got an idea there. Try your background check files on two other SOC men. Tucker and Hanson. I don't know their first names."

Her fingers blurred across the keyboard, the red ruby ring on her ring hand glimmering. "That will be easy enough. Yes. Here they are."

She read the highlights of these files to him and when she was done, he had what he was looking for.

He said, "They served in the same Army Ranger unit in Iraq and in Kosovo before that. Those are both killing grounds. Those three—Price, Tucker and Hanson—didn't meet at SOC on the job. They came to the job knowing each other, and have enough military training between the three of them to undertake God knows what if they have the proper hardware."

"Their prior connection could be quite innocent."

"Uh-uh. These aren't innocent guys, Mei. They're hardcases. They have shark eyes and my spine feels like little men with cold feet are running up and down it every time one of them glances at me. Crazy, huh? But that feeling has never been wrong."

"What will you do next?"

"I guess for now the first priority is to get back on the job and find Kelly Jackson."

He stood from his place beside her at the laptop screen. She rose with him and with one slight shift of her slim, muscular body there in the small alcove, they were against each other. He started to step out of the archway so she could pass and he was about to mumble an *excuse me*.

She said, "Would you like to . . . stay here awhile? I could make us some tea."

She said it in a little, tentative voice that was so unlike anything she'd exhibited before, he felt an ache tug at his heart, and that wasn't all. Hell, he was a man, wasn't he? This close up, looking down into those brown eyes of hers with their delicate lashes, the classically sculpted Asian features and nice figure made her lack of Western fashion irrelevant. She moistened her lips with a tiny pink tongue. A nervous gesture at making herself vulnerable with the invitation, or an erotic nature, perhaps artfully concealed or subliminally suppressed, expressing itself? Either way, right now she represented desire incarnate.

McCall was not sure what he felt, or what he should say.

"You've, uh, changed your mind about Americans then?" *Keep it light,* he told himself.

"I've changed my mind about you," she said. "I had perused your file, naturally. You are a man of impressive skill and experience, Taggart McCall. I was impressed with the way you conducted our interviews and the manner in which you treated the black girl, Tyrona . . . but the way you took command on that subway platform in an emergency and performed as you did, guided by the will to help and the wherewithal to accomplish it. You were, that is to say, you are . . . most impressive." She rested one of her hands on each of his shoulders. "You are most desirable. I want you."

There it was, he thought. The subtle command. Maybe they were alike in that regard, each accustomed to directness and this time it came textured with the sensuality of a touch that sparked him as if she had electrodes hidden in her palms while the timber of the whispered words was of the innocent sensuality of a virgin.

He thought about Rose Campbell and embers within him of something like love that had stirred during their time spent together in Beijing. He thought about her feelings.

He said, "This isn't the Mei Chen I've become accustomed to."

"Is there not a colloquialism in your country that says one cannot judge a book by looking at its cover? Let's stay here for an hour or so, McCall. No one will miss us. We deserve it."

Her left hand stayed on his right shoulder, the palm of the other hand drifting south across his chest. She lifted her parted, moist lips toward his for a kiss, the little pink tongue visible.

And God help him, but hell yeah, he was a man. As she leaned against him and he felt her breasts against his chest, damn if he couldn't help but form a picture of her nude with those smooth, firm, round hips and legs that would be muscular like a dancer's legs and her breasts—yeah, he could feel them as if they were already naked, firm and up-tilted with hard nipples poking holes in his chest and she had a bottom that would be sweet to grab so he could . . . yes, he was a man. He couldn't help the stirring of his libido as her lips came within a fraction of his. The fingertips of her right hand grazed across his belt, trailing fire, continuing south, stroking him.

He took her by each arm and eased her back, not forcefully but with conviction.

"Sorry, Mei. I, uh, think we'd better get back to the Green."

"You do not find me attractive?"

"It isn't that. Believe me, it is not that."

"It's the woman, Rose. You and her—?"

"Yeah, me and her. Sorry, and thanks for the offer. I'm flattered, Mei. But back home I'm what they call a one-woman man."

The sultry undercurrent subsided like a blast of cold air. "I understand. You are a man of honor."

"Thanks for understanding."

"I do not understand," she said in her normal cool, crisp manner. "I accept." She turned from him and extinguished the stick of incense. "Very well then. Let us return to the task of locating Kelly Jackson."

CHAPTER 25

There was no way for Kelly to keep track of time.

There was only the utter darkness of being blindfolded, the aching muscles from having been bound to the chair for an extended period of time, and the closeness and vague threat of another presence. She had tired of working her wrists to loosen them from the clothesline. The pain told her she was only grinding away at flesh with no hope of loosening her bonds. Panic was a barely concealed beast that lived inside, her stomach muscles quivering, tightening and loosening and tightening again in spasms of fear.

But she was realizing for the first time how the long road of training had toughened her. She had not done well in Beijing and, knowing that her last chance to bring home gold was slipping through her fingers, she had allowed herself the indulgence of sliding into self-pity and putting her emotions before the ultimate goal toward which she had focused her life. She had allowed her losing streak to get the best of her. But by not breaking down and emotionally falling apart in front of this person in this close place, wherever they were, by not blubbering for mercy or pleading—which she wanted to do, if the truth be told!—she had come to understand just how tough she was. She willed herself to breathe deep and measured, and attempted to start some sort of dialogue with her captor, or guard, who had removed the duct tape from her mouth without speaking a word.

She had asked, "Just please say something," which had been

met by stone cold silence except for the regular sound of the other's normal breathing. It sounded like a man.

The second time, she judged it to have been perhaps a half-hour later, she said, "Do you speak English?" Again, no response.

Except that he lit a cigarette.

She endured the smoke until it made her cough, and then she attempted conversation for a third time. "Please, could you stop smoking?"

No response.

So she lost track of how long she sat there. He smoked cigarettes nonstop, so two new sounds were added to her dark world, the click of his lighter and the audible exhalation of his smoking. It could have been an hour; it could have been four hours. She was incredibly thirsty.

At times her heartbeat thundered in her ears, then she would talk herself into calming down, reminding herself that she was an athlete who competed at a world-class level and—except until Beijing!—usually won, so she could take being blindfolded and tied to a chair. If this were about killing her, then she would already be dead. So what was this about? A kidnap for ransom? She hoped it was that, cut and dried. There were perverted sickos out there and she hoped to God that she hadn't fallen into one of their hands.

Eventually, nature took its course.

She said, "Whoever you are . . . if you speak English, I need to pee." As was usual, a full bladder had diminished every emotion except irritability. "I don't know how long you expect me to sit like this and not pee. I'm a girl. I have to pee even if you don't speak English."

His chuckle startled her.

"At last," he said in a conversational tone that managed to sound both smooth and dangerous. "You have said something worth responding to." He spoke with a heavy Chinese accent.

"You have to pee even if I don't speak English. This I like. You are a witty girl, eh?"

"Yes, well now that I've amused you, would you kindly start by removing this blindfold?"

She wanted to scream, *Get this frigging thing off me!* But she had broken the ice and now must keep her fear and outrage under wraps.

He said, "I will do this."

And just like that, the blindfold was gone.

The man flung the blindfold aside and returned to a chair identical to hers, its front legs raised a few inches off the floor because he sat tilted back against the wall. It was the man who had lured her here, but he had changed both in appearance and demeanor, no longer the mild-mannered, humble father seeking a favor for his disabled child. There was a natural curl to his mouth that gave him a permanent sneer. He was dressed in black, his hair worn in the trendy, spiked style.

The room was a ten-foot-by-ten-foot square of high, blank cement walls. A single light bulb burned inside wire mesh attached to the ceiling. There was one door, across from her. She had the impression this was an unused storeroom. *But where?*

She gulped hard, hoping the gulp didn't sound as loud to him as it did inside her head.

"Thank you. Really. Thank you! I really do need to pee so bad."

She was exaggerating. There was pressure making its presence known, but she could have gone another hour easy. Still, that slight pressure had given her this idea. Now she wondered what she could do about it.

His sneer grew and he said, "So now you pee. You start now and do it."

She gulped again and she thought, *Uh oh.*

"Please, avert your eyes, won't you?"

183

He chuckled again and lit another cigarette, speaking as he exhaled smoke, the cigarette bobbing from in his mouth.

"And why should I?" Lewdness glinted in his eyes from behind the veil of cigarette smoke. "I will watch you urinate. I want to watch."

Her mind raced. What could she say? What could she do? She had found a way to get the blindfold removed. Could she find a way to . . . to what? Something flittered into her mind like a leaf carried in on a breeze. She and the girls on the team, and other female athletes her age that she met at events, lived mostly cloistered lives, sacrificing everything for the strict regimen of training, the younger ones like Kelly always under the watchful eye of their trainers, backers and security. But that didn't mean there weren't opportunities for girls to get together and laugh and talk and gab about everything under the moon and the sun and sometimes those conversations were XXX-rated. A girl could learn a lot that way. This guy was a kinky sicko and this was the only chance she had . . .

She lowered her chin in a subtle gesture of submission and looked at him through fluttering eyelashes.

"And what makes you think I wouldn't enjoy that?"

The front legs of his chair snapped to the floor.

"Huh?"

"I said, I don't mind if you watch."

He surveyed her as if for the first time.

"Is that so?" The lewdness dripped like oil from his words. His eyes caressed her. The cigarette, dangling from the corner of his mouth, was half ash. He said, "Then do it. Let me see you pee, little American girl."

She thought, *All right, Kelly. You've gone this far, girl, don't stop now. The vamp approach is working. Go for it!*

She said, "Please don't make me soil my clothes. Have some mercy on me."

The pervert was enjoying himself immensely. "And why should I?"

"Well . . ." Again she batted her eyelashes. "You would see more. You'd like that, wouldn't you?"

His eyes narrowed. His lips grew moist. He did not reply, but he was thinking about it.

Her heart hammered against her ribcage like someone repeatedly kicking her from the inside, and she felt herself breaking out in a cold, clammy sweat that she hoped didn't register as paleness. It was important that this perv thought she might really be into it. She nodded at a coffee can, next to his chair, into which he had been dropping his chain-smoked cigarette butts.

"I can pee in that. Just untie me long enough for me to squat. You," once again the flutter of eyelashes, "won't be disappointed."

He stepped forward and, as easily as with the blindfold, a twist here and a pull there, the clothesline fell away. His cigarette smoke stung her eyes and clogged her nostrils but she kept from coughing. Quite the contrary, with the clothesline not binding her, she felt like a bird taking wing. He stepped away and eased the coffee can toward her with the pointed toe of a suede boot.

He laughed. "I wish I had a camera."

She saw in him not a hint of human decency. What choice did she have? She had never peed in front of anyone since she was a baby! She gingerly drew the can toward her like the repugnant object it was, placing it between her ankles. She squatted and reached to shift the material at her crotch.

He watched her closely, absently drawing a cigarette from the pack in his breast pocket. Holding the lighter in his other hand, he shifted his eyes from her only for the instant necessary to place the flame of the lighter against the tip of the cigarette.

185

She came up at him lightning fast, pivoting with blinding speed, gripping the can in both hands and straightening out her arms. It was only a coffee can but the conditioned strength of her muscles and the pent-up rage driving the blow connected to knock him off his feet, depositing him in a corner. She sprung for the door, twisting at its handle and yanking the door inward.

She bolted out, hearing the man scrambling to his feet after her, muttering something to himself in angry Chinese. She was in a windowed corridor that curved with the architecture of the building, one side nothing but windows, the other side lined with closed doors.

Sunlight flooded in. It was very quiet.

She sprinted off to the right for no particular reason, the sunlight animating her after the chill of her imprisonment. She glimpsed the smoggy Beijing skyline from on high and even in her panicky flight, the view registered as almost identical to the one from where she'd encountered Taggart McCall earlier.

Then the man was upon her, tackling her around the ankles, bringing her down to the tiled floor.

CHAPTER 26

Dan Price and his human shadows, Tucker and Hanson, were stepping out of Dan's office when Rose Campbell walked by on her way back from her afternoon break, which she'd spent sitting outside in the shaded patio area, where she sipped diet cola and thought about Tag McCall.

She really had behaved like a jealous lover when they'd met with Mei Chen, but that was past and done as far as Tag was concerned because she had apologized. Rose had a good feeling about Tag; he would not mess around with that little Chinese iceberg even if she thawed out an invitation to sample her charms. Rose trusted Tag, but that said, trust didn't come easy for her. She knew men.

She and Dan Price nodded to each other the way co-workers will when unintended eye contact has been made. Price turned to join his two men who were crossing the lobby, Tucker and Hanson taking point to "clear the way" for their boss, conspicuous as always with their macho strut, the all-black attire and openly worn sidearm. And then they were gone, and she was standing there in the hallway, not yet visible to her co-workers at the dispatch station. She stood opposite the closed door to Dan's office. No one was in sight . . . and she knew his numbers to the door keypad, which would allow her to enter the office.

A few days ago, she had similarly happened to be passing as Dan was tapping in the numbers. She'd been wearing flats that day, and he hadn't heard her approach. Her eyes had seen the digits his index finger tapped before he was aware of her presence. He had stepped into his office, unable to know for sure what she saw. She'd told Tag about it the next time she saw him, in the afterglow of one of their lovemaking sessions, in fact. He'd urged her not to try to gain entry to Price's office because he could well have other surveillance measures, and nothing was worth her getting caught. Sound advice from the man she was falling in love with—or, let's be honest, the man she *had* fallen in love with!—and she followed his advice for the first few days.

Until now.

She *had* to do it. She had to do it. The Olympics were practically over. A good person, a dear friend, an honest, hardworking nobody in the grand scheme of things who had sacrificed her life for . . . that was the question, wasn't it? Why had Jody Simms died? Was it a terrorist act, the way Dan Price claimed? If so, why did she and McCall think something about that didn't ring true?

She glanced up and down the hallway. It was one of those inevitable lulls in human traffic, and it would be over any second. She must *act.* Jody . . .

It took less than a handful of seconds for her to tap in the numbers and she was inside, drawing the door shut behind her.

The overhead office lights were on. Curtains had been drawn over the row of windows that gave onto the patio.

Rose felt furtive, guilty. Her pulse raced. A quick tug on each file cabinet drawer. Locked, as she'd expected. But she had to try, and fast. Very fast. She went through the things on his desktop without finding anything suspicious. She had not expected to find anything. She was crazy to be doing this, but something had to give in the case of Jody's death. She could not leave Beijing without knowing that she had given everything toward that goal, even if commitment overruled common sense.

The desk had a row of drawers on each side. She went through the other row and, on the bottom of the bottom drawer, beneath manila folders, she found a magazine.

It was a glossy, garish sex magazine. The text, what little there was, was in Chinese. But the multitude of color photographs was graphic enough: a variety of women in dominatrix costumes. Some of the layouts were the usual girl-girl stuff, but other pictures had men posed (or caught!) in various acts of erotic submission.

She wasn't overly shocked. She'd read enough articles in *Cosmo* and seen enough reality TV to know that everyone had their kinky side. So Mr. Squeaky-Clean All-American Dan Price had one as well beneath all of that alpha male bullcrap. She possessed a healthy appetite between the sheets, but had never considered herself whatever kinky was supposed to be. She just preferred good old-fashioned man–woman lovemaking. The magazine did not shock her, nor did it arouse her or otherwise interest her. She was about to replace it when something slipped out. A glossy 8 × 10-inch snapshot that wasn't part of the magazine fluttered to the linoleum floor. She stooped to retrieve it, almost idly turning the photograph over for a look.

The sound of a key being fitted into the outside door pierced her consciousness like a bullet.

Oh no! *Oh no!* Price was outside, coming in via the outer doorway instead of retracing his route through the lobby. *Oh, my God.* Now she must really move fast. Something made her slip the photograph inside her blouse, inside her bra.

She caught the briefest glimpse of a masked woman seated on what looked like a throne, but there was no time to note anything else about the picture. She could think of nothing else now except escape. She replaced the magazine exactly as she had found it beneath the manila folders in the bottom drawer. She had never moved faster in her life than when she darted for the hallway door and let herself out.

Wonderfully—miraculously—no one was in sight as she stepped from the office. She strode swiftly in the direction of the dispatch station. Midway there, employees happened to appear from either direction, walking along purposefully about their business, but by that time she could not be connected to Dan Price's office in their minds.

Across the office she'd left behind, in the outer doorway that led onto the patio, Dan Price stood with his hand on that door handle, watching the opposite door click shut behind whoever had just withdrawn. With a small smile, he crossed his office. He could smell the trace of her perfume. He would look at the surveillance footage. The camera was placed behind the tiniest hole in the wall, well above eye level, behind his desk, and took in his entire office. But he knew who the culprit was.

He had somehow sensed what was going through her head in the hallway in the instant they'd made their brief eye contact and once out of the lobby, he had run around the side of the building to catch her. Hell, he'd been waiting for something like this. It only confirmed his suspicion that yes, she had copped his keypad code a few days ago when she'd similarly passed him outside his door.

It didn't much matter that he had missed catching her in his office. Her scent was enough. Confirmation was enough for now. For that matter, things could have become more complicated had he cornered her. Rose Campbell would have to be dealt with, and this was not a job he would defer to Tucker and Hanson. The nosey bitch had been getting under his skin from the start, her and that McCall son of a bitch. Well, McCall's time would come soon enough. McCall would be dead by this time tomorrow. And yeah, as for Miss Rose Campbell, he would take care of her personally.

The mission was ready to go down. The moment of implementation was almost at hand. Forget military assault terminology like "shock and awe." Nothing but stomp-ass blood and thunder was about to come down. That was predetermined. And the funny thing, the great thing, the perfect thing was that no one except those in the cocoon of elitism who were his targets would even know it was happening. The perfect crime was about to be initiated. And nothing, no one, was going to stop him.

As Price activated the camera monitor on his computer, a thought struck him and for the briefest instant, he knew cold, irrational fear. This too was confirmed.

The picture of Mistress was gone!

It was a slow afternoon at the lobby dispatch desk, with even the Olympic attendees slipping into routine as to movement and activity, little of it requiring SOC attention.

This was not a good thing for Rose, since it gave her too much time to think and the more she thought, the more she came to know the frigid touch of an eerie, unpleasant sense of foreboding. She had screwed up royally. It couldn't get much worse. She wanted to call Tag but for all she knew, their cell phone traffic was being monitored, and certainly Price would have the dispatch station's land lines monitored, just as Chinese security would be monitoring SOC communications.

She must meet with Tag as soon as possible. Price wouldn't dare try anything here as long as she was in public, on her job, but her shift wouldn't go on indefinitely. The first thing she got off work, she would call Taggart via a public pay phone.

The picture hidden inside her blouse felt as if it were searing her flesh.

CHAPTER 27

There was next to no conversation between McCall and Mei during their brief return trip together to the Olympic Green, as if nothing had happened; as if there had not been the close encounter in her home, the open invitation of the ultimate physical intimacy. Her expression was again of stone, a stern automaton of the state, her manner and sparse conversation terse and aloof, as usual. McCall was okay with that. In one way, he would have preferred that she had not come on to him, but on the other hand, her advance gave him something more to think on. Had her sexual advance been purely because of his virile animal magnetism? Or had Major Yang instructed Mei to learn as much about what McCall knew as possible, using any means necessary?

Animal magnetism?

He felt queasy, with a nauseous chill that wouldn't let go. Tightness was in his chest, a strange, numb ache around the area of his heart. No pain, but it would come and go at approximately fifteen-minute intervals. Something he ate, he told himself. Keep pushing. He knew he was lying to himself, but he would keep pushing.

From the end-of-the-line subway station it was a short walk to one of the Green's many international buffets, where McCall had asked three people to meet them, using his cell phone before catching the subway. Within minutes they approached a big corner table in the busy restaurant. Food scents from the steaming trays of the buffet seasoned the air.

Kelly Jackson's mother had lost her sparkle, as if she and her husband had reversed roles. McCall had previously sized her up as the drive and focus that had driven their daughter to this pinnacle of achievement, and her husband had come across as the modest guy content to remain in the background. McCall remembered Mei commenting on this after a previous interview with the Jacksons. But now Candace emanated a worn-down demeanor. There was no vivacious smile. Crow's feet he hadn't noticed before were visible at the corners of her eyes and mouth. Her husband sat with one burly arm around her, holding her close. She looked glad to be held.

There were soft drinks in front of them on the table. Andrea Cometti sipped white wine from a long-stemmed glass, while Temerov nursed a Heineken. Apparently no one had an appetite.

When McCall and Mei reached the table, Candace greeted them with, "My daughter . . . is there any news about Kelly?" Her voice too had lost its sparkle, and was tight with restrained emotion. "Please tell me that you have some good news, that she's all right."

Her husband held her a little closer. "Now, Candy, she's only been gone a few hours."

"I know. But she's supposed to—"

Mei Chen regarded Candace Jackson with the same disdain she'd registered with Mrs. Jackson's earlier image. "We are retracing our steps in the investigation."

McCall softened this by adding, "Sorry, but we haven't got any new leads on Kelly. But we're working on it, and that's why we're here. We wanted to speak with the four of you together in the hope of getting a more complete picture."

Boris Temerov said, "A picture of what?" He inhaled a hearty draft from a glass of beer and wiped the specks of foam left in his beard with a brush of the back of his bear-like paw. "We sat down to await you here just minutes ago. Andrea was just telling us that you spoke with Kelly's friend, Tyrona."

Candace nodded. "Yes, that was good work," she told McCall and Mei. "If anyone knows where Kelly is, it would be Tyrona." She started wringing her hands in her lap. "Oh, I hope my baby's all right."

Steve Jackson said, "There, there, honey. Everything's going to work out fine, you'll see."

Andrea Cometti looked straight at Boris and said, "I told you what Tyrona told these investigators. But I didn't tell you what I told them."

Candace said, "What do you mean? What did you tell them?"

Boris's shaggy brows drew together above his dark, glaring eyes. "I know what she's about to say." He turned to the Jacksons. "She's about to say that—"

Andrea interrupted him coolly, "I was about to tell them that I saw you and their daughter having a lover's quarrel."

Steve Jackson drew up straight. "A what?"

Candace blinked dully. "What are you saying, Andrea?"

Andrea said, "I speak plain enough. Everyone knows that Boris and I have long been lovers, and that we have grown apart only recently. Grown apart? Hardly. Boris's head was turned from me by Kelly."

Candace smiled strangely, and said in a mild voice, "But that can't be true. We trust Boris. We entrusted him with our daughter years ago to train and direct her. He would never . . ." She lifted a sad gaze to the bearded bear across from her. ". . . you would never take advantage of our little girl, would you, Boris? I know you wouldn't." She sounded unconvinced, like someone who did not know who or what to believe.

Her husband withdrew his comforting arm from around her. The fingers of his hands were curling into claws.

He asked Andrea, "Are you saying this son of a bitch violated my little girl?"

Boris rose from his chair. "Yes, my good man, that is what this witch is saying. And it is entirely false, completely fabricated. This is a jealous old woman."

Andrea shrieked. *"Old?"*

Candace dropped her eyes, wringing her hands in her lap. "So that's why Kelly ran away. That's what's caused her to perform so poorly. Oh, why didn't I see this coming? How could I be so blind?"

Steve Jackson snarled, "You son of a bitch, I'm going to kill you," and he flung himself at Temerov with both clawed hands reaching for the Bulgarian's throat. "I'll rip your goddamn head off, you child molester!"

McCall stepped between them with enough physical presence to halt Jackson with a palm to the man's chest.

McCall said, "Chill. Mr. Jackson, stop acting like your daughter's a minor. She's an adult. Maybe you should start thinking of her that way. And we don't know if any of this is true."

Candace did not lift her eyes. She said, "It's true."

Steve snarled again. "You're damn right it's true. Temerov, how long has this been going on? Where is she, damn you?"

One of Andrea's eyebrows arched as she surveyed Boris, giving her a demeanor of callous, dominant triumph. "Yes, Boris. I too should like to know how long this sordid business has been going on."

Temerov said, "You bitch. You lying, scheming bitch."

Mei said, "Mr. Temerov, do you or do you not know the present whereabouts of Kelly Jackson?"

The big bear huffed. "I certainly do not. Mr. and Mrs. Jackson, I assure you that this woman is only making despicable, totally untrue accusations."

Steve Jackson stepped back, but he did not sit down. "I wish I could believe you. When Kelly's back with us, I'm going to ask her straight up. She won't lie to me. And if what Andrea says is true, Boris, I'm coming after you with a gun and I'll find you and by God, I'll kill you."

Mei ignored this. She said to Andrea, "What about you? Do you know the present whereabouts of Miss Jackson?"

Andrea blew a thin stream of cigarette smoke pointedly into Mei's face. "Of course not. Why would I?"

Mei's only visible response was a slight narrowing of the eyes.

She said, "Then we're finished here. This interview is at an end." McCall noticed that she said this pointedly, without conferring with him even with eye contact.

Candace said, "But what about Kelly? We have to find Kelly. What will you do next?"

McCall said, "I know it's difficult, Mrs. Jackson, but you'll have to be patient. You'll be the first ones we call when we have anything to report."

His cell phone beeped. He didn't recognize the number on the readout. He thumbed the connection. "Yes?"

A young woman's voice, sounding like that of a teenage girl, said, "Is that you, Mr. McCall?" The Chinese accent was noticeable, but the words were spoken in self-consciously precise Oxford English.

McCall felt a quiver at the base of his spine that vanquished the nausea and sharpened his every awareness. *General Yu Bin had a teenage daughter.* At the table, the Jacksons were being prompted to their feet by Mei Chen and were withdrawing with no words of parting for Andrea and Boris, only dirty looks. Boris and Andrea, still exchanging heated words, appeared oblivious to this. McCall turned his back on this scene.

"Yes, this is McCall."

General Yu Bin's voice was clear enough across the connection, but sounded ragged, speaking in a whisper.

"Is this really you, McCall?"

"Yeah, it's me. How did you manage to track me down?"

A slight chuckle. "I couldn't tell you if I wanted to, my friend. My dear daughter has a way of exploiting computers that is really quite impressive, and should serve us well when we settle in a new home. I hope I have not inconvenienced or endangered you with this call."

McCall glanced over his shoulder. The Jacksons had left. Mei now stood between Boris Temerov and Andrea Cometti, addressing them as they stared daggers at each other, Andrea retaining her haughty demeanor, complete with coolly arched eyebrows, while Boris was red of face, like he wanted to tear her limb from limb or at least strangle her. McCall turned from them again to speak into his cell phone.

"You're the one in danger."

"I can no longer wait, my friend. My time has run out. I must directly approach a representative of your government and know that my family will be protected."

McCall mentally sped through his file of events scheduled for the day.

He said, "The swimming finals at the Aquatics Center. The U.S. ambassador and his family are attending. They'll be heavily guarded. I'll get you close enough and the ambassador's security force can take it from there."

"Thank you, McCall. Thank you!"

McCall added, "And I don't care how clever your little girl is, we've got to break contact right now."

"Yes, Major Yang has eyes and ears everywhere. But where—"

"The northeast entrance of the Aquatics Center. The event is about to begin. The ambassador's party will be in place. There's no room for error on this. How soon can you make it there?"

"Ten minutes."

"I'll see you there," said McCall.

He broke the connection and turned. Andrea Cometti was striding off in one direction, her head held high, prancing through the crowd like the diva she was, while Boris Temerov was joining the pedestrian flow, lumbering away from the restaurant in the opposite direction. McCall dropped the cell phone into his pocket. He had to disengage from this case and do it fast and unobtrusively, yet the immediacy of this group interview still held him in its grip.

Watching the retreating figures of Andrea and Boris, he said to Mei Chen, "This could be what we call an inside job. That means—"

"I know what it means," said Mei. "You suspect that the Cometti woman or Temerov is responsible for the disappearance?"

"Hell, I'm not sure what to think just yet. Anything is possible. Kelly Jackson is worth a lot of money, enough for those two to fake a breakup and all the rest of it while they both have Kelly stashed someplace with an accomplice watching her, and they're just waiting to make a ransom demand, not revealing who they are, of course. The only thing that stops me from thinking that is the hate and anger between them looks so damn real. I can't see them working together on a deal like that."

She said, "You raised the possibility that none of the woman's accusations are true, that there was no affair between Temerov and the girl."

"Andrea Cometti is a scorned, spiteful woman. She'd say anything to get that Bulgarian in deep. But if he is hiding Kelly somewhere . . . why? Why would Kelly vanish and not Boris, if they were having such a torrid, scandalous affair? They'd disappear together unless they had a fight and she left without him, or tried to."

Mei said decisively, "I am going to follow Cometti."

Andrea had nearly vanished into the sea of Olympic attendees passing by the restaurant; she was still visible only because of her regal walk that made her stand out even at a distance.

McCall said, truthfully, "You may be onto something there."

"What about you? You cannot come with me. You will follow Boris?"

"No, he's no kidnapper." McCall patted his cell phone. "I've got more office politics to deal with."

"Dan Price again?"

"Mei, we've got to get hustling."

She acknowledged this by abruptly wheeling about and angling off in the direction last seen taken by Andrea Cometti.

McCall waited until Mei Chen was lost from his sight, then he turned and made up for the precious lost time by breaking into a double-time jog in the direction of the Aquatics Center.

He felt fine.

The queasiness, the weird tightness in the chest, was gone. Something he ate, that's all it was. He would see a doctor when they got back to the states. *They* . . . he and Rose. But right now he had a missing gymnast to find, a girl who reminded him of his daughter. And a defecting Chinese General with a wife and teenager daughter in tow.

There was a lot to do, and no time to lose.

CHAPTER 28

With the relay swimming event minutes away from starting, there was only a smattering of people loitering about and passing through the northeast entrance to the Aquatics Center.

McCall drew up at the foot of the towering, glittering structure. He would have preferred there be more people around. The entrance would be closely watched. Cameras were visible on metal poles, trained on the entranceway and panning back and forth to include the surrounding vicinity. Attentive eyes would be monitoring. More passersby would have provided some human camouflage for when he met the General and his family to escort them inside. This had to go down without a wasted second or wrong step, and an extra helping of luck for them to make it through that entrance and in to the U.S. ambassador wouldn't hurt either.

General Yu Bin was nowhere in sight. He would be even more cautious than McCall, considering that it was his life and the lives of his family that were at stake.

Adrenaline streamed through McCall. These were the moments for which his training and natural instincts had equipped him, the razor's edge when time was like a piece of elastic stretched to the breaking point, ready to snap. And yes, he felt like a million bucks. This was the sort of thing he was born to do. *Come on, General. Make your move. They've got my picture in their files too. Where the hell are you?*

The General emerged at a normal gait from around a line of

cherry blossom trees. He was holding hands with his wife on his one side and his daughter on the other. To McCall, they stood out amongst the sparsely populated surroundings because he noted their darting eyes and the effort they were putting into *not* appearing furtive and desperate.

McCall approached them. They intersected just outside the entrance, not slackening their pace for handshakes or introductions. The General kept walking and watching. The daughter was wide-eyed. Her mother radiated stoic resolve. The four of them strode at somewhat more than a leisurely pace.

The General said, "It's good to see you, McCall. You have my undying gratitude."

McCall said, "Let's not talk about dying. Tell your women to be ready to drop and seek cover at my command. Trouble could come from out of nowhere at any time."

Yim-Fong said, "My mother does not speak English, but I will translate," and she did.

They passed the cameras, entering an airy, noisy area where stairways and escalators carried people to various levels while the entrance itself gave onto a busy, colorful arcade of shops and cafés. There would be cameras in here too and there was no sense in trying to avoid them. There was no turning back now. They plunged ahead. The crowd became noisier and more dense when they drew near to the gate McCall was looking for. He flashed his SOC ID at the ticket taker and they were admitted.

Inside, seventeen thousand fans were making a lot of noise. The brightly lit swimming pool and the relay teams poised to start were postage stamp-sized from this distance. Giant screens broadcast closeups of the athletes to the rows-upon-rows-upon-rows of fans. The attendant hoopla created an ear-pummeling cacophony, the arena quaking with collective anticipation.

McCall told the General, "We've got to get down front."

The General nodded wordlessly. He dropped his wife's hand

so that his hands were free. He positioned himself shoulder to shoulder with McCall and they forged on, mother and daughter close behind them. Reaching the front row, McCall's ID was again necessary.

McCall caught first sight of the ambassador, a classic portrait of diplomatic decorum even in this overcharged, raucous environment. Next to the ambassador were well-heeled Americans guarded by an obvious security force of granite-faced men who stood poised with their arms clasped before them, a pistol on each man's hip, waiting and watching for trouble.

The General didn't need to be told that this man was their destination, nor did Yim-Fong, who was guiding her mother by the hand. Mrs. Yu looked about vaguely, disoriented by the loud surroundings.

The crowd was really dense, down this close to the front, this close to the pool. They were separated from the banks of TV cameras and sports announcers from around the world on one side and on the other by the front rows that were jammed with spectators. The ambassador and his party were now only intermittently visible, this close in, beyond a sea of bobbing heads.

And suddenly there was movement from either side, a simultaneous shifting of bystanders, and two ski-masked figures stormed forward from the sea of faces. McCall got the impression that one of them was a woman, though a bulky black sweater made it difficult to be certain in this rapidly unfolding moment. They had been two normal appearing civilians, but had tugged the masks down over their faces, protecting their identities as a government hit team after angling in on the General in a synchronized go-for-broke final attempt to stop General Yu from reaching freedom. They came in at him with drawn knives.

202

Yim-Fong screamed, the sheer terror in her voice rose above the surrounding cacophony, turning heads. Her mother whimpered pitifully. The General stepped and assumed a protective posture, facing the assailant nearest him.

McCall grabbed for his gun, shifting to meet the oncoming knifeman from their opposite flank, while behind him he saw the swipe of a blade that refracted shafts of light from the TV lights. The General tried to dodge, but grunted in pain. A splash of blood. Then the second attacker was seizing McCall's wrist before he completed the turn to face him and the pistol was adroitly twisted from his grasp. He rasped a curse and rammed a knee between the ambusher's legs.

The assailant howled in agony and stumbled away, both hands grasping his crotch. His knife dropped to the floor. McCall followed through with a right cross to the jaw and a left hook, with an uppercut to the solar plexus. The man doubled over and sank to his knees, wheezing.

McCall raised his fist to finish the job, but the first assailant, the one he thought might be a woman, grabbed his arm from behind and spun him around. A small fist popped McCall in the face hard enough to knock him back a step. This assailant charged forward, grasping the knife for a downward plunge. McCall's left fist jabbed twice, tagging the attacker on the point of the chin and the tip of the nose. The head bobbed from the stinging punches, and McCall swung a hard right for the jaw. The assailant blocked the punch with a slim, muscular forearm and rammed a fist into McCall's stomach. A left hook sent him staggering back into his first opponent who had just managed to drag himself up from all fours. McCall promptly clapped both palms to this man's ears.

The attacker bellowed in pain as his head seemed to explode. He clasped both hands to the sides of his skull and crumpled, unconscious.

Strong fingers seized McCall from behind. He struck out with an elbow, catching his attacker in the jaw. This assailant swayed, caught off guard. Blood sprayed from the mouth of the mask. McCall struck again with a left and then a right that caught his opponent squarely in the bridge of the nose and this one, who might have been a woman, went down and stayed down.

McCall paused to yank off the mask, half expecting it to be Mei Chen. Nothing would surprise him at this point. But they were the features of a woman he did not recognize, either from having met or from his mental mug shot file. He sighed briefly in relief and turned back to the General.

General Yu Bin held his left forearm with a clenched right hand, stemming a trickle of blood caused by a slash of his assailant's knife. The sleeve of his jacket was ripped where he had blocked what would have been a fatal under-jab to his heart. His wife and daughter were fussing over him.

The ambassador's security force exploded into action with the speed and force of a professional basketball team hustling down court. The granite-faced men closest to the ambassador held their positions, covering him with their considerable bulk, their hands filled with weaponry. The other half of their unit stormed in to seize control of this situation, establishing a human perimeter around the scene. Their ranking officer came straight to McCall and the General's family.

"Drop the piece, pal," he advised McCall. "What the hell is going on?"

McCall saw no reason to antagonize. He dropped his pistol, but he didn't give them the wrong impression by raising his hands.

He said, "This is General Yu Bin and his wife and daughter. The General would like a few words with the ambassador."

Dan Price had never knelt before anything or anyone, except to pay homage to Mistress.

She sat regally before him in the high-backed chair in the candle-lit room, her trim legs crossed, wearing her black leather mask, studded with diamonds. Dominatrix black leather caressed her from the top of creamy breasts to just below her hips, concealing her treasures from her slave's eyes. Black boots ran to mid-thigh. She regarding him haughtily.

He knelt, naked, before her. She let him touch himself while he told again of mother bringing home the johns when he was a boy, of doing this alone in bed while he listened and watched. But they found him one night, and she had whipped him, and from that day on he had never been able to perform as a real man unless Mistress was treating him the way she was now. She never let him finish.

"Stop what you're doing," she commanded. "It is time, slave."

Dan groaned with exquisite frustration. The tension gave him focus.

"Yes, mistress."

"The Premier has arrived. He and his guests are comfortably ensconced in their private box. The time has come to strike."

"Yes, mistress. We are minus fifty-seven minutes and counting."

"And what of Taggart McCall and the woman, Rose Campbell?"

"They are about to be taken care of."

"*About to be?*" The regal tone bristled with contempt and displeasure.

Dan Price had always seemed a stable, highly competent professional on the outside and that's because he was. But in deeper, darker ways, that outer life was a charade for him to hide behind. His inner self was of a restless, ruthless, hungry nature, yet he moved through life always excelling but never satisfied; always thinking he could be doing something more, make one big outstanding strike and be richer than God and never have to worry again, but knowing also the bitter truth. He lacked the imagination to conceive and carry out something of that magnitude.

This was how Mistress controlled him. She was the only person who ever had or could or would. She owned him in the one place in his world that gave him true, unbridled pleasure, but these games they played started only after he first met her professionally upon his arrival in Beijing. She wasted little time in getting him alone and presenting him with a brilliant plan she had conceived. But she needed help. And she wasn't flattering him. For her idea to be manifested, the resources he could provide were indeed vital. He considered it from all angles. Yes—*hell, yes!*—it *could* be done. And damn if they weren't about to do it.

She said, "Kiss my boot, slave." As he obeyed, she said, "Tell me what you will do to McCall and the woman."

He was panting. He decided not to tell her about Rose Campbell having searched his office, and confiscating the picture. "The Campbell bitch gets off work in twenty minutes. I'm having her followed. I'm seeing to it myself. And that will take down McCall, too."

She stood abruptly. A cape had been draped across the chair, and she wrapped herself in it with a grand gesture to stand there staring down at him with contempt, the cloak clinging to her poised figure like a second skin.

"See to it then. Perform your task well, and I will reward you when next you kneel before me. Be gone."

"Yes, mistress."

As was their custom when she concluded their games, he withdrew without gazing upon her. Unbelievably aroused, he dressed quickly.

When the world next saw Dan Price a few minutes later, he was again the confident All-American whose icy commitment to purpose glittered in narrowed, determined eyes.

That was the last McCall saw of the General, who was hustled away, along with his wife and daughter, after exchanging a few words with the ambassador. A follow-up hit team sent by the Chinese was feared. The General was obviously worth any cost to them, and that was good enough for the ambassador to fast track getting the Yu family out of the building to someplace safe.

The General sent McCall a friendly, natural military salute, which McCall returned in kind. Then the General diverted his eyes to look straight ahead, his arm again around his wife's shoulder as they were escorted away by some of the ambassador's security force. The General's wife was walking with a more assured bearing. Their daughter was practically dancing with anticipation of a new life. Then they were gone.

McCall was detained first by the ambassador's security, and then, after Dan Price cleared him via cell phone communication, some other plainclothes American guys had their turn with him. McCall guessed them to be CIA. They wanted to know what he knew about General Yu Bin. Twenty minutes of Q&A along those lines, and another phone verification from Price, and they handed McCall back his cell phone and wallet and told him he was free to go.

No one said thanks. He didn't even get to meet the ambassador.

McCall's cell phone beeped within minutes of his reclaiming it. The prefix on his caller ID was for the public pay phones throughout the Olympic Green.

"McCall."

Rose said, "Tag, it's me."

Something was wrong. He knew her well enough to tell.

"Rosie, is everything okay?"

"Everything is not okay. I have to see you, Tag. Drop everything and come meet me right now, okay? I have something to show you."

"What have you got, Rose?"

"I don't want to take time telling you about it, dammit. You should be here now. I'm pretty sure they're on to me. I think I'm being watched."

"You mean under surveillance? By who?"

"I can't be sure." There was a catch in her voice, a jerky, repeated pause when she spoke that hadn't been there before. "I was walking straight to this pay phone from the office but along the way I saw Tucker, then I passed Hanson and, I don't know, I've got a feeling. We've got to meet in a public place. I think I'm safe as long as I stay with the crowd."

"Let's meet at our table."

"Yes, that's perfect. The table where you met Jody. Hurry, Tag. I won't feel safe until you're here. I love you."

"I love you too, Rose. I'm on my way."

CHAPTER 29

McCall checked his watch for the fifth time in four minutes. Around him, the restaurant buzzed with the murmur of dozens of conversations in as many languages.

No Rose.

She should have been here, waiting. He'd checked the number on the pay phone at the restaurant entrance, and it matched the readout on his caller ID when she'd called. She had phoned him from here. Why wasn't she here now, waiting? The women's public restroom at the back of the establishment? No, not for this eternity of five minutes that he'd sat here after she had urged him to show up ASAP.

Something was wrong.

He tried her cell phone number again. He disconnected when her automated answering message clicked on. It was the third time he'd dialed the number since arriving at their table.

Something was definitely wrong.

Rose thought she'd be safe if she stayed with the crowd. That was good thinking, but was it enough? A lot can happen in a crowd that it doesn't see if their attention isn't drawn to it. He had long ago learned the universal truth that most people are simply too involved in themselves—their appearance, their thoughts, the sort of impression they're making—even if of the best intentions, or were otherwise involved in whoever they're with, to pay attention to what's going on around them. Human Nature 101, easily exploited. Someone leans over, appears from even close by to speak in a friendly manner in Rose's ear, there could be a gun placed against her side and whispered instructions for her to stand and do exactly as she's told or she would die on the spot. They had walked her away from this table.

Rose was in jeopardy.

It could only be Dan Price and his goons, Tucker and Hanson. Something was going down, and it was happening now, and somehow Rose had uncovered something vital that would explain everything . . . just the way Jody Simms had.

The thought froze him to the marrow.

But if that was it, why had Price facilitated McCall's release from custody after McCall turned over General Yu? Wouldn't he rather have McCall tied up in bureaucratic red tape while Price went on with his plans? Price wanted McCall "on the street," maybe because he thought that would make McCall easier to kill. But . . . *why?* Could it be tied in with the disappearance of Kelly Jackson? The dark undercurrents of apprehensive Mr. and Mrs. Jackson, the surly earthiness of Boris Temerov, and the haughty bitchiness of Andrea Cometti could lead anywhere. Was Dan Price tied in with any of them, and how? And Major Yang, and Mei Chen . . . he must make sense out of it.

His cell phone beeped. A row of asterisks appeared across its readout, something he had never seen before.

He answered, "McCall," and was surprised at the ache of apprehension he heard in his voice. He told himself to be hopeful. They were holding Rose as a hostage, bait to lure him. At least she was alive.

Dan Price said in his ear, "Do you know who this is?"

"You son of a bitch." McCall's voice grew taut with a rage that melted the ice, his blood turning hot. "If you've touched a hair on that woman's head—"

Price sighed theatrically, a real smug son of a bitch sneer snickered across the connection. "It's not like you weren't warned off, you stupid son of a bitch. You and Rose had plenty of opportunities to back off but you just couldn't stop snooping, could you?"

"Where is she? I want to talk to her."

Price snickered again. "She's waiting for you, guy. Sublevel Section 6."

"Is that where you are now? Is she with you? Put her on, Price. What the hell?"

Price had broken the connection.

A hallway, tile-walled, well illuminated by overhead lights, wrapped around the circumference of the stadium's subbasement. The roar of the crowd and the soccer match in progress was like faraway yet constant thunder down here. The hallway was empty because every employee was presently occupied with his or her appointed task during the game.

McCall had paused to reconnoiter at the bottom of a narrow cement stairwell, his pistol up and ready in a two-handed grip. He peered with one eye around the corner. There was only the silence and the bright overhead lights, and a row of personal lockers along one wall further down to his right. McCall eased around the corner and started toward the lockers.

The soft *putt-putt-putting* of a small engine broke the silence, accompanied by a clattering sound, approaching from his left beyond a bend in the wide hallway. He returned to brace himself against one wall of the stairwell.

A blue golf cart putted by with a clattering wagon in tow that was stacked with boxes destined for concessionaires in the stadium. The golf cart and wagon passed the stairwell and the row of lockers before vanishing around the far bend in the hallway. Its racket diminished, then was gone.

The chilly, aseptic silence reclaimed Sublevel Section 6.

McCall retraced his steps toward the lockers, his sensory

awareness probing ahead and around him like invisible antennae. The butt of the pistol was sweaty against his palm, despite the piped-in chilly air. He hesitated at one end of the gray metal lockers. One of them, in the precise middle of the row, was ajar no more than an inch. The golf cart driver, probably like anybody who may have chanced to pass by in the past few minutes, had either not noticed or not cared that one of a row of lockers was slightly ajar.

McCall noticed, he cared, because something was very wrong and he did not want to experience what he knew was about to happen. But what choice did he have? When he reached the locker, continuing to hold his pistol in both hands, his eyes panned to the left and right. Someone could be pressed to the wall around the opposite end of the lockers. He used the toe of one shoe to nudge open the locker door the rest of the way.

Rose Campbell toppled from inside the locker, her body collapsing to the floor with a sodden *thud!* Someone had wedged her into the locker, and her corpse had been kept in place by the door.

So many things quaked through McCall's mind. The sheer horror of it. He had the impulsively random thought that she would not have liked anyone to see her with her hair so mussed. He thought of how they were falling in love and suddenly in the blink of an eye she was gone, leaving only this lifeless shell behind. A length of plastic clothesline was wrapped tightly around her throat. Her eyes were wide orbs of frozen agony. Her tongue lagged obscenely from the corner of her mouth.

McCall knelt beside her. *Oh my God, Rosie . . .*

Still holding his pistol in one hand, he closed the lids of her eyes with his other hand, and was about to close her mouth before reporting in, when there was the suggestion of movement behind him, one of his sixth-sense awareness antennae responding to danger. He rushed to stand and come about, but was far too late. He'd been had.

The bastard *had* been pressed behind the row of lockers. The millisecond of numbing horror that had transfixed McCall at this brutal discovery was the distraction he'd been waiting for. He sapped McCall behind the left ear.

McCall's world exploded with an all-consuming, blinding flash of pain. Reality ceased to exist for him as he was swallowed by a black infinity of unconsciousness.

His first waking awareness was that someone was knocking on a door. They were knocking real hard. In actuality, someone was knocking on the door of his unconsciousness; someone who had him expertly pinned to the floor with a knee to his chest while a hand was methodically slapping him, the palm across one side of McCall's face, the backhand to the other, repeatedly until finally his eyelids fluttered.

The light overhead was blinding at first, but gradually shadows in the wide, bright hallway began to take shape. A Chinese SWAT officer was pinning him and slapping him. McCall tried to sit up. The knee held him down.

From beyond McCall's line of vision, someone said, "It seems that every time I encounter you, Mr. McCall, there is violent death in the vicinity."

"Major Yang, sorry to see you again. As a matter of fact, I can't see you. Permission to stand."

"Granted." Yang issued an order in Chinese.

The SWAT man promptly rose and stepped aside to rejoin his teammates. As yet no bystanders had congregated, indicating that McCall had not been unconscious for very long. Major Yang and his SWAT team had just arrived.

McCall started to his feet easily enough, and then a wave of vertigo overcame him as he regained his full height. The bright hallway whirled around him like a Ferris wheel. He supported

213

himself with one arm against the nearest wall and heard himself mutter a curse.

Yang was saying, "There was Opening Night when the Simms woman and Captain Li were killed at Dock 7, then later behind the club on Sanlitun Lu."

McCall said, "As I remember that night in that alley, you were the one with the dead body."

The hallway's walls and lights began to stabilize, returning to normal.

"It's true. My man, Chin Qian, and his assistant were moving a body."

"Classified Bureau of Internal Security business, I understand."

"Precisely, though given your role in the defection of General Yu, of which I was just informed, you may be interested to know that the body you saw being disposed of was that of Mr. Marvin Helman."

"Never heard of him."

"He was an American CIA agent entrusted with facilitating the defection of General Yu. I ordered him eliminated. That should have made it easier to intercept the General, having removed his cover as it were. And it almost happened until you became involved, Mr. McCall."

The world had steadied itself, but for some reason McCall remained leaning against the wall, supported by the one arm and staring at the floor, unable to summon the strength to gaze upon Rosie.

"And why are you telling me this classified information about the murder of an American agent?"

Major Yang smiled thinly. "Merely to emphasize that you have been a thorn in my side; one that I am about to remove. Why don't you look at the body, McCall?"

He did so. They hadn't even gotten around to covering her

yet. The taste of bile burned at the back of his throat. He consciously squelched his nausea. And yet he could still be objective, clinical when viewing the empurpled rope burns around her neck and throat, inflicted during the final moments of her struggle for life as the throttling length of clothesline had been twisted mercilessly from behind; the length of clothesline was nowhere in sight.

He said, "There was a length of clothesline around her neck."

Major Yang lifted a clear zip-lock evidence bag, inside of which was the length of clothesline. In the bright overhead lighting, McCall saw traces of blood smeared upon its plastic whiteness.

"It may have been around her neck when you were strangling her, Mr. McCall, but this length of clothesline was in your hand when we arrived and found you unconscious beside her body."

Other people began arriving, the crime scene forensic crew and several stadium workers now milling about beyond the taped-off perimeter.

McCall said, "Somebody knocked me unconscious after they killed Rose . . . Miss Campbell."

"She's the woman who was with you in the alley that night."

"This is a frame-up," said McCall, "and you're in on it, aren't you, Major? You're in with Dan Price."

Yang ignored this. He nodded at two men of the SWAT team who sprang, one to McCall's either side. Holding a submachine gun in one hand, each gripped one of McCall's arms just above the elbow.

Yang said, "You will come with me for interrogation. I will warn you, McCall, it won't be pleasant for you. You are under arrest. The charge is murder."

215

CHAPTER 30

Kelly Jackson's head jerked up again as she fought off slipping back into the fitful half-sleep that kept trying to claim her.

There was a strange, infinitesimally small sort of vibration that had started pulsating through the floor. She wondered if perhaps she wasn't being held in some upper reach of the Beijing National Stadium. It could have been any massive sporting event in any of the oversized venues, but surely the 91,000-seat Stadium would be one of the few sports structures on earth with capacity sufficient to actually, subtly vibrate to the roar of the crowd and the unbridled collective human energy of the event, shivering through every inch of its mighty structure.

These were the sorts of thoughts that had been occupying her in-and-out state of consciousness since the man had hauled her back into the tiny room and thrust her into the chair, retying her with the clothesline so that she was bound and helpless as before. There would be no escape now. At least the Chinese guy hadn't blindfolded or gagged her again, as if her impudence and determination had earned her at least that much.

After she was securely bound again, he returned to his chair, leaning it back against the wall, and resumed chain smoking, blowing the cigarette smoke toward her face. He chuckled when the occasional stream of harsh blue-gray smoke irritated her throat enough to reflexively cough, and that was the only communication that passed between them. Engaging the creep in conversation would only result in him abusing her verbally in some way and she had little heart for that. Being tackled by him and dragged back into this dungeon was an ordeal that had deflated her as surely as if the wind had been kicked from her lungs. She wondered if he noted the subtle vibration around them, as if they were in the belly of a stirring monster. He gave no indication of anything like that, so she let it go.

Ultimately, though, the snail-like passage of time, the physical discomfort and one too many clouds of smoke exhaled in her face wore down both her defenses and her resolve.

"Please . . . can you tell me how long this will last?"

The front chair legs rejoined the floor.

"Ah, she speaks. I did not care for you trying to strike me," he said in a cordial, reasonable voice, "but it was understandable, given the circumstances. I have chosen to forgive you."

"Why are you doing this? My parents will pay—"

"My time and effort has already been amply bought and paid for." The prominent curl to his mouth that was a natural sneer became more pronounced. "Paid in advance, of course. Chin Qian always gets paid in advance."

"But who is paying you?" Kelly forced herself to stay resolute in her defiance. "My parents will double whatever you're being paid. Really. My dad owns a car dealership back in the States. But who are you working for? Tell me, damn you."

He laughed and started to say something.

The door opened inward abruptly, startling them both. He leapt to his feet. Andrea Cometti stepped into the room, regal as ever even in this squalid setting of a young woman tied to a chair beneath a single light in a bare room. Chin scampered to close the door behind her as if he were lackey to a queen.

Kelly's spirits lifted with a spontaneous, reflexive squeal of joy and relief at seeing someone she knew. "Andrea, you found me!" She had grown accustomed to seeing Andrea with Boris Temerov during the past few years. "You've got to help me!

Thank God. I don't know what's going on, but—"

Andrea backhanded Kelly across the face.

The slap carried the brittle *crack* of a small-caliber pistol shot. Kelly's head snapped back, an explosion of pain springing tears to her eyes. She blinked the tears away and bit her lower lip to stifle an outcry.

Andrea's eyes were steely. "Yes, I'm going to help you, Kelly." Her voice was icy. "I'm going to save you from the clutches of a perverted old man, and I do mean Boris Temerov."

Kelly said, "But Andrea, I don't understand! There's nothing like that going on between Boris and me. He's my trainer and my mentor but nothing more. Oh my God, you don't think—"

"I know what I saw," rasped Andrea, "you wicked little thief. Boris said he was leaving me because I was domineering and controlling, but that is my nature. I am a strong woman. And I will not be made a fool of by a tart like you."

"But I've never done anything to hurt you," said Kelly. "Why are you keeping me like this? Who is this man?"

"This is Chin. I went into the city and made discreet inquiries. I was looking for a man of Chin's talents and a willingness to take on any task no matter how illegal. In fact, Chin makes his living hustling in the Beijing underworld. He is a very slick and tough customer, is that not so, Chin?"

Chin's eyes, cruel and unkind, roved over Kelly's body, making her skin crawl.

"It is as you say, madam."

Andrea glared at Kelly. "Silly slut, don't you yet understand? You and Tyrona and the women's gymnastics team have another two events scheduled. Suspicion and the cloud of scandal have already descended upon Boris. He will be ruined, and so will you."

"You're, you're not going to hurt me—"

"No, not in a physical sense, unless you force Chin to further restrain you. But you will miss those events, and when Chin sets you free and you reappear, he and I will be long gone and there will be nothing to link any of this to us. Most people will prefer to believe a scandal about you and the trainer old enough to be your father." Andrea nodded with satisfaction. "You will both be punished."

J. Bob Wiley didn't know very many big words, but his favorite, of those he did know, was serendipity. He just liked the sound of it. The dippity part mostly, and because he liked the sound of this word when he first heard it, he had gone on to do something he rarely did. He had gone to the dictionary.

The gift of finding agreeable things not sought for.

He liked the sound of that, too.

It could only have been serendipity that brought the plumber across J. Bob's path when J. Bob entered that public restroom. J. Bob didn't know anything about soccer and he cared even less. Seemed to be a lot of running around and girly kicking of the ball, least that's what it looked like.

He was ready to take on the ragheads, ready to walk into their private box and start blasting. This match had their big shots, the Iranian delegates to the Games, gathered just one flight up. Two soldiers guarded the stairway leading up to that level. The Chinese Premier and his guests also had a private box up there. The elite would arrive and depart via secured private elevators. J. Bob wasn't sure what to do next.

Serendipity occurred when he happened to walk into a public restroom. Though there was capacity attendance in the stadium, there were enough well-placed and designated public restrooms that occasionally an individual facility might become temporarily unused, as was the restroom into which he stepped. The rest-room—three stalls, five urinals, tile walls and marble floor—was

unoccupied except for a plumber crouched before one of the sinks.

The plumber's back was to J. Bob. He was struggling to stem a dripping leak from one of the faucets by applying wrench to pipe beneath the sink. The echoes of J. Bob's footfalls drew the plumber's attention around. He was not Chinese.

That's when the plan burst into J. Bob's mind. The Olympics hiring people had not drawn from a strictly Chinese labor pool.

The plumber returned to his task. J. Bob reached down and picked up the heaviest wrench from the man's toolbox. The plumber started to turn toward J. Bob again. *This had to be done fast and he would have to be damn lucky to pull it off, but it was serendipity, damnit!*

The head of the wrench caught the man right in the right temple and there was the sound of an egg breaking. He fell over sideways as if overcome with a sudden urge to nap. With another short, hard swing, J. Bob indented the forehead. There was not much blood.

J. Bob replaced the wrench in the toolbox. He sat the dead man up, slipped an arm under each of the body's arms and dragged it to the nearest stall. Sitting the corpse on the commode, he stripped off the man's blue coveralls, peeled off his slacks and stepped into the coveralls, zippering them up the front. The fit was a size too small but would not be noticeable at first glance. At least, he hoped not. He hurriedly managed to fit the dead man's legs into his discarded slacks. He bunched them and the dead man's undergarment down around the corpse's ankles. J. Bob locked the cubicle and squeezed himself out from underneath the stall. From the outside, it looked like just another customer was using the john.

Picking up the toolbox, J. Bob the Plumber started out, but first he had to stand aside for three busily chatting Asians coming in. Then he left the dripping faucet and the dead man behind.

CHAPTER 31

In the specially designed, equipped and fortified private box reserved for the Premier and his chosen guests, Agent Luo Cong stared out at the vigorous soccer match from behind the smoked glass of this sanctuary of power. The wall-to-wall windows provided a view of the playing field that was second to none.

Luo was head of security for this event, and was convinced that it would be impossible to breach the precautions in place to protect the Premier and his esteemed guests.

Present in the box besides the Premier and his wife and interpreter were the American Secretary of State, the American ambassador to China, and their respective wives.

Luo had agents stationed outside the box where a small anteroom gave access to stairs, a restroom and the elevator. The stairs and elevator were secured from below. A short hallway following the contour of the stadium in either direction was shared with a few other VIP boxes such as the furthest one, occupied by the Iranian delegation. Luo had one more agent with him here in the Premier's box. Each agent on the protective detail wore body armor.

The box was furnished for maximum comfort: oak paneling, thick carpeting, soft, deep-seated leather divans and chairs. A young woman was tending a wet bar off to the side. The lighting was indirect, the murmur of pleasant conversation, warm, cozy.

It was strange, seeing the expansive view of so many people

out there in the stands making all their noise while up here the roar of the crowd was muted to a droning hum, something like a movie on a giant wraparound screen with the sound turned way down.

The Premier was politely raising his glass of wine to a toast made by the Secretary of State.

The door to the anteroom opened.

The head chef appeared, accompanied by what appeared to be some members of his kitchen staff: three round-eyes, which struck Luo as odd.

The first waiter was a tall, heavyset, muscular man with black hair worn short, touched with a hint of gray at the temples. He carried a tray and wore a deferential, apologetic expression as he stepped in. But there was something about the man that tripped a warning buzzer in Luo's subconscious. *Those aren't the eyes of a waiter.* Behind this one Luo saw the chef, wheeling in a table, followed by another waiter carrying a tray. One of the SOC security men was visible behind them, dressed in black, armed with silenced machine gun—but he was not Luo's man!

This all happened in a matter of milliseconds.

Luo reached for his weapon and started to snap a command at the agent in the owner's box with him. Too late. He couldn't believe how fast it happened.

The instant they crossed the threshold, the "waiters" dropped their trays and whipped out automatic 9 mm pistols from beneath their jackets. The second waiter opened fire on the Chinese security agent near the Premier. The first slug caught the man in the chest, knocking him back a few paces, kicking the wind from his lungs, but he remained standing thanks to the body armor worn beneath his suit. Tucker fired twice more. His second round clipped the agent's thigh, spinning him around. The third bullet blew off the back of the security man's head, splattering a portion of the smoked glass with blood, oozing brains and little white chips of bone.

With his own gun half-cleared from its concealed holster, Luo realized that the first "waiter" was already tracking his pistol on Luo. The tall, heavyset man, who had instantly triggered alarm bells in Luo's subconscious, fired. There was an orange-red flash from the muzzle of his pistol. Luo's world ceased to exist, his body sprawling across that of the other agent.

Tucker gave a rough shove to the chef, an elderly Chinese man in chef's white who retained a sense of dignity as he was herded over to join the assembled hostages. The chef had been their Trojan horse, their ticket in. Hanson and Tucker each held a gun covering the men and women who were pressed against a far wall. There was wide-eyed horror and fear there, centered on the heavyset man, who now stood behind the Premier.

Dan Price held his 9 mm pistol with casual familiarity, pressing its warm muzzle to the back of the Premier's head. Beyond the windows the drone of the soccer match continued unabated. A haze of gun smoke wafted with the cigarette smoke in the box. The Premier was a smoker.

Well all right, thought Price. *I've done it.* That is, he'd gotten this far. This was where the real deal went down and right now in the Premier's private box, this thing was definitely under control. His control. And he was going to keep it that way. Things were going beautifully. And why shouldn't they? They'd trained him to be the best. A government trains you. Sends you into jungles and deserts and urban war zones around the world on secret ops. And that's only the beginning. Then things go wrong and all of a sudden you go from being the hidden power behind diplomacy to a nasty little embarrassment that has to be swept under the rug, and you're told to go away and be a good soldier and here's your pension and thanks. Now get lost. But he wanted more. It wasn't in Dan Price to "get lost."

Once he'd bought into the plan, he'd used what he knew and who he knew to put this together, and everything had stayed on track despite the obstacles that had presented themselves first in the person of Jody Simms. It didn't matter, really, what that overzealous New Breed bitch had gotten hold of, only that she had told him that something paramilitary was about to go down; it would only have been a matter of time before she tracked it to him, her boss, and so he had acted on the spot and still did not regret it, despite the subsequent meddling from Taggart McCall and Rose Campbell. That too had been squelched. Yeah, this was going like clockwork.

Price removed the pistol from the back of the Premier's head. The Premier continued to sit stoically, dwelling in some inner place of peace and patience. Price addressed the hostages, gesturing with his gun to indicate the pair of corpses near where the Premier sat impassively.

"I hope this clarifies the urgency of your situation. Only your best behavior is going to be good enough."

The American Secretary of State eyed him icily and spoke in a voice that matched. "You're a cold-blooded killer. What in God's name—"

Price said, "Shut up or I'll kill you too, Mr. Secretary."

There were startled outcries of alarm. The ambassador's wife screamed.

The ambassador's Adam's apple bobbed up and down as he said, "There's no reason to kill anyone else. Nobody left here is a threat to you."

Price made a quick assessment of the assembled hostages. The men and their spouses, and the young woman who'd been tending the bar, indeed did not pose a threat. They were civilians, no matter how high-ranking the men were. The American ambassador was right. The box had been secured.

At a nod from Price, Hanson swept glasses and liquor bottles off a table and replaced them with an aluminum case that had been secreted beneath the wheeled-in table. He snapped the case open. Two dime-thin computer screens popped up into view. The base of the case housed elaborate keyboards. Hanson switched on the computer. The screens flickered.

Price plucked an envelope from an inside pocket, walked over and handed it to the Premier's interpreter, a studious-looking woman in her mid-twenties.

The Secretary of State was staring over her shoulder. "What is this?"

"You've won the lottery," Price said sarcastically. To the interpreter he said, "Open it and read it."

She did so.

The ambassador was looking over her other shoulder.

He said, "It's nothing but a list of numbers!"

Price said, "Those are the numbers of thirteen bank accounts in seven countries. The sum of one billion dollars will be transferred to those accounts before this soccer game is concluded." He looked again at the stocky, elderly man seated impassively before him. He gestured with his pistol and added, "Or the Premier dies. Tucker, I want you to backtrack. We've scrambled the tac nets for the security forces involved and everyone else, like those Iranians, should be in their box. Make a sweep. Kill anyone who doesn't belong. And you, Miss," he concluded, addressed the interpreter, "you'd better hip the big cheese here to what's going on. I don't imagine he wants to die, so he'd better start initiating the transfer of funds."

Getting upstairs to the VIP level was easier than J. Bob Wily thought it would be—at first.

The soldiers, guarding the stairway, spoke English and J. Bob made that work for him, fervently insisting that someone in the

Iranian party had phoned Maintenance about a plugged toilet in their private box. The soldiers, armed with submachine guns, knew nothing about this and consulted with their duty officer via lapel microphones and earpiece receivers while J. Bob, wearing his blue Olympics maintenance department coveralls and holding his toolbox, tried to appear impatient, and that didn't take much acting.

He was so close to slaughtering ragheads, he could taste it. The duty officer at first denied access but through the soldiers, J. Bob argued with the duty officer that there was no mistake; that he had been sent for. Communication followed between the duty officer, at some unknown location, and the Iranians; things quickly became garbled, helped by J. Bob remaining adamant that he had been ordered here, that he was overworked and in a hurry. Through lack of communication, amid considerable confusion, it was decided that the plumber should advance.

Another pair of soldiers, also armed with machine guns, was dispatched to guide him to the upper level. They looked tough enough and in earnest but they could each not have been more than twenty years old. They led him upstairs, along a curved hallway, one soldier to his either side. To their left was a glass wall overlooking the Beijing skyline. To their right was a blank wall with the occasional closed door of polished wood.

Well before they reached the Iranians' box, the soldier on his right surprised J. Bob by halting him with a tug on the arm. The soldier opened a door and stood aside for J. Bob to gaze in.

It was a cramped, two-stall, one-urinal men's room.

J. Bob said, "But—"

"You look at this one," one of the soldiers barked at him in clipped English. "There no problem with ragheads or any of the others. But I use this one today. Not work."

J. Bob decided that what worked once could work twice. He

set down his toolbox.

"Okay."

Then he swung up the large wrench and smashed one kid soldier in the temple, hearing that breaking sound again. The soldier fell against the other one, bumping him off balance, slowing his attempt to bring his submachine gun up and around while J. Bob quite easily relieved the first soldier of his weapon.

J. Bob triggered a short, silenced burst that stitched the soldier from belt to throat, splashing the tiled walls of the restroom with blood like swirls of red paint. The *chug-chug-chug!* of the machine gun sounded loud, but a glance up and down the corridor revealed no one in sight. The military had established the outer line of security. Now that he was inside, he realized that their own security units must protect the individual VIP boxes—the Iranians, and the Premier's box further on.

Everyone was engrossed in the game on the field. Good enough. Maybe he'd blow away some chinks when he was done with the ragheads!

He shoulder-slung each of the machine guns and dragged the soldiers' remains into the restroom. No need to be fancy with these two, the way he had been with the plumber. He was *in*. He started in the direction of the Iranians' box.

A lumbering figure approached from around a corner about twenty paces ahead of him, which surprised J. Bob, bringing him up short. In a heartbeat he registered the man's Kevlar vest, a sidearm worn on each hip; a formidable, stalking figure. J. Bob saw the submachine gun in the man's hands. He saw the grim expression.

J. Bob thought, *Uh-oh.* But if he'd been able to bluff his way past those chink soldiers, he would surely stand a chance with another American, which this man in black stalking toward him obviously was. J. Bob raised both of his hands, with palms outward, leaving his machine guns to dangle by their straps from his shoulders, so as to express no hostility or aggression.

J. Bob said, "Howdy there, hoss."

Tucker squeezed off a single round without slowing his advance. The bullet clipped away one third of J. Bob's face. When Tucker stalked past him, J. Bob's body had skidded onto its back and was shuddering with death shivers. Wincing, Tucker looked away. Death had voided J. Bob's bowels. Tucker continued on.

Kelly said, "Andrea, is there a*nything* I can do to talk you out of this?"

Andrea straightened from checking the knots in the clothesline that bound Kelly to the chair.

"No, nothing. You will suffer your public humiliation like the evil little wench you are. The tabloids love serving up trash like you to the masses."

"Please don't. It would destroy my mom and dad. They raised me to be a good girl. I swear you're totally wrong about everything you think about Boris and me."

Andrea pretended not to have heard.

"I will leave now. I must accompany Tyrona for a series of interviews. My alibi is airtight, you see."

Chin remained standing in deference to Andrea's presence. He leaned against a wall, a cigarette dangling from the corner of his mouth. There was a vague, subtle insolence to his manner.

His cell phone rang. Chin answered, spoke briefly in rapid-fire Chinese and folded and pocketed the cell phone.

Andrea regarded him with her chin raised, an imperious glint in her frosty eyes. "I was under the impression that I had bought your time, Chin. You will stay bought until we are through here. No personal business, understand?"

Chin straightened from the wall. He dropped his cigarette

into the can beside him and said, "As a matter of fact, Miss Cometti, that telephone call was business and it concerns you."

"Kindly explain that remark."

"Yes, ma'am." There was the purr of satisfaction in his exaggerated civility. "That was the man I work for. Major Yang."

This confused Kelly. For a moment, the muscles of her arms relaxed in their constant straining against the clothesline.

"Major? You mean like in the army? I don't understand."

Chin ignored her. He stared straight at Andrea Cometti. In his right hand he held a pistol, held down against his outer thigh. From his left hand dangled a set of handcuffs, which he extended to Andrea.

"Here, put these on. I am detaining you for Major Yang."

The door suddenly burst open, slamming against the wall from one powerful boot kick, and Tucker stood there like a futuristic death machine in black, filling the doorway, startling the three of them out of their immediate drama. Eyes widening in surprise, Chin stupidly started to track his pistol up on Tucker, who sniggered as he fired a half dozen rounds that blew away parts of Chin's torso. Chin gyrated wildly as each slug caught him, dancing to some insane, unheard music. His blood and brains speckled the tied-up girl and the cool number standing over her.

The stately brunette yipped once from behind a hand, her eyes wide saucers. The bound girl was biting her lip, her eyes closed against the horror, leaning so far back in her chair she was ready to tip over.

Tucker raised Dan Price, speaking into the nearly microscopic mic on his lapel.

"Commander, I've got a wrinkle."

"What kind?" Price's words clipped in Tucker's ear.

"Uh, that missing gymnast, Kelly Jackson. I found her and some other broad. I had to cap a guy."

"Well, well," said Price. "Get back here pronto, and bring them with you."

CHAPTER 32

McCall said, in the most reasonable tone he could muster, "You're not telling me that you really think I killed her?"

He and Yang sat facing each other across a cluttered desk in a small, windowless office requisitioned by the Major. There was a computer on the desk. The distant, raucous enthusiasm of fans in the stadium stands, cheering on the soccer action on the field, shimmered through the mighty stadium structure even as far as this remote cubicle, located somewhere in the outer reaches of a vacated administration suite.

McCall had been escorted in none too gently, kept at a distance from the few people he glimpsed during his rushed journey here from Sublevel 6. The SWAT team was posted directly outside a single, closed door.

Major Yang regarded McCall at considerable length. "And why shouldn't I believe that you murdered Rose Campbell?" The harsh fluorescent overheads revealed no stress or emotion about him. His features were smooth, as unreadable as Mei Chen's countenance had always been. He said, "The length of clothesline found on you—"

McCall gestured impatiently.

"It's an obvious frame-up." He indicated the tender, throbbing lump behind his left ear, which Yang had already inspected. "What about this? You think I conked myself after strangling a woman I felt deep affection for? That's crazy."

232

"You went into shock. On occasion, traumatic stress will overwhelm a murderer after he has perpetrated his crime. You lost consciousness and struck your head when you fell."

"Balls. You've read my file."

Yang conceded this with a nod. "Thoroughly."

"Then you know I'm no goddamn rookie. Where's Mei Chen? Ask her if she thinks I'm capable of cold-blooded murder. She saw Rose and me together. Bring Mei in. Let's talk to her. You trust her judgment, don't you?"

Yang said, "That remains to be seen. Mei Chen has been debriefed and reassigned. She cannot help you. No one can help you, McCall. Except me. I hold the power of life and death over you. What do you think of that?"

McCall said, "Screw it. I just want to get my hands on the bastard who killed Rosie Campbell."

He couldn't blink his eyelids without seeing her dead on the floor of that subbasement, as if she mattered no more than a discarded piece of tissue. And now someone else was going to die real soon. The someone who killed Rosie. They were going to die hard when he tracked them down. There would be no place on earth for them to hide, certainly not in a stadium, no matter how majestic and oversized. He was playing it cool because he had to, but his heart was racing.

Yang said, "So you maintain that Dan Price telephoned you and summoned you to where you found Miss Campbell's body?"

"Of course I maintain it. That's the truth."

Yang leaned forward. "I believe you. I've been testing your mettle, McCall, prodding to determine if you were the sort of man I could trust. I believe I can help you. We can help each other."

"You're talking in circles, Major."

Yang's posture straightened in his chair. "I know who killed

Rose Campbell. I don't have proof but at this point, that hardly matters."

McCall echoed, "At this point?"

"Yes. You have been a painful thorn in my side in the business over General Yu. I endured a severe reprimand from my superiors only an hour ago, and will likely face demotion."

"Tell me Dan Price is the one I want."

Yang responded with a slight nod. "As you know he is. Or he had one of his men do it while he stood by and watched. You and the Campbell woman were suspicious of him. As was I. That first night at Dock 7, the way Price drew you into the investigation was an obvious attempt to distract me."

"I'm having a hard time figuring you, Major."

Yang said, "I too was suspicious of the circumstances surrounding the death of Jody Simms that night. As with the case against you, I sensed that it had been manufactured to be airtight. And it might have passed muster had not Mr. Price drawn you in. But like you and Miss Campbell, I could uncover no proof against Price, no motive. And so, like the two of you, what could I do?"

"Rose found or did something. That's why Dan Price killed her. She uncovered something that tipped his game."

Yang produced a pack of cigarettes, offering one to McCall. When McCall shook his head, Yang lit his cigarette, exhaling a stream of smoke toward the overhead lighting panels, away from McCall.

He said, "Yes, that is what I believe also. Miss Campbell uncovered something incriminating, just as her friend Jody Simms had. Perhaps it was the same lead, perhaps not. I suspect we may never know. Both women were killed to silence them."

"You said you could help me. Can you help get my hands around Dan Price's neck?"

"I said we could help each other. This, you see, is where matters converge."

"How so?"

"There is the matter of General Yu's defection. You will appreciate that this was not only a professional embarrassment, but a personal one as well. I was assigned to prevent the General's defection. Largely because of you, I have suffered great embarrassment and loss of face. In China, this is not a matter to be taken lightly. Do you appreciate this?"

McCall considered the matter briefly and shook his head. "You're acting like I owe you one because of all the trouble I caused. I don't see it that way. I didn't ask for the General Yu business. That came *at* me, literally."

Yang's eyes grew somber. "I have no option but to redeem myself. McCall, you killed two of my men."

"And you killed an American CIA agent. But you know what? You guys all knew you were getting into dirty, shark-infested waters when you took the plunge. But not me and not Rosie Campbell. I've done my time in bullet alley, but I'm too old for this. I'm no secret agent. I thought this was going to be a walk-through security assignment that happened to be in Beijing at the Olympics. Sounded like fun. And here I am in way over my head, and I know it. But Major, this murder charge you're trying to frighten me with, I think I've got a good chance to beat it so I'll call your bluff. If you know my file, you know about my connections. I still have friends from the old days who owe me favors. Powerful friends. You go ahead and redeem your own goddamn self. I want Dan Price and nothing else."

"In your anger, you have taken leave of your common sense."

"So stop wasting time and tell me something that will change my mind."

"I can do better than that. I will show you."

Yang shifted the flat computer screen so they could both see it. The screen was dark with an innocuous screen saver. Yang speed-typed an access code and suddenly they were watching black and white television. McCall recognized the participants. This was the feed from a hidden camera, positioned near the ceiling of an expensive private box, capturing a stark tableau.

His pistol dangling nonchalantly in his right hand, Dan Price lounged on a bar stool in an attitude of arrogant command, leaning against a wet bar with a view of hostages clustered in a corner. Beyond him, the soccer game progressed on the field below the massive windows.

One hostage sat apart from the others, in a table chair near Price. The bulky figure of the Chinese Premier sat with his back rigid, his large hands folded in his lap, staring straight ahead at some fixed point known only to himself.

The rest of the hostages huddled together in a corner. Tucker stood holding a machine gun, covering them. Hanson sat at a laptop computer, eyeing the screen intently. The American Secretary of State and the American ambassador to China stood like statues behind their seated wives, doing their best to maintain their composure. The ambassador's wife was weeping into her hands. Kelly Jackson sat next to her. Andrea stood with the men, directly behind Kelly. A bloodless mask of strain and horror had replaced Andrea's habitual haughtiness. Two young women completed the group, one's uniform attesting to her having tended the wet bar in the box, and a mousy Chinese girl who was probably the Premier's interpreter.

McCall returned his attention to Kelly. She looked mussed-up but unharmed. *Kelly! What the hell!?* He averted his eyes from the PC screen with effort.

"Is this a live feed?"

"Yes. Much needs to be explained," said Yang, "but the salient facts are these. About forty minutes ago Dan Price and his two men stormed the Premier's box."

"I would think your Premier would have security measures

equal to the American President's."

"He does. Much will come to light, I'm certain, in a postmortem investigation. There could only have been complicity at the highest levels of security."

"What are their demands?"

"A massive transfer of my government's funds, which is in progress as we speak. In an emergency session, the Politburo voted to negotiate with the criminals."

"Price must have had himself quite the foolproof plan."

"Quite," Yang conceded. "They somehow gained access to a private kitchen and used the chef as a, er, Trojan horse, to gain entry. Two of the Premier's security men were killed in the takeover of the box."

"What's Kelly Jackson doing up there? Has she been there the whole time she was missing?"

"We're uncertain about that. Price sent the man, Tucker, on a search and destroy sweep of the immediate area around the box before we were alerted and rushed to close them off. A dead man was found when our troops moved in. The man had been shot to death, but he in turn most likely killed two soldiers. He was heavily armed, and his presence there is suspect as well. Of course, there has been a complete media blackout regarding any and all of this. When Price's man returned, he had Kelly Jackson and a trainer, the Cometti woman, with him. We found an unused storage room with another dead man inside. It's been a bloodbath. Miss Jackson was apparently being held against her will, it appears, by the Cometti woman."

McCall returned his attention to the PC screen. "That's crazy."

"Nonetheless, they joined the other hostages. As an afterthought, Price demanded an additional half million dollars from the girl's parents. Mr. and Mrs. Jackson are presently attempting to raise that money, but thus far have been unable to do so."

McCall felt his jaw muscles tighten. "And if they can't?"

"There have only been . . . vague threats before Price ceased communication. He could harm her, of course, or he could take Miss Jackson with him when he and his men extract."

"How would they do that, exactly?"

"Considerable planning seems to have gone into this, as well as considerable connections. A helicopter is waiting on a landing pad outside the stadium. With a gun to the Premier's head, and using the other hostages as shields, they will take the private elevator outside the Premier's box to a lower level, march the hostages to the helicopter and they will be allowed to escape." Yang winced.

McCall said, "So that's the secret Price has been killing to protect. What sort of operation is underway to rescue the hostages?"

"A fierce debate is in progress concerning exactly that." Discomfort lingered in Yang's voice. "Another of our SWAT teams has been mobilized. There is an air duct leading to the Premier's box, via which a commando rescue mission attack might be launched."

"That can't be accomplished quietly," said McCall. "They'll make too much racket in their approach no matter how trained they are."

"You are forgetting," said Yang, "we are dealing with Chinese design. The air ducts are extremely well insulated. Sound will not be a problem."

McCall tugged irritably at an earlobe. "It still sounds to me like a bloodbath."

"Quite right," said Yang. "In Munich in 1972, it was the rescue attempt that killed all of the hostages. Our Premier is a much-loved public figure."

McCall couldn't stay seated any longer.

"Let me guess, Major. You have a way for me to somehow get

in there and execute a surgical strike, is that it? You want the precision a massed assault most likely would not accomplish."

Yang said, "The immediate area—except for the box itself and its anteroom—which unfortunately includes the private elevator—is sealed off. As we speak, a SWAT team is poised at an air duct awaiting the order to initiate. However, I could get you into that air duct system from a point well removed from the sealed-off area. You could squeeze your way in and crawl through the system to ultimately access the Premier's box from another angle without the SWAT team being aware of your presence. You could effect the hostages' rescue before the order is given for the SWAT unit to strike."

McCall said, "I get it. I pull off this long shot and you come out a hero because it was your idea. You're redeemed. But if the element of surprise isn't enough, I'm just a crazy American who went maverick to avenge the death of his fiancée and you're left to pick up and rearrange the pieces any way you like. You're slick, Major."

Yang rose, regarding McCall eye to eye.

"We are losing valuable time. The money transfers are nearly complete and when they are finalized, Dan Price will undertake his escape and our opportunity will be lost."

McCall shook his head, no. "Forget the insulation. I'm not only a foreign devil here, I'm a damn big foreign devil. I don't care how much insulation you've got, Price and his goons will hear me coming."

"Not," said Yang, "if you're wearing a wetsuit."

"A what?"

"They call it that because it resembles a scuba diving suit. It's designed specifically for utilizing architectural design in urban combat. Your American military special ops units surely have a counterpart, at least in prototype. The suit is of a specially designed material that actually excretes a lubricant patina that allows the wearer to soundlessly negotiate such angles of approach as are provided by, say, an air duct, with a relatively minimal degree of effort. The SWAT team is wearing them." Yang paused to smirk at something he read in McCall's expression. "Well, *gwai-lo,* aren't you going to say something like damn clever, you Orientals?"

McCall chuckled dryly. "I'm thinking it."

On the PC screen, Tucker was covering the hostages. Hanson sat at the laptop. And Dan Price was grinning smugly to himself like he ruled the world, his heist going off without a hitch, checking the action of his pistol while the Premier sat before him, a stoic, human mountain. The hostages remained a frozen tableau.

Strangely, as McCall was about to shift his eyes from the screen, Kelly Jackson happened to choose that precise moment to idly glance up directly at the hidden camera, unaware that she was making direct eye contact with him. McCall's heartbeat was no longer thundering against his ribs. An icy objectivity settled in.

"Okay, let's do it. I want my gun back with that wetsuit. And a flash-bang grenade off one of your SWAT team boys."

CHAPTER 33

He felt the weirdest sensation of a child returning to the womb as he left the world where people walked and sat and talked with room to move. The air duct, on the other hand, was true confinement.

After the slight physical effort of gaining entry, the coolness of the duct walls pressing in against McCall combined with the inevitable sensation of claustrophobia to create a cold sweat for the first minute that he was completely inside the duct system. It was a tight fit. He forced his breathing to remain steady and deep. The fresh air blowing through dried the sweat on his brow. The black wetsuit felt like a second skin. In fact, he barely felt it at all except for its eerie, gliding outer slickness that allowed him to effortlessly and soundlessly advance. After several minutes of working his way along the narrow space, his body temperature returned to normal.

Behind him, Yang was refastening the screws that held the outer vent in place to prevent detection of this maverick action. Before leaving the office, the Major had drawn up blueprints of this section of the stadium on the computer, indicating the route through the air duct section that would take McCall to the Premier's box.

Several rooms away, the military SWAT team had not made its move yet. They stood ready to insert into the duct system from another point of entry, but the go order had not been given.

Yang had not only returned McCall's pistol—which presently rode snug in its holster at the small of his back—and acquired a flash/concussion grenade, but he also handed over a small flashlight attached to a band designed to be worn on the head, another requisition from his SWAT team. Yang then dismissed the soldiers, assuring them that the prisoner was secured. With the SWAT team redeployed, Yang used his authority to hurry with McCall up several flights and through three security checkpoints to a conference room with a chandelier, a broad, long table lined with chairs, a stunning panorama of the city—and not a soul in sight.

After locking the door, Yang led McCall to the air conditioning vent. It was at this point that McCall donned the tight-fitting wetsuit, which he had been carrying in a sack. The officer had slid over a chair, stood on it and went to work with a Swiss Army knife. Within seconds he had removed the vent cover. Stepping down from the chair, he placed the vent cover on the table.

McCall stepped onto the chair, still testing the clinging fabric of the wetsuit to find that it in no way hindered his natural movement. He gripped the frame of the opened vent, and hoisted himself up for a look-see. The flashlight's beam had revealed the air duct to be approximately three feet by three feet in dimension; a narrow crawl space of four metallic walls, cool to the touch.

The tiny flashlight on his forehead functioned literally as a headlight. He had commenced working his way along the narrow space toward the Premier's private box, some twenty meters ahead. He had memorized the route through this cool, dark labyrinth. It was slow going, although not particularly difficult once he got the hang of it and overcame the initial surge of claustrophobia. He used his feet, knees and hands for traction, advancing in a crab-like fashion. Driven as he was—*Dan Price*

242

was the son of a bitch responsible for Rosie's death and now the homicidal bastard held Kelly Jackson's life in his hands; Kelly, who reminded McCall of his own daughter—he experienced no physical discomfort in his scramble through the series of air ducts, although his breathing sounded abnormally loud to him in the confines of this closed environment.

By the time he paused to douse the light, drawing up just short of the vent to the Premier's box, he had grown relatively at ease and adept at movement within the cramped quarters. McCall filled his right hand with the grip of his pistol, his left with the concussion grenade.

He peered through the vent.

The expectancy of imminent violence was so real in the plush private box, Kelly thought she could almost hear the ticking of a time bomb. The only thing left was wondering when it would explode and who would die.

It seemed unlikely that there could be any other outcome, stranded as she was here with these hostages. She recognized the Premier, of course, one of the most powerful men in the world, who sat at a table near a wet bar where one of the three intruders sat on a bar stool and alternately fondled his pistol and practically cooed to it as if the handgun was a pet. Sneering, he would aim his pistol at the Premier's head. Then there was the intruder who sat before the laptop computer, his submachine gun resting beside the laptop on the table. And the one Kelly was most concerned about, the one who had brought her and Andrea here after he shot Chin, and who was now the one assigned to keep an eye on the hostages; a seedy specimen, outfitted all in black and heavily armed like the others.

This seedy man held his machine gun pointed steadily at Kelly and the others where they had been herded against a window-walled corner. His eyes mostly remained divided between Kelly and the girl who sat next to her, an attractive young woman whose crisp white blouse and dark vest and trouser uniform suggested that she had been tending the wet bar when the trio of commando-types had first staged their assault. The seedy one's eyes gleamed when he looked over Kelly and the other girl, undressing them with his eyes slowly, savoring each moment.

What a stunning chain of incredible events that had brought her to this razor's edge of time that crystallized in her mind the present and the past few hours.

My God, had she really awoke this morning in Beijing with her biggest worry being that she sucked so incredibly as a supposed world-class gymnast? Death, or possibly rape at the hands of a slavering gunman, now stared her dead-on in the face. When had it turned so crazy that she ended up in this? The blow-up in front of her parents and Boris? That had led to the scene alone with Boris and then a private conversation with Taggart McCall not more than a hundred yards from here.

That conversation was the last breath of sanity before the madness unfurled. First duped by the Chinese man, Chin. Bound, at his mercy and, it turned out, at the mercy of a merciless bitch named Andrea Cometti. *My God, my God, my God.* Insanity then went crazy. She witnessed Chin shot to death and she and Andrea were brought here. She and that horrible woman had not spoken since being roughly ushered in at the point of a machine gun. The vicious, spiteful things Andrea thought about Kelly and poor old Boris, whose worst crime was to be overbearing. And the terrible things Andrea had done! Kelly thought, *She almost deserved what was happening to her. But what about me? What have I done to deserve being thrust into this? Why is this happening to* me?

The only sound in their richly carpeted, poshly upholstered prison was the quiet weeping of the Secretary of State's wife and the gentle clacking of the keys of the laptop. The roar of the crowd in the stands beyond the smoked glass was nothing more than a faraway background noise.

Kelly inventoried the placement of the participants one more time.

She had already determined that the man seated on a stool at the bar was the man in charge. He emanated an aura of danger that all but reached out and clawed out at you. The Premier remained impassive. And there were the pair of dead men on the floor. Blood that had soaked into the carpet was beginning to coagulate. Her gaze traveled on. She needed to look anywhere else so as to avoid any accidental eye contact with the perv with the machine gun who was licking his chops like she was a piece of meat. Her eyes swept along the ceiling, and then to the short passageway that led to the anteroom and the elevators they had passed when she and Andrea were led in.

Because Kelly happened to be looking in that direction, she was the only one to see the cover of an air conditioning vent drop from the ceiling under a sharp kick of a shoe briefly visible from inside the air duct. The vent cover rattled to the floor, drawing everyone's attention. A ball-like object dropped from the hole in the ceiling.

Movement to Kelly's left caught her attention. While everyone else was startled into reflexively glancing in the direction of the disturbance—including the gunman at the laptop and the one watching the hostages—their leader was leaping from his bar stool to grab the Premier by the collar of his jacket. He thrust the Premier of China bodily out of sight behind the bar and followed in a headlong dive.

This was good enough for Kelly. She averted her eyes from the direction that held everyone else's attention, closing her eyes, burying her face in the crook of her arm a split-second before the deafening, blinding blast.

McCall dropped through the vent while the grenade blast still resonated. He landed in a springy, bent-kneed combat crouch, the 9 mm up, seeking his first target, taking in the scene at a glance. The hostages stumbled about blindly, hands to their eardrums, dazed under the effect of the concussion grenade. They would regain their senses in short order. The Premier and Dan Price were nowhere to be seen. *Damn!* Kelly Jackson seemed okay. He selected his first target. Hanson was storming up from the table, the laptop computer forgotten, blindly seizing his submachine gun, although he was stunned, nearly senseless. But Tucker stood already on his feet, unmoved from where he'd been covering the hostages, as if his sturdy frame was rooted to the plush carpeting. Tucker was shaking his head to clear it. He'd held onto his machine gun and so he became target number one.

McCall took him out with a headshot that made Tucker a dead man, but the merc reflexively jerked the trigger in his death spasm. His machine gun unleashed a blistering firestorm even as his knees met and he wilted. McCall dived to the floor, his mind crying *Be safe, Kelly!* He saw Hanson catch a half dozen rounds that kicked him off his feet, heavy rounds that pulped his chest and puked globs of red mud from gaping exit wounds in his back. Then the gunfire ceased. The bullets had only riddled Hanson, the wall and the bar behind him. Everyone in the hostage group appeared to have escaped injury.

McCall got to his feet. Kelly was standing steadier than those around her. When McCall reached her, she pointed urgently behind the bar. McCall nodded and, cautiously at first, he gazed around at the area behind the bar. Then he flung himself at the closed trap door in the floor that was now revealed where it had been concealed beneath an elegant woven throw rug.

He was pawing at the sealed-shut trap door, becoming frantic with the realization that Dan Price had eluded him with the Premier as his hostage, when the pain inside burned up and down his left arm just long enough to warn him of what was about to happen.

He thought, *Oh shit, no!* Then the pain exploded in his chest like a mule kick, knocking the wind from his lungs just like in his shower that morning. His moment had come. *He was having a goddamn heart attack!* It was the last wholly lucid thought he experienced.

The pain and the contracting pressure were flaming spears plunging into him, crushing his chest. He heard himself gasping for air. He looked up and saw Kelly Jackson leaning over him, saying something.

Then everything faded to black.

CHAPTER 34

When her name was announced, Kelly Jackson bounded into the performance area, struggling to maintain her focus.

Stay on automatic pilot, she kept telling herself. *You've come this far and nothing matters now except winning this one last event, being in this moment, existing as if nothing has gone before and nothing after will matter. All that matters is winning right here, right now.*

The horrific echoes of combat and violent death hammered at the invisible walls she had constructed around her mind. Her unspeakable personal ordeal, of which the public remained ignorant, her aching questions about so much—What had it all been about, the horror that had exploded in the Chinese Premier's exclusive viewing box? How and where was Tag Mc-Call?—it would all have to wait. She and the other hostages had been rushed away from the carnage before she could learn of McCall's fate. It had been nothing but confusion.

The moment of truth came shortly after she was reunited with her family. It was a foregone conclusion that she would be rushed to a hospital, canceling her final appearance. But she refused all but the most rudimentary medical attention.

Boris Temerov was present at the private reunion. The normally hearty, bearded bear was strangely reserved, staying in the background. Her mother was wan, not glowing with her usual forced ebullience, and her father, while overflowing with joy and relief, had pointedly avoided looking at Boris, as he normally would have during such an extraordinary moment. A strange clarity descended upon Kelly to reveal the strain of a deep divide that had not been there before between her parents and her trainer. Had her mother and Boris ever had an affair? Had her father become aware of it? And what would happen next? More for her to sort out . . . later. She would confront them. She must know the truth. But not now. Not now.

What is a champion? She knew the answer. She was the answer. A champion perseveres to victory.

Her appearance elicited a rousing cheer from the capacity audience that filled the cavernous arena, serving to reinforce those invisible walls that blocked out everything except driving determination.

McCall sat propped up in bed against the headboard, watching television. Shafts of sunlight poured through the window, intensifying the stark whiteness of the hospital room and its sparse furnishings.

When Major Yang entered and started to address him, Mc-Call motioned for the major to hold the thought. He wanted to watch the conclusion of a televised ceremony. He did not want to miss seeing a gold medal being draped around Kelly Jackson's neck. The high-definition television screen caught the medal beaming almost as brightly as Kelly where she stood with the other gymnasts, basking in the cheering that poured over them from the stands at the National Stadium.

McCall thumbed the remote and the TV screen *clicked* and went dark. He and Yang were alone in the room. McCall took a deep breath and exhaled slowly. His brain was clearing for the first time since the "episode." In fact, his mind was pretty much clear and he felt fine.

Angina pectorales, had been a grim-faced Chinese doctor's diagnosis. McCall was having chest pains because he was not

249

getting sufficient oxygen to the heart due to a blocked artery. They gave McCall some temporary medicine and urged him to see a heart specialist as soon as he got home.

Yesterday he had been too spaced out on whatever drugs they'd pumped into him to want to do anything but stay in bed like he was told. He watched the Games on and off, slipping in and out of lucidity, only halfway aware of doctors and nurses coming and going, tending to him and talking over him in Chinese as if he weren't there; as if he was already dead. Unbelievably sleepy, he was awake enough at one point to comprehend what the doctor told him in English about his condition. Then things became uncertain and fuzzy again. Someone entered his room at intervals: Major Yang, his authority and manner causing the doctors and nurses to make themselves scarce whenever he showed up. He would stand there and watch McCall, and then leave and return later, waiting for when McCall would be ready to talk.

McCall's mind had wandered, swooping and landing and arcing like an eagle against an American landscape, and he thought of Rosie. The sight of her dead body kept returning to him, opening wounds in his soul. It was Rose's soul soaring against that American sky. Those were the sorts of thoughts rippling across his semi-consciousness. *Rosie, Rosie. Oh, forgive me. Goddamn . . .*

A cheery bouquet of flowers had been placed on a counter on the other side of the hospital room. The accompanying card read *Get Well, Best Wishes, Mei Chen*, rendered in a delicate, lilting hand so at odds with the edgy, professional side she showed the world. McCall was not surprised, not after that side of her complex personality had revealed itself to him in the intimacy of her apartment following his delivery of the baby on that subway platform. These thoughts brought a stark reminder of his mortality. He was certainly doing his part to maintain the balance, bringing a new soul into the world on his way out. One in, one about to check out. Sounded fair enough.

Such was the state of mind that had prevailed until this morning, when the fog between his ears began to clear.

Major Yang stood near the closed door, hands clasped before him. "Your doctors assure me that your interest in the Games is a healthy sign." The attempt at opening with a conversational tone was brittle, lacking in conviction. "I am told you will be leaving tomorrow."

"I may be leaving at any minute," said McCall. "I'm feeling restless. We've got things to talk about, Major." He nodded at the television. "That set's been on around the clock and I haven't heard squat about a bloodbath up in the VIP section at the Stadium."

"And you or no one else ever will," said Yang. "Did you expect otherwise? Too much is predicated on the outcome of these games for China, her allies and yes, her enemies. Yes, there have been problems and trouble at the Games . . . but a gun held to the Premier's head? Your Secretary of State and ambassador and their wives subjected to terrorism at a personal level . . . no, that will never go into the history books, nor even a hint of it."

"Sort of like history in general," McCall observed. "I was never much of a conspiracy theorist . . . until I joined the Secret Service. And you've just made me a believer for life."

"All involved," said Yang, "that is to say the highest offices of your government and mine, extend through me their most heartfelt gratitude and appreciation for your role in this, and for your cooperation in keeping this forever Top Secret. The Premier in particular wished to come here to visit, to shake your hand, but of course security concerns countermanded even his request. As for your own government—"

McCall thought of being drummed out of the Service after the Camp David fiasco that ended his government career, which led to the breakup of his life, his divorce, the loss of a good wife and daughter in large part because so many doors had been slammed in his face. He thought of the tough Q&A at CIA hands after he'd turned over General Yu.

He said, "I know about my government. Tell me something I don't know. What happened after I took my nosedive?"

"The hidden trapdoor behind the bar was a secret escape route that, strangely enough, even the Premier was unaware of. His bodyguards who died in the assault were the only ones who knew."

"Dan Price knew about it."

Yang nodded. "And he knew his way out of it. The Premier was quickly located by one of our SWAT teams thanks to a GPS chip imbedded in one of his molars. But Dan Price, I regret to say, escaped."

"In other words that son of a bitch was smarter than anything or anyone either of our governments could throw at him?"

"Up to a point, yes."

"And how did he get away? You told me he had a helo waiting."

"We arrested the helicopter pilot and he claims to know nothing about why he was hired. He was shown official documents that stated Dan Price had clearance and was operating with complete sanction of our government."

"Cheeky bastard," said McCall.

"While our SWAT units were busy with the helicopter, Dan Price apparently rejoined the masses of people in the stadium who knew nothing of the dire situation," said Yang, "and thus managed to escape by the simple expedient of walking away. Every minute of surveillance video is being pored over but so far, nothing. The helicopter pilot claims to have had no knowledge of the hostage extortion plot."

"I believe the pilot," said McCall. "Buddy Dan would keep

everything compartmentalized. The pilot's lucky. Price intended to leave him somewhere with a bullet in the head after he'd performed his task." He thought of Rosie lying dead on a linoleum floor. "The bastard isn't leaving any living loose ends behind." He broke that chain of thought and said, with another nod at the TV, "Kelly Jackson came back strong."

"A remarkable young woman." This time the major's voice bespoke true sincerity. He said, almost wistfully, "The resilience of youth. Her parents and her trainer, I'm told, tried to dissuade Miss Jackson from participating in the final round of competition, but it was as if her ordeal inspired her to renewed greatness. She acquitted herself admirably."

"Let's talk about that ordeal," said McCall. "What about Andrea Cometti?"

Yang strode over to the window to peer out and down at the emerald green, manicured hospital grounds.

"That unpleasant person is presently in the custody of the Chinese government. Your ambassador is protesting, of course. The Politburo is expected to hand down a decision regarding jurisdiction today or tomorrow. In the meanwhile, Miss Cometti is enjoying Chinese hospitality, although not of the same class and comfort as yourself, my friend."

"Friend?" said McCall. "Don't get carried away, Major. A word like *friend* makes me nervous when guys like you use it. You don't have friends, is my reading. You've got your job, and you think you're playing it cagey. But I'm an old tiger in the same jungle, friend, so why not tell it to me straight?"

Yang's shoulders twitched in an indifferent shrug. "There does seem little call for subterfuge at this point. The fact is, I was aware of Kelly Jackson's plight before she was kidnapped."

"You are a man of many secrets."

"Then allow me to divest myself of some. Andrea Cometti engineered the kidnapping of Kelly Jackson. She did this out of

253

---

spite as a spurned lover, to discredit and humiliate Boris Temerov and Kelly Jackson in the eyes of the world."

"No secrets there," said McCall. "Your government is going public with all of that, and with the death of some racist nut, in order to deflect media heat from what you and I know happened up in that VIP box."

Yang said, "Ah yes, Mr. J. Bob Wiley. What sort of a name is that, I ask you?"

"It's a cultural thing. Major, how did you know about the Kelly Jackson kidnapping before it happened?"

"Quite simple. The man the Cometti woman selected as her accomplice, a scoundrel named Chin, was working for me; a denizen of our underworld, such as it is. I have many like him on the streets of Beijing and in the provinces. Informers, some of them, and others who pose as bait to lure the unwary shark."

McCall said, "In my country they call that a sting. So the Cometti woman nosed in the right or wrong circles after she got to Beijing and someone steered her to your man, Chin. And you let her go ahead with it? You didn't try to stop it?" McCall's eyes narrowed. "You put Kelly Jackson's life in danger. We're not friends, Major."

"I assure you, Miss Jackson was not for a single moment in danger. Chin's orders were to let nothing happen to her. We would have staged a rescue and arrested the Cometti woman in due course, if Dan Price's gunman had not taken Chin by surprise and gunned him down when he took the women hostage."

"You were looking for an excuse to imbed someone in the Special Operations Command. The kidnapping was perfect for your office to assign an operative to cooperate with the SOC. The operative was Mei Chen."

Yang said, "You and I have discussed Dan Price. I did not trust him from that first night when the Simms woman and

Captain Li were killed. And there was the matter of General Yu Bin, who would certainly contact your organization to defect. It was my good fortune that circumstance provided the General with you."

"So I'm investigating Kelly Jackson's disappearance with Mei Chen," said McCall, "and the whole time she's filing daily reports to you on what she knows about me and the General and whatever she can dig up on Dan Price and the Simms business. Tell me, Major, did you order Mei to offer herself to me sexually when she and I were alone in her apartment?"

The lack of an immediate response from Yang—droll, dismissive or otherwise—spoke volumes to one attuned by nature and training to nuance in conversation and behavior. Yang's bearing grew more erect while he remained at the window, gazing out. When he turned, he eyed McCall with a new look that McCall could not identify at first.

"I was unaware that Mei had, er, so offered herself to you."

What McCall had seen was the flicker of jealousy, quickly extinguished beneath the same mask of impersonal, arrogant competence that Mei Chen had worn.

McCall said, "I see it, Major. You're in love with Mei Chen."

Yang appeared to notice the flower arrangement on the table for the first time. He picked up the accompanying card and stared at the inscription for a long time. Then he replaced the card.

He withdrew an envelope from an inside breast pocket of his jacket. "We have been intercepting and inspecting your mail, of course. I'm sure you understand. This arrived today, mailed from the Olympic Green. It was sent to you by Rose Campbell."

This arrested every nerve end in McCall.

"Let me see that."

"This is what happened," said Yang. "Dan Price's men, Tucker and Hanson, were closing in on Miss Campbell after she quit her work shift on her way to meet you. She had found something incriminating and knew that Price would stop at nothing to intercept her and retrieve what she'd found because if it was made public, everything would come toppling down for Dan Price because it would start a line of inquiry that could only result in his arrest for the murder of Jody Simms and Captain Li. Before they could intercept her, she mailed this to you."

McCall remained with his hand outstretched. "I said, let me see it."

Yang handed him the envelope.

"The saying is a picture is worth a thousand words, is that not so? Well, gaze upon the picture in that envelope, McCall— the picture Rose Campbell sent to you during the final minutes of her life—and everything will be explained."

CHAPTER 35

Candlelight bathed a low-ceilinged bedroom.

She sat in a high-backed chair. Viewed from the corner of a ground-level window, left open against the humid, sultry night, the wavering golden glow of the candles imbued the black leather of her dominatrix costume with a shimmer, as if the narrow strips of leather were a living caress across barely concealed breasts and hips. She wore thigh-high black leather boots. Her arms rested on the chair arms. A short whip curled down from her right hand. The mouth, revealed by the leather mask, was a garish crimson slash. The eyes were steely. She sat erect, not moving, and alone in the bedroom.

McCall's nostrils caught a trace of incense that he recognized as the same musk scent that Mei Chen had lighted when they were alone in her apartment. The candlelight glowed off a ruby ring, her only piece of jewelry, that decorated her left hand. McCall remembered noting that ring the day they met.

Crouched beside him, Major Yang leaned close in the darkness. He breathed in a nearly inaudible whisper, "She's magnificent."

McCall and Yang both held their pistols ready.

McCall whispered, "She's one of the two brains behind the biggest heist in a hundred years."

In the photograph that was inside the envelope Yang had shown McCall at the hospital, Mistress Mei was sitting in that same chair, wearing the same getup. The camera had clearly caught the same ruby ring. And Dan Price was clearly visible in the photograph, kneeling before her, kissing one of the boots. *Rose had somehow acquired the picture. She would have made the connection instantly, recalling the ruby ring from when she met Mei, even though the dominatrix in the photo was masked.* It was enough to get McCall out of his hospital bed and into street clothes.

Yang had located Mei Chen through computer tracking that linked him to this cottage owned by a distant relative of Mei's who, in all likelihood, was unaware that these partners in crime, Mei Chen and Dan Price, had chosen this cottage to lay low for a few days, until some of the initial heat subsided, when their money would buy them safe passage out of China and they would be home free.

Yang had explained, during their drive here, that he had reconnoitered the cottage and surrounding residential neighborhood of one-acre lots, and had verified the fugitives' presence. The hitch was that Major Yang was keeping this to himself, permitting only McCall into his confidence. With the capture tonight of the two most wanted criminals on the planet, solely at his and McCall's hands, Major Yang intended to not only redeem himself but to put himself on a career advancement fast track. But he wanted McCall along.

It was too much for one man, McCall had to agree. McCall wanted Dan Price to settle the score for Rose Campbell, and Yang wanted to apprehend and hand over to the Politburo a traitorous bitch who had not only helped mastermind the heist, but had in the process betrayed her trust as an agent under Major Yang's command and forever sullied his record.

Yang whispered, "How long must we wait?" He was accustomed to being the man in charge, not having to cooperate with others. "Would it not be better if—"

McCall didn't like conversing, even in a whisper. The lilting music from inside was the only reason they chanced not being heard. Mei could not see them. She sat with her chin lifted, with that air of regal anticipation burnished with eroticism.

McCall said, "We're waiting until Dan Price shows up. We've got nothing if he escapes."

Yang's attention was glued to Mei Chen.

"As you wish."

Blinding light suddenly flooded the area, freezing everything around the window in its harsh silver glare. McCall and Yang whirled, jerking up their arms to shield their eyes from the glare.

Dan Price's voice said from behind the lights, "Hold it right there, you goddamn Peeping Toms. Drop your weapons."

As they let their weapons drop, McCall growled, "Well, at least the wait's over."

"Smart guy," said Price.

The lights went out. The stygian gloom of night reclaimed this corner of the suburban world. The splash of blinding light had been brief, but effective. From behind the bank of floodlights, Dan Price's retinas would retain a precise placement of McCall and Yang and for them, the damage had been done, their night vision obliterated.

McCall kept his eyes closed in an attempt to speed up reclamation of his night vision.

"Now what?" he asked.

Beside him, Yang stood unmoving, silent as a post.

Price could be heard stooping to retrieve their dropped handguns.

Price said, "Now the both of you march your sorry selves into the house. I'm holding a silenced submachine gun in my right hand, balanced on my hip, and my finger's on the trigger. Do as you're told or I'll kill you here and now."

Night slumbered around them, the residential tranquility undisturbed by the brief flash of light. Cicadas chattered.

Somewhere, a dog yawped.

With Price prodding them from behind, they shuffled along the side of the house. McCall allowed Yang to assume the point position. McCall's heartbeat was regular. By the time they reached a back stoop, his night vision had begun to gradually return. Ahead of him, the major was fumbling in the dark before he found a door handle, which he pushed inward. McCall stepped after him into the darkened house, followed by Dan Price, who kicked the door shut after him.

Secret Service procedural training included response tactics if you fell into a hostage situation exactly like this one, always a distinct if remote possibility in an agent's line of duty. There was life, so there was hope. *Stay vigilant, receptive to and prepared to seize the first opening that presented itself and run like hell with it. Run? Hell . . .*

They little more than shuffled through the stale-smelling kitchen, proceeding tentatively into a musty, dark living room where the shapes of sheet-covered furniture bore witness like mute, ghostly sentries. Yang led the little procession to a hallway that branched off from the living room, drawn toward the doorway of the candle-lit bedroom, beckoned there by tendrils of musk. Price herded them into the bedroom. He stopped just inside the bedroom door, where he could equally cover McCall and Yang.

She was waiting for them; her booted feet planted squarely, hands on her hips, the whip dangling from one clenched fist, a vision of exquisite, haughty grandeur in the waving golden glow of the candles.

Opened suitcases, one stuffed with Euro dollars, were visible on the dresser and against one wall.

McCall said, "Hello, Mei. I'm glad to see you've put aside that asexual cog-in-the-machine personae, but isn't this kind of extreme in the opposite direction?"

Her back arched. Her chin lifted. Insolent breasts thrust against their skimpy leather restraint. Steely eyes swept with disdain across McCall and Yang before glaring at Dan Price.

"Slave, why have you not executed them?"

Price tossed their pistols onto the bed and resumed holding the machine gun, aimed at them with both hands.

"I wanted to bring them inside," he said in a voice McCall had never heard from him, somehow remaining masculine in timbre yet becoming submissive, almost meek. "In a neighborhood quiet as this, even a silenced machine gun could cause a disturbance at this hour. And it would be good for us to know who else knows about our little hideaway."

Mei regarded Yang with distaste.

"That one has always wanted me. It has blinded his common sense." She sneered at McCall. "And this one thought he admired me, and dreamed that he too might be allowed to possess me."

Price growled deep in his throat. "What do you mean? Did something happen between you two?"

McCall saw his angle then, but he couldn't automatically run with it the way his training had taught him. This called for some finesse, a setup before making the life-or-death, go-for-broke attempt at turning the tables.

He said, "Well well, Dan. Everyone has a kink, they say. Shouldn't be much of a surprise that a control freak like you would get his kicks from being told what to do by a woman."

Price motioned with his machine gun. "Don't confuse fun and games with the real world, pal. It was Mei's plan initially, yeah. She came to me with the whole idea worked out. But *I* put it together and made it happen and now the two of us are richer than God and no one's going to take that away from us, are they, babe?"

Mei yanked off her leather mask and tossed it aside.

Unmasked, she radiated an even colder fury.

"Why do you wait, damn you? Kill them."

They were giving McCall words instead of bullets. He must exploit this. A question had been aroused in Price's disciplined mind, apparent in the briefest facial tic in his otherwise granite features. McCall must use words to buy time, and there were details yet to be revealed.

He said to Mei, "After we finished interrogating the Jacksons and Boris Temerov and Andrea Cometti, you didn't go off to investigate Andrea. You went directly to hook up with Price, to help him initiate the assault on the Premier's party."

Yang nodded. "It could only have been accomplished with help from the inside." He addressed Mei. "Were there others like me among the Premier's security force and staff, who helped you because they thought—" The briefest pause. Yang gulped hard and resumed, "—because they thought they were in love with you?"

Mei sneered. "Hardly love, you fool. Two of the Premier's security staff and one of his advisors are numbered among my worshipful slaves. They hear and obey."

"I am a fool," said Yang, "in the matters of the heart. What man is not? I'm sure you were practical enough to make video recordings of these accomplices playing your role games, in case additional persuasion was required. Those videos will tell us who the traitors are."

Mei laughed, an unpleasant, grating sound. "You are a bigger fool than you know. You will not leave this room alive, either of you." She glared at Price. "I order you to annihilate them. Obey me."

The struggle raging within Price was apparent in the whiteness of the knuckle of his trigger finger, curved around the trigger of the machine gun aimed at McCall and Yang. The bond between him and this woman was potent enough to test the strength of will of this muscular little dominatrix-clad tart. Price stayed his finger from squeezing the trigger.

This was the opening and McCall played it.

He said, "Yeah, I've had your precious little mistress and I didn't have to play any stupid games to get her. She took me up to her apartment. She wanted to find out if Rose Campbell and I had told anyone else that we were investigating you." He did not add that, in telling Mei that no one else knew of their investigation, he had in effect sealed Rose's fate when Price and Mei went about covering their tracks. He said, "Mei was willing to do anything—anything—to get me to talk, and she did, buddy . . . and she didn't mind it a bit, did you, babe?" he asked her.

Dan Price held the machine gun pointed at Yang and Mc-Call, but his troubled eyes swung on Mei.

"That's not true, is it? I mean, you wouldn't—"

She snapped her whip, an angry *crack!*

"Silence. Do not speak to me in this manner. Hand me the gun and I'll do it myself."

Price said plaintively, "It is just that—I need to know. Did you give it up to this smart son of a bitch?"

"You know she did, chump." McCall sharpened the edge in his voice. "She didn't tell Major Yang about it and she didn't tell you. What a tangled web we weave. Ask the Major. Your mistress was obeying *his* orders too. Wasn't she, Major?"

With the trace of a smug smile, as if about to comment, Yang scratched the back of his neck. Then his arm thrust forward, straightening with lightning speed.

The blade of a knife, that had been sheathed beneath his collar at the back of his neck, glittered in the candlelight, expertly flung at Dan Price. Price took the blade, buried to its hilt, squarely in the throat. His arms jerked reflexively up to grasp at it. He was instantly apoplectic, his eyes wide with surprise and alarm, and then he started spewing blood like a crimson fountain, stumbling back one, two, three paces and pitching to the floor where, spasmodic on his side in a fetal position, he gagged on his blood, blood-slippery fingers unable to withdraw the knife handle protruding from his throat.

Mei hissed like an angry cat, drawing her arm back to snap the whip with a violent practiced flick of her wrist. The whip laced around Yang's ankles. Mei gave a tug that yanked Yang off his feet. She dropped the whip and dived for the bed and the handguns there but took only one step before McCall intercepted her. Then he had her, pinning this diminutive, hissing lioness to the wall with a hand to her throat. She ceased struggling physically but her eyes narrowed fiercely. Mei strained to pull air through her constricted larynx.

Dan Price's coughing, the sounds of his death spasms on the floor, had subsided. A weird stillness prevailed. Yang could be heard disentangling himself from the whip hobbling his ankles, and then he was checking Dan Price's vital signs.

"He's dead."

McCall eased off just a bit, enough to allow Mei's dangling feet to find a little purchase.

She hissed at him. "What are you going to do now, round eyes? Are you going to kill me? Would that satisfy you?"

"No," said McCall, "I've got something better in mind. The Major's going to arrest you. I want your country's justice system to have its way. Maybe you'll get lucky and they'll execute you. A quick bullet to the back of the head."

"That would be too good for her," said Yang in a tight voice.

"I agree," said McCall. He met Mei's fierce, unblinking eyes, inches away, with a fury of his own. "My guess is they'll sentence you to a labor camp where you'll be worn down to an old woman within five years, if you last that long. You'll be worked to death within ten years, Mei. How does that sound, beautiful?

Was it worth it?"

She blinked twice and the hate remained, but the ferocious resistance had gone away.

She said, "Kill me." in a quiet, beseeching tone, no longer domineering. "Do me that favor, McCall. End it for me, here and now."

"I don't owe you any favors," McCall said. "I owe you for Rose Campbell."

He lifted her completely off the floor by the throat with his left hand, and KOed her with a short right jab to the jaw. The back of Mei's head hit the wall. Her eyes rolled back in their sockets. McCall stepped away and let her drop.

She was snoring gently.

Yang called in for backup.

EPILOGUE

Two weeks later. A rural hillside cemetery.

He waited until the mourners were gone. Then he waited for the grave-digging crew—who had remained discreetly out of view during the funeral service; two black men, working with a backhoe—to complete their task. The racket and exhaust fumes of the machine violated the atmosphere, but after their departure quiet reigned again, except for the *drip-drip* of moisture from the willow trees and a tentative chittering of cicadas now that the rain had stopped.

McCall quit his position near the stand of willows and walked down to the grave. His hair and somber gray clothing were both damp. He had not sought shelter from the rain.

The headstone was in place. The humid air was redolent with an earthy aroma; the freshly packed rich soil of the grave. He knelt on one knee. The damp earth soaked through the knee of his trousers. He reached out a straightened right arm and rested his hand on the gravestone.

"It's me, Rose. I came to say goodbye."

He closed his eyes and let his head droop, allowing free rein to his emotions. He'd always thought of headstones as cold, but this one felt warm to his touch; warmth that traveled along the length of his arm and through him. He remembered laughing eyes and a beautiful smile that brightened whenever she saw him walking toward her. He remembered a generous purity of heart, her loyalty and tenacity and tenderness—and yes, the

266

earthy, passionate heat—and most of all he remembered the way she followed her heart, ready to take a chance on new love with an old tiger named McCall.

He said, "We got 'em, hon. Price and Mei Chen. We were right, you and me. We were right about each other, too. I know you're up in Heaven, Rose. I'll be along one of these days . . . if they let me in."

He thought of Dan Price. He thought of the limp, lifeless body of Rose, murdered halfway around the world from this simple and decent place of her upbringing. Dan Price had not gone to the same place as Rose Campbell. Wherever the soul goes after this life, there had to be one place for the loving and another for those who would hate and kill for lust and greed. McCall wondered where his soul was bound.

He felt warmth upon his back, and looked up.

Shafts of sunlight had broken through the clouds. The grassy hillside of the cemetery sparkled with moisture, as if adorned with handfuls of scattered diamonds. The black thunderheads were graying, lifting from the surrounding hills. The storm had passed.

For Rosie, the games were over. The Games in Beijing, and the games that were the dance of life. A tear eased from the corner of McCall's eye and he didn't brush it away, but let it trickle its way down his cheek.

He was heading to Southern California where he had a grow- ing daughter. The lawyers had worked things out. And he would see the doctors when he got there. There had been no more heart incidents since Beijing, but he understood that he was liv- ing on borrowed time. He understood, more than ever, that everyone was living on borrowed time. He felt worn out, weary to his soul, but he would not scrimp on whatever borrowed time remained for him. He'd seen an American hero named Kelly Jackson overcome her trauma and self-doubts to handily sweep the final competition she'd participated in Beijing. If a little five-foot bundle of kid female like that could overcome all of her obstacles and return home with victory, then a beat-up veteran of life named McCall would find what it took to best live the rest of his life.

He stood from the grave and his right hand dropped to his side.

"Until next time, Rosie."

He turned and walked away, carefully negotiating his way down the grassy, wet incline.

ABOUT THE AUTHOR

Stephen Mertz has traveled the world as an adventurer and writer. His novels, written under a variety of pseudonyms, have been widely translated and have sold millions of copies worldwide. He currently lives in the American Southwest, and is always at work on a new novel.